Burning Out

KATHERINE MAY

snowbooks

Proudly Published by Snowbooks in 2009

Snowbooks Ltd.
120 Pentonville Road
London
N1 9JN
Tel: 0790 406 2414
email: info@snowbooks.com
www.snowbooks.com

British Library Cataloguing in Publication Data
A catalogue record for this book is available from the British Library.

ISBN: 978-1-906727-39-0

Printed in the UK by J F Print Ltd., Sparkford, Somerset

Part One

Last night I dreamed of a room that overlooked the sea. I had never been there before, but I knew it well. I could hear music coming from somewhere, so I began to search for it. I looked in every corner, in every cupboard and drawer, but all I found were shells and stones. Beneath my feet, the floor was strewn with sand.

The more I hunted, the more vague the music became. I could never quite identify it. Before long, it had vanished altogether, and everything was silent. I felt a gust of cold air on the back of my neck, and I turned to see that the music had escaped through an open window. In its wake, there was nothing but salty air, and the room felt clean, new and empty.

That's how I knew she was dead.

Time to tell our story, then, now that it no longer matters.

But where should I start? At my beginning or hers? Would it, I wonder, make any difference either way? Life has a funny way of repeating itself; it weaves its way into circles, and I can't find the beginning anymore.

We've got time wrong. We like to think of it as a continuum, a march of progress, an arrow striking into the future. We believe that history is cumulative: a slow pile of lessons learned that will one day reach critical mass and reveal, grandly, The Way.

But it's not like that at all. It's trial and error. We don't learn a thing. The needle hits the centre of the record, and we lift it off and play it again.

Dungeness is misty this morning. The tough, grey grasses that prickle all over my front yard are thrown into relief against the whiteness of it all, as if they mark the end of the world. On days like this, it's a comfort to believe that everything stops at my garden fence, that there's nothing beyond it. It might as well be true.

It's quiet here, at the end of the world. It's like everything's been stuffed up with cotton wool. Here, indoors, without the noises of the outside intruding, I can hear each new minute marked by the clock, and the dog sighing as he dozes beside me. If I sit still just for a few seconds, I can hear the low boom of my pulse. Until last night, these were the times when the link between us was strongest, when the silvery thread that joined her and me drew taut between us, and I would feel the presence of another living, breathing human being at the end of it. But I now know that won't happen again. The thread had worn thin, and last night, it frayed into nothingness. All that remains is my heartbeat, alone.

It won't be long before the mists roll back into the sea, and the rest of the world will return: the black hulk of the power station will fade into view, and the rush of the waves will come back. I'll be able to hear the wind again. As soon as the fog goes, the owl-screech of the miniature train will echo over the gravel, and will bring with it crunching feet and curious gazes, a parade of faces to peer into my front window, their eyes shielded from the obscuring daylight with cupped hands. Time was that they would see me in here and withdraw, embarrassed; nowadays they're more likely to call in other faces to stare at me. I'm the exhibit they were hoping to catch. They press cameras up against the glass and pulse bright light into my room. I'm a source of fascination to them, living here like this, when everyone else has surrendered to those neat condominiums in town. This thin woman in her tatty, black hut, who they see scrubbing about in her garden to pull up what little she can grow; whose clutch of chickens they chase when they hobble out of their run; whose dogs they tease when they growl and bark against their daily intrusion. I must have found my way into a guidebook, I suppose, or perhaps they're just drawn by the unfamiliar yellow glow of a wood fire in the afternoon. Who knows how they live now. I withdrew from it all so long ago that I barely remember what my own time was like.

Don't pity me. There are other visitors, kinder ones. Besides, I'm a practical woman, and this is the life I choose, cast out here between the marshes and the sea, picking out what living I can from the gaps in the shingle. So what if they come to poke and stare, to shout rough comments over the fence like terrified schoolboys? I've got enough here, on my own, to do without their approval, and I'm thankful for it. Rather this than the world that they have, the eternal flicker of bright screens and the endless deluge of chatter and information.

Too much information makes you stupid. It's the great paradox of modern life. It crowds the front of your brain with so much useless stimulation that your own thoughts get pushed to the back. This fatted proletariat are in thrall to it, and the only thing that stops them from knowing it is their own lethargy. Nothing is kept from them. They have access to the facts like never before, but they are so glutted with the surface of things that they don't dig any deeper. There is simply no space left after their daily flood of glamour and gloss, the gossip that masquerades as news and the idiocy that masquerades as intelligent comment.

Who wants to know about it anyway, the layer underneath? Come hear the bad news! I am here to spread the gospel of desolation! Listen to the lament of our final days on this earth!

Yet some people do. A surprising number of them, so I'm told. They pick up my missives from this empty part of the world, and they pass them on. For years now, they have given life and vigour to my rhetoric; they have spread my word like true disciples. But they barely know me at all. Behind everything, although I never even realised it myself, was another story, the one that started it all. Now she's gone, there's no reason not to tell it.

So I'd better find a place to start, before the world comes back. And it's obvious, really, where to begin. It's a moment I don't remember, but she did, and so I've seen it many times.

For Violet, it all began like this:

ONE

As the train left behind the uncertain edges of the London sprawl, Violet noticed that the sky had turned a smooth, ominous lilac-grey. The clouds hung low and heavy, lending everything a yellowish tint, an enclosed darkness.

A snowy sky. London had never seen snow since Violet moved there ten years before, but she recognised the signs from childhood winters spent willing it to come, listening intently to the radio in the hope that school would be closed for the day. She felt the familiar leap in her stomach, the sense of open anticipation at the liberties snow would bring. It was as if it were all ingrained in her, or that it was reignited now she had returned.

By the time the train pulled in to Stonehithe station, the tingling sense of nostalgia that she had carried with her since the previous evening was mingled with pure, childlike glee. She nevertheless felt her body recoil from the cold as she stepped out of the overheated train and let the doors close behind her. When she walked out onto the street, she was shocked by the sheer violence of the wind that rushed out from the sea and into her face, making her eyes stream. Snow was gathering in all the untouched corners now, and was sitting on the railings that lined the promenade. She staggered across the pavement, against the force of the weather, and climbed into the back of a waiting taxi.

The heat inside the cab made her flush, forcing her to pull off her coat and scarf. She handed the driver a sheet of paper with her destination – a church hall at the far end of town – printed on it, and hoped that this would substitute for conversation.

Violet made a rule of not talking to taxi drivers, nervous of the way that they could steal great chunks of her time by forcing her, out of politeness, to maintain the stream of conversation. In her handbag, there was a pair of earphones especially for this eventuality, which were plugged into nothing at all, but which hopefully gave the impression of her being out of bounds. She inserted them into her ears now, conscious that she really ought to be making calls ahead to the researchers she was meeting, or checking her emails on her mobile phone; but with no-one there to witness her doing these things, she saw no reason to bother. Just for ten minutes, she could allow herself the pleasure of savouring the quiet hum of the engine and the muffled rhythms of the wheels rumbling over the road, while she gazed out of the window to see what she could recall of this transformed landscape.

There was a vaguely-remembered familiarity to everything: the shops, the seafront, the rows of empty hotels that lined it; yet it was all so distant that she felt as though she was driving through a place that she had only ever seen in a dream. As the taxi passed along the main road that cut through the centre of town, Violet saw streets that she had neither forgotten nor remembered in the years since she left. She found that this information had been archived in some arcane part of her brain, ready for the moment she needed it again. She wondered how long it would have taken for this internal map to be erased forever.

The snow was now falling in finer, faster, more deliberate flakes, which seemed readier to pile onto the snow that had already settled. It was winning the battle against the passing cars and feet, whitening the streets despite their interruption. The taxi crawled up the hill that led away from the promenade, and Violet could now see that the lawns and roofs of the houses were carrying a thin veil of white that made them look blank, disguised. Excitement had settled in her like the snow; she knew that, if she were asked, she would have to look martyred and complain about the inconvenience of the stuff, the way that the world seemed to stop for it, that she was too busy to put up with this sort of disruption, but in truth this was what she loved about it: the way it disrupted everyday life, the way it transformed not just the landscape, but the people living in it also.

She wiped the steam from the window with the back of her hand and pressed her nose up to the glass, trying to enter the scene outside, to be part of the snow.

"Sorry about this traffic, love." The taxi driver leaned back in his seat so that he could watch Violet from the corner of his eye. She looked past him to see the red glow of dozens of brake lights stretched out in front of her, and then turned to see a long tail of steaming cars behind. Beyond them, she caught a glimpse of the sea; even through the obscuring snow, she thought she could make it out, prowling blackly at the horizon.

"Is this all just because of the snow?"

"Bit of a prang somewhere, I reckon. Right weather for it. These people, they don't change the way they drive, even when it's like this. Drive like it's a sunny day." He shook his head and squinted out of the windscreen as if he believed that he could see straight through the line of traffic if he stared hard enough. Violet noticed for the first time that he was wearing a shirt and tie. She looked around the cab. It was spotlessly clean, and scented a sickly lemon from the air-freshener that hung from the rear-view mirror. On the dashboard was a No Smoking sticker, and next to it, fluttering slightly in the breath of the heating vent, was a photograph of three neat schoolgirls, smiling down over the gear-stick like benevolent icons. The driver was old enough to be their grandfather, but the greenish tint of the photographs, the crisp blue shirts that the girls wore and the tidy alice bands that held their hair in place, suggested that the picture must be at least thirty years old and that the girls, now, were older than Violet.

"Looks like the girls' school's been sent home." Violet looked around her and saw that teenagers were beginning to trickle down the street, younger girls at first, hauling heavy bags and walking with earnest speed. The driver changed his grip on the steering wheel and tutted. "When I was at school, we had to go in, whatever the weather. I remember sitting lessons in my duffel coat." He smiled, rubbed his immaculately-shaven chin. "*And* I had to walk home, snow or no snow. No-one came to pick me up. This lot," he nodded towards the window, "get treated like babies."

Larger groups of girls had begun to appear now, swarming in tight clusters, linking arms against the snow, laughing into it, letting it drift into their mouths and eyes. Most were wrapped up in overbearing scarves, trying to chatter through them, blowing out clouds of white breath like seasoned smokers. Some girls came past in conspiratorial pairs, acting out the espionage of teenage life. Most of them wore woolly black tights, but some, as was clearly the fashion, wore thigh-high socks that exposed mottled stretches of freezing flesh with every movement of their short skirts. Soft ankles bent painfully sideways over heels that were too high.

Violet thawed a little. "This used to be my school," she said.

The taxi driver nodded and inched the car forwards. "Had you down as a Londoner."

"I am now." Violet peered out at the girls. The crowds were beginning to thin out; the big groups had all gone, and the remaining ones were walking alone. She watched a girl with a cello case and a home-knitted hat for a while. "I grew up here, though."

"Back to see your folks?" The traffic was loosening up, and the taxi was moving forward in regular bursts. Violet realised that she had been drawn into the conversation that all her precautions were supposed to avoid. She sighed.

"No. They moved away when I went to college. This is the first time I've been back." The car made a burst of progress and stopped next to a girl who was sitting on a wall, her legs wrapped around a gaunt man of about twenty, kissing him elaborately. The taxi driver averted his gaze. The girl came up for air, smirked, pulled back a strand of hair that had crept across her cheek and had snared itself in the corner of her mouth. A group of younger girls walked past, giggling. One of them poked two fingers into her mouth and retched. The taxi moved on. "Actually," said Violet, "I'm here on business."

"Oh," said the taxi driver, and switched on his radio. "I'm going to listen out for the traffic report," he said, "Hope it won't interfere with what you're listening to." Violet was confused for a few seconds, then she flinched and removed the silent earphones. She wondered how she must look to him, this clean man, with his whole pristine empire packed into one Mercedes saloon. She suspected that he wouldn't approve, that the tangle of electronica that she dragged with her into the car would later make her the butt of some joke or other with the three gym-slipped daughters and the wife that produced them.

He inched up the volume control of the radio, angled his head to indicate that he was listening. "I think it's clearing up now," he said. Violet nodded and gazed back out of the window.

The snow was falling ever harder, more purposefully, in small aggressive flakes that produced delicate thuds as they hit the roof of the car. They were dry and hard like soap powder; the wind was whisking them along the paths and corralling them into any corners it could find. Violet had forgotten this street in the years she had been away, but now she remembered it in snatches. There was a time when, having walked its length every morning and afternoon for seven years, she had known every front garden, every lamp-post, every crack in the pavement as landmarks that tracked the progress of her journey to school.

They were getting nearer to the school, passing the long hedge at the edge of the hockey pitch, which was now barricaded behind a violent steel fence. By the gates, a few girls were still milling around, waiting for lifts that were most likely stranded further down the hill.

One of them caught her eye. She was older than the others, seventeen or eighteen, and was chatting with another girl, shuffling her feet to keep warm. Violet smiled and remembered the sense of leisure that came with a snow-day, the delight at having snatched back a small pocket of time. The girl was dressed in a herringbone coat with a black fur collar. It reminded Violet of the old coat that she took to wearing in the sixth form, with its nipped-in waist and horn buttons. On her head was a Russian hat that she had to cling onto to prevent it being stolen by the wind. The girl could almost be her, at that age. Watching her, Violet was overtaken by the notion of how the musty coat must smell, and how the freezing air must be biting into her bare wrists, exposed because her sleeves were too short.

The taxi moved forwards. Now, perhaps ten metres from the girl, Violet tried to get a sense of what she looked like, but her face remained elusive. Violet could only see her own features on it: high brows, a thin mouth, cheeks that flared red against the cold. She smiled, surprised at herself, falling for such an obvious psychological trick, projecting her own life onto this stranger to such an extent that she even saw her own face. There were times when the characters in her dreams had continued to haunt her bedroom long after she had opened her eyes. Violet blinked to try to clear the illusion. The girl's face stayed the same.

The taxi hauled on another metre, so that Violet found herself level with the girl. Her stomach lurched. There, just a few footsteps away, was herself. She was so close now that there could be no question. It was as if she was looking into a mirror, and seeing herself ten years ago. Every movement the girl made - the way she rubbed at her neck with her gloved hands, the way she nodded as she laughed, the way she fidgeted with her bag and her coat - gave Violet a dragging sense of recognition, a kind of déjà-vu that didn't simply shake away as the moment passed. She felt sick, light-headed, frozen. She pressed both her hands to the cold window as if she could touch her.

The taxi moved forwards, and Violet twisted around in her seat so as not to lose her view. She caught one last glimpse of the girl (getting into the front seat of an old car with a loud stereo) as the taxi passed through the temporary traffic lights that had been holding them up; then, the girl disappeared from view.

"More blimmin' road works," said the taxi driver; "it's a wonder there's any road left, all the digging they do."

TWO

Violet pushed two Nurofen through their thin blister pack and placed them carefully on her desk. For good measure, she added a two probiotic pills to protect her stomach lining from the effects of the painkillers. She eyed this neat rank of white lozenges for a few seconds, savouring their clean, white air of salvation, then she scooped them all up into the palm of her hand. Their glazed surfaces clashed together, a glassy shuffle. Her eyes smarted with tiredness; her arms were heavy and unwilling to move. She tossed the pills to the back of her throat and flushed them down with three deep gulps of water.

While she waited for the resistant rush of nausea to subside, she pulled a tissue from the box in front of her and held it against her mouth. The cold water made slow progress down her gullet. It wouldn't take long. Everything would be fine. She opened her desk drawer and counted out five brazil nuts from a chrome storage jar. She lined these up, too, and ate them one by one. Selenium, zinc, magnesium, copper and iron. If she was careful, she could get three bites out of each nut, making fifteen mouthfuls to be chewed slowly.

She leaned against the soft back of her chair and let it absorb her weight. Every joint and every muscle ached, and she could feel the hypnotic crunch of sleep dragging at her. There was no reason she should feel as tired as this. She had taken precautions, had carefully ensured the quality of her sleep, the precise balance of her meals. It was just lethargy no doubt, brought on by too much time sitting down, too long in front of a screen. The heating didn't help; it was all very well for keeping the winter out, but it also dried the air, trapping her in a daily battle against sandy eyes and chalky skin, static hair and a parched mouth. They needed more plants around to boost the levels of oxygen in the air. She would buy one, the next time she was near the sort of shop that sold them.

She drew in a deep breath and stretched, working each muscle in her torso in turn. Standing up, she checked her grey trouser-suit for creases, brushing pieces of nylon fluff from the neat, straight trousers and shaking out the jacket. She took another couple of Nurofen, checked her messages, and then set about tidying her desk. This was an action she undertook several times a day, not to soothe herself with new-found order, but to fill time, to make sure that she had an excuse to remain in her office for as long as everyone else. She looked around the room: through the glass partitions, she could see at least a dozen of her colleagues still at their desks, typing furiously into their consoles, or speaking into phones, laughing as if it was a show of bravado. She was profoundly irritated by this. Tonight, of all nights, she should have the privilege of being the last one in the office, a reward for returning to work after a day visiting the researchers, but most other people were still here anyway, and appeared to be in full swing. She had planned to send a few emails out, hoping that the recipients would notice the time-stamp and would therefore have to acknowledge her exceptional commitment, but it seemed pointless now, if everyone else were doing it too. How did they all find enough to do to keep them busy until this hour? As time went on, Violet found that her work took less and less time to complete, so that, outside of meetings, when her time was being strictly used and demarcated, she was increasingly casting around for activities that would make her look busy.

Perhaps that was what everyone else was doing, surfing the internet and calling friends in other offices, just so that they weren't the first ones to leave. Violet stacked up the mass of company prospectuses that she had left splayed across her desk with deliberate haphazardness before leaving that morning, and stowed them neatly on her shelf. She then harvested her collection of pens and pencils and dropped them into the leather pot that she'd brought in herself to try to personalise her work space. There was nothing else to tidy. She was running out of things to do. Her inbox was empty and she had read every document that Marcus had passed down to her, even the ones that didn't need actioning for another month. She couldn't leave yet, not with everyone still in full flow. And not with her mind like this, turning over and over that image she'd seen.

Her own face, out of time.

Herself.

THREE

You can do it! You're King of the World!

As Violet pounded uphill on the running machine, feeling the pull in the backs of her calves and the ache in her knees, she read the series of messages that scrolled across the screen in front of her. She wondered, not for the first time, whether there was any point in entering her sex, age, weight and height into the console before she started running, if she were still to be referred to as a male throughout her run.

Next to the digital count of the calories she was burning (surprisingly few, although it was compelling to watch the number rise, imagining the foodstuffs it represented), was a small video image of the track she was supposed to be following, an alpine forest trail lined with lush pines. Occasionally, to add interest, the program would allow her to startle a deer or a pair of rabbits, but, given that the same deer and rabbits were startled at the same point in every run, this no longer held much enchantment for Violet.

She had been running, full-pelt, her feet rebounding off the rubber track of the machine, for thirty minutes now. Ten to go. She glanced around at the rows of men and women that surrounded her. It was like looking into a sequence of mirrors, the same matt black running machines repeated again and again down a long row, mounted by the same jolting bodies. She could feel her own body pounding in time with the others, forming a part of the continuous beat of the room. Everybody in step. Everybody marching to the same tune.

There were moments when Violet lost herself in this room, when she felt her body surrender utterly to its communal rhythm and would forgot herself, her place in the world. At these moments, she was capable of indulging so completely in her own thoughts that, when she regained control again, she would feel afraid that she might have unconsciously spoken, gesticulated or pulled a face in a manner that gave the rest of the room a glimpse into her interior landscape. Most of the time, she was only too aware of the bodies that surrounded her. There were the usual faces she knew, people she passed in corridors or stood with in lifts; people with whom she had endured brief seasons of contact when their working paths had crossed.

Violet's breath felt weighty now, hot and painful to draw in. She swigged from her water bottle, feeling the moisture being absorbed so quickly by her tongue that she was instantly thirsty again. There was an odd contrast between the heat of her body and the coolness of the air around her, as if the physical products of her labours were being drawn away before she even had a chance to experience them. Looking around her, at the men who were running immediately to her left and right, she saw that they were red-faced and sweating, their loose tee-shirts ringed with deep patches of wetness, and yet she could smell nothing of them, could hear nothing above the drone of the machines. She had a surreal sense that they were not wholly there, that they only existed enough to engage her visual sense. Far from carrying the taint of heaving human bodies, the air in the room smelt clean, saline, faintly floral, like damp laundry fresh from the washing machine.

Newhouse Image's staff gym only really came into its own at times like this, the hours after eight or nine pm, when its employees gradually began to detach themselves from their workstations and make their way reluctantly home, the day's tasks being completed. Many of them, Violet concluded, simply descended into the basement most nights to delay the return to domestic life for just another hour. There was even a persistent rumour, which never seemed to be out of circulation amongst the staff, that their gym attendance was being covertly monitored, and that this was the reason they all had to swipe their staff cards on the way in. Violet found it hard to believe that anyone in the company would have the time or energy to undertake this type of surveillance, but she suspected that a gentler form of observation nevertheless took place, the kind that arose from having one's face seen down there each night by one's superiors, which she felt could do her no harm. If the time at which she left the office each night was little more than a competition to see who would blink first, then her sessions in the gym were quite literally the survival of the fittest, a gladiatorial contest that took place each night, in which employees paraded their strength, stamina and energy before a mildly interested audience. If nothing else, it notched up another hour on-site and filled another hour before bedtime in which Violet was not alone in her apartment.

At nine-thirty, streamers and champagne corks burst across the screen of the running machine. *Congratulations!* it said, *You made it!*

Violet jogged to a standstill, wiped her face and chest with a towel, and moved onto the mats to start her stretches.

FOUR

She couldn't go home. She was wired, twitchy, her brain reeling with circular thoughts and wild speculations, and the very idea of returning to her flat made her feel claustrophobic. The London night was brown, stained by the lights that bled from the office blocks and reached into the sky. She hailed a taxi outside her office, and gave the driver an address on the other side of the river. As they pulled away, she glanced behind her to see the glow of Newhouse Image's foyer disappearing around the corner, gaudy and yellow.

The roads were almost empty in the city. The taxi passed a series of glass-clad skyscrapers, illuminated for the evening; St Paul's; a shiny black Thames; the carnival lights of the South Bank. Violet watched them all wash over the windows of the cab, this night-time city, eerily perfect without its untidy swarm of human bodies. It was so dark and quiet, so pristine, that it seemed unreal, as if it were a glassy reflection of itself, a polished impression that, in a rare moment of stillness, had peeled away from the real thing and now stood alone. She was a part of this place now, and it was a part of her; she had fully imbibed its principles, its attitude, its smartness and its surface gloss. It was barely different to how she had imagined it, all those years ago, when she had set it as her target, the place she would escape to, away from the low ceilings of her hometown. The city had met all her expectations; it was her lifestyle that had diverged, being free of the glamorous circle of friends, the outings to theatres, bars and restaurants that she had imagined.

They had passed now from the glowing parts of London into the darker places, where all-night kebab shops lit the empty streets and kids still hung around outside them at this time of night, kicking cans and begging fags from strangers. Violet could see the reflection of Canary Wharf and her sparkling sisters in the rear-view mirror, hanging over this part of London like an unattainable dream. Soon they entered an industrial estate, a cluster of corrugated warehouses that she knew from daytime visits were brightly coloured, but which were grey and ugly at night.

"Here, please," she said as she spotted the familiar façade, still lit for night-time visitors like herself, and so showing its gaudy orange and black paintwork: *U-Store – Peace of Mind in M³*. The taxi driver didn't offer his card for the return journey, but he waited courteously while she swiped herself in to the lobby and let the door click securely behind her.

Violet followed her memorised route to her own storage compartment, her footsteps echoing as she walked down the long, wide corridors. She wrapped her coat around her in defence against the still, cold air that smelt of dust and paint. To her left and right were rows of orange doors, each with a number. Hers, she knew, was the second from the end, one of the smaller units crammed into the rear of the building.

She unlocked her door, and was relieved to close and latch it behind her, away from the stiff silence and shadowy light. This place was rarely empty, populated at all times by lone men and women like herself, who would scuttle past her in the corridors, offering an embarrassed smile if they ever met at all. Violet had no idea what they might do in their individual cells, what compelled them to visit so regularly. But then, she supposed, they probably wondered the same thing about her. When she moved in, the manager of the place, a thin man with spiky hair and a red shaving rash, who was sweating profusely inside his orange nylon shirt, had gossiped that they had one client who came several nights a week just to sit and read, alone, away from his house-mates. He had, according to the manager, nothing but an armchair and a blanket in his room. He looked embarrassed after he'd told her this, and had hurriedly added that clients were, of course, welcome to do whatever they liked with their units, within reason. Violet had assured him that she had a flat of her own to read in.

The first time she had seen the room, it had been nothing but an empty cube, painted floor to ceiling in a pale buff, so that it felt like stepping into an enormous cardboard box. Violet remembered noticing how the light was clean and exact, illuminating every corner of the room with clinical precision. Today the light was straining to creep around the contents of the room, casting long, craggy shadows across the pale floor. Lining every wall were cheap Ikea shelves, and filling the shelves, stacked neatly so that there was no risk that they would landslide in her absence, were a mass of brown document boxes, each of the same size and shape, a squat oblong. There was a date on each of them, noting the day that it had been filled and consigned to the shelves, but there was nothing to differentiate them other than that.

More boxes were stacked on the floor by the shelves, but empty and still folded flat; next to them was a wad of white tissue paper. Violet bought both of these things regularly from a website that seemed to sell little else; she had lost count of how many boxes she had bought by now – perhaps one hundred, perhaps two.

The final thing in the room was an old folding garden chair with an orange and brown flowered seat, which Violet had found one day leaning against the wall in the corridor.

She had been suspicious of taking it at first, in case its owner had simply mislaid it, and would angrily knock on her door within minutes of her carrying it in. But when she noticed it in the same place three days later, she decided that it was probably fair game. It held an alarming air of decay, its worn seat being polished and bobbled by years of use, and Violet was always slightly nervous of sitting on it, imagining that it might excrete puffs of dust at the least provocation. Still, it had been a useful find, and moreover one that saved her from having to sit on the cold, concrete floor while she pored over her collection.

She unfolded the chair now, setting it beside a group of boxes that dated from several years ago. Selecting a box at random, she pulled it out from beneath two others, and placed it on her lap, feeling its heaviness against her legs. The lid resisted being lifted off at first, sealed by a weak vacuum, but she jiggled it around until it released its hold, and then put it on the floor under her chair.

Inside were dozens of small bundles, each wrapped neatly in its own coat of white tissue. She lifted one out, weighing it her palm for a few seconds before carefully unfurling the paper, unfolding it over and over until it finally surrendered its treasure, a grey, kidney-shaped pebble, cut by a zebra-stripe of white quartz.

She slipped it out of its paper and wrapped her fingers around it, stroking its rounded perfection with the flat of her thumb. Opening her hand out again, she caught a nip of its scent, concentrated: a dark, salty mineral smell, which she knew would hang on her skin all night. She placed the stone back in its wrapper, moulding the paper around the cold, hard form, and then rolled it back up to create a thick, white duvet around it.

Placing it in the lid of her box, she unwrapped another: a flat, black slate with an oily sheen, its edges bevelled to reveal its thin layers. This one seemed to have a warmth of its own, and her eyes drank in its fluid colour, but it was angular and awkward in her hand. She wrapped it back up again, taking pleasure in creasing the tissue around its sharp edges. She wished, as she had many times before, that she had developed some kind of a system for recording where she had found each of these objects. It seemed too late to start one now. The third wrapper held a diamond of worn brick, pale pink and pock-marked. In the next, a frilled oyster shell, golden and nacreous on the inside. She continued through the box in a trance (a lump of chalk with a configuration of deep holes that made it look like a face; an ammonite fossil that she'd bought from a market stall one Sunday morning; a tall whelk shell, with one side broken away to reveal a spiral twist on the inside), enjoying the unsteady rhythm of unwrapping, holding, turning over, wrapping again, until the box was empty.

Her gathering of stones had graduated from the little pocketfuls of pebbles that used to cluster around her bedroom, to become a formal collection, a kind of record of her life that needed to be boxed, arranged and stored in a facility like this. She certainly didn't have the room for them at home, but more than that, she felt slightly furtive about her stones, slightly ashamed of the obsessiveness that prevented her from throwing them away. She would have hated her cleaner to come across them.

Finding stones was never something she intended to do, but she had ways of tricking herself into expeditions for them: a shortcut through a building site whose soil had been freshly turned over, or a trip to a shop so near to the Thames that it was a shame not to wander along its banks. No matter how much she pretended to herself that she didn't go out looking for them, she could never bring herself to throw them away. Each stone represented a unit of imagination for Violet, a spark of fantasy that had ignited in her mind when she first spotted it. She had stones in her collection that looked like things (a smooth seal, a heart) and stones triggered different instincts, a love of colour or weight or texture, an appreciation of weight or lightness.

Of course, her collection had changed over the years, as the trips to the seaside that made today's box possible petered out. Nowadays, she had to settle for the London equivalent of the sea-worn stones and shells that had been her starting point. There were stones in London, but they tended to be pieces of concrete and mortar; the more interesting finds in the city arose from the spoils of human occupation. Her most recent box contained a marble, a shard of willow-patterned china and a length of copper pipe, oxidised to a startling sea green. Each of these carried an extra association to their beauty, having once been touched by human hands in some way, and perhaps even owned, loved, cherished. She loved to hold her London stones and imagine their history, the tales that surrounded them, the people that had owned them. Some of her objects would have been lost accidentally, falling out of pockets and bags, and therefore lamented, whilst others would have been deliberately mislaid or cast out, perhaps in sorrow or anger. She had once found an emerald engagement ring in a gutter near Regent's Park, but she had left that one, feeling it to be beyond the scope of her collection.

Her eyes stung and her fingers were stiff from the cold room. It was getting late – too late for another box tonight. She eased the lid back on today's selection (May - August 2001), and replaced it back in its chronological order on the shelf. Next, she dialled the number of the only taxi firm that she knew in the area. *Twenty minutes,* she was told. Violet sighed and said she would wait for it, her hand already reaching for the next box.

FIVE

The staff at Newhouse Image were unusually solicitous today, slowing by Violet's desk every time they passed to cock their heads in mock-concern and ask her if she was alright. It was clearly understood that this was not an expression of actual worry, but rather an expression of noticing, a means of relaying to the whole of the prick-eared office that Violet was off-task.

This was not for want of trying on Violet's part. Whatever task she began, whether it was replying to her small list of emails, or scrolling through her budget spreadsheet in search of adjustments to make, she would always realise, five minutes later, that she was picking at her nails or staring into space.

This morning, after waking every hour throughout the night with her heart fluttering and the breath shallow in her lungs, her journey to work had seemed strangely unfamiliar. The doors of the tube had stopped three feet away from where she had stood in anticipation of their opening, and later she had found herself disoriented by the bright lights and the winding passages of Bank; routes that she took every day without thinking were newly mysterious to her, and she was almost knocked over by a slick-haired city boy as she stopped to read a map at the junction between two corridors.

On the train, she felt a queasy mix of sleepiness and panic, so that her eyelids would draw together every few minutes, and the grainy dreams that she had been having all night would creep in again. She would lose herself in these for a few moments – these visions of the girl infiltrating every place she knew, sitting at Violet's desk in her office, reclining magisterially across the Italian leather couch in the lobby of her apartments, lying next to her in her bed, sitting opposite her, now, in the tube – before dispelling them with a jerk, terrified that she might have slept too long and missed her stop.

Her inattention, however subtle, was clearly creating something of a stir, or so she was forced to conclude from the sheer number of people who had found a reason to walk past her cubicle this morning. She began to wonder whether she had been the subject of an email that drew everyone's attention to her slightly dazed state. In her less rational moments, she feared a darker conspiracy was at play, that perhaps she was inadvertently broadcasting her own confusion and distress, and that the others were catching the scent of it, and swarming like wasps over weakened prey. Either way, she realised that this must be some kind of a sensation, the idea that she was showing a crack in her ambitious, busy façade. They must be sensing an advantage already; it didn't take much encouragement. She thought of how she herself had seized on the news of pregnancies, illnesses and divorces in the past, how her first consideration had always been of how she could turn things in her favour, and she felt dizzy.

She was hungry, thirsty, tired – that was all. She could remedy this weird malaise, this sagging of the soul; it just took concentration, will, obedience. She must apply herself to her work, battle through it; the mists would clear once she settled her mind to a task. She picked up the phone to call the marketing manager of their smallest client. Just a courtesy call, to check how things were progressing, to make sure all parties were happy with the current levels of provision. She was on top of things. Ultra-efficient.

A face appeared over the unsteady wall of her cubicle, accompanied by a tentative, sing-song voice.

"You alright?"

The work experience girl, whose name Violet could never remember, smiled with all her teeth, and edged around to Violet's side. "I got you a nice cuppa," she said, and set it delicately down by Violet's mouse, as if she would be startled by too great a noise. "I thought you could do with a bit of this as well." She placed a small yellow spray-bottle by the tea. "It always sorts me out when I'm flagging."

Violet gazed at this patronising act of invasion. "Rescue Remedy?" she said, hoping, but clearly failing, to denote some level of disgust.

"Yeah, you spray it under your tongue. It helps with, like, stress and stuff."

"I'll do without it, thanks." She wanted to say, *How dare you stand here and diagnose me with stress? How dare you appear at my desk and offer me consolation as if I need it?* Instead, she pushed the bottle back towards the girl, and, after looking into the cup, pushed this away as well. "I don't drink anything with caffeine in it. Or cow's milk. Sorry."

"Oh," said the girl, continuing to hover at Violet's side as if she were expecting a special exemption.

"I'm sure Marcus will drink it. If he's not busy. You can earn brownie points with him instead." She gave the girl a significant glance. The bottle and mug were removed in silence.

It was only 11.45, but she could wait no longer. It must be hunger that was doing this to her. She prised open the plastic lid of her prepared lunch, unfolded her napkin and tried to drum up the motivation to eat any of the tofu salad that awaited her, a damp tangle of shoots, buckwheat noodles and sesame seeds surrounded by shreds of glassy mooli.

Violet's meals were delivered daily by a company called *relish!* Every morning at six, or eight at weekends, three meals would be delivered to her door on the kind of segregated plastic trays that airlines use. *Relish!* undertook to care for Violet's every nutritional need: her meals were perfectly balanced and calorie-counted. They were organic, free of wheat, dairy, processed sugar and salt, low in saturated fat, and designed to fit in with her busy lifestyle. There was no need for Violet to do a thing, other than eat them.

She split in half the disposable chopsticks that were taped to the lid of the box and shunted the salad around its tray, before opening the next box and doing the same with the clump of soggy spinach that she found there. There was nothing about this meal that appealed to her; in fact, the thought of its insubstantial wetness in her mouth made her stomach lurch.

A flush of fever passed over her. She needed to eat something; she had read all about the importance blood sugar levels. Perhaps she was hypoglycaemic.

She looked at the salad again, and still couldn't bear to eat it. She could already taste the grainy noodles, the soft, bland tofu, the chlorophyll bitterness of the spinach. Her mind was filled, as it often was, with images of other, forbidden dishes, things she had eaten as a child: spaghetti bolognese, roast potatoes, hot buttered toast. She could almost taste their richness, their fullness; her mouth watered at the prospect of its own satisfaction. She must resist them, as she always did. What was the point of taking such care over her diet if she faltered whenever she got a bit tired? This was the time when she needed *relish!* the most. She imagined her longings for unhealthy food as the little devil on her shoulder that could be repelled by a single mouthful from a well-constructed, nutritious menu.

And yet the thought of the meal in front of her was now unbearable. She stacked the two cartons of food inside each other, wrapped them in their plastic bag and threw them in the bin. The work experience girl leaned over the partition between their desks and said, "Not hungry?"

"No," said Violet, "I've decided to go for a walk."

SIX

Piccadilly Circus at lunchtime was intimidating and alien, full of people that Violet did not recognise or understand. Without the wilful flow of the crowd of commuters that surged through it in the mornings and evenings, it felt sordid and empty, risky somehow. People milled around the streets listlessly, examining maps or watching the whirling lights on the billboards. Violet had long ago stopped noticing the illuminated signs that hung above the square, but today they seemed to attract her attention, bullying her into noticing their pulsating messages.

She wondered if this was their vision of London, these strangers; whether it was any more to them than the tawdry glitz of Piccadilly Circus, the fixed smiles of Madame Tussaud's, the cheap leather in Camden market.

Groups of golden-skinned lads lounged against the lamp-posts in loose-haired clusters, their clothes too colourful, their lack of anything pressing to do too obvious. They scuffled and laughed, feigned obliviousness to the drab natives and called out to girls across the street who were also tourists, flagged up by their neat backpacks and the way that they walked, their heads up, ready to meet the eye of anyone who tried to meet theirs.

Their lack of anonymity infuriated Violet. They didn't seem to care whether or not they were identified as tourists. It was if they had their own little dimension of London, something exclusively theirs. How did they get the right?

It had taken Violet years to feel this comfortable, and still she shied away from these gregarious displays lassitude and otherness.

She found herself angry as she followed a giggling pair of Japanese girls down the street. They lingered at the windows of tourist shops (*House of Cashmere, Glorious London!*) carrying Fortnum and Mason's bags filled with pale turquoise boxes of tea. They chattered, laughed, pointed openly at the statue of Eros; when a worker in a suit collided with them they apologised in English, and then chattered excitedly in Japanese about the experience.

Everywhere she walked, people got too close. In the routine flow of commuter bodies, Violet never minded this; there was a kind of trust between her and her fellow travellers. They were honest people, or at the very least were seeking greater fortunes than Violet could offer them. But here, at midday, she trusted no-one. People pushed past her to make faster progress along the street, or simply failed to follow a straight course, swerving across the pavement to bump into her sideways, setting her off balance.

She had heard things about the pickpockets around here. One of her colleagues had gone for lunch with a client a couple of months back and found that his wallet had vanished from his pocket by the time he got to the restaurant; the admin girls, too, abounded with stories of mobile phone snatches, bags that vanished from under toilet cubicles and knifepoint muggings in broad daylight. She pulled her handbag up to her chest, stuffed her scarf in above the contents and fastened the zip over the top of it. Still she worried about creeping fingers that could enter, invisibly, and frisk the contents. It would only take a few seconds, she knew, and there were so many things to divert her attention.

She glanced into the shops on Piccadilly as she passed, taking in high piles of pastel-coloured macaroons, Japanese confectionary in the shape of rosy peaches, vast Persian rugs and displays of country tweed. After the Ritz, the street opened up, and she saw the black railings of Green Park. She crossed the road and walked through the gates.

She had only been there once before, when she was new to the company and had so little to do that it was impossible to even fake working through her lunch hour. At the time, she had been excited by the proximity of London; she vowed to herself that she would make the most of it, book weekly visits to the theatre, catch all the latest exhibitions, spend her weekends drinking coffee in chic cafés and trawling the antiques markets. When she got back to the office, Marcus had laughed at her and said, "An hour for lunch? You'll be joining a union next!" Violet took lunch at her desk after that.

That day was early September, and the park had been full of people enjoying the late summer sun. Today, the great expanse of grass that stretched before her was drenched in winter mist, as if the pure white sky had fallen a little to obscure it. Here and there, the whiteness was broken by the black crag of a bare tree, but even these were muted, their starkness faded to grey in the near distance, so that they looked as though they were being erased.

Few people went to the park on a day like this, and the temperature seemed to drop a few degrees as soon as Violet entered, lacking the busy heat of the bodies collected on the streets.

She wondered if she should take a walk around the perimeter, to exercise away the spell that hung over her like the freezing mists around the park, but the thought of reaching the Buckingham Palace crowds at the other side horrified her. Instead, she followed the path into the centre of the park, where it felt darker, deeper, with knobbly trees and a tall Victorian lamp post fighting against the gloom. Here, she located a thickly-painted bench by the path, but found that it was damp from yesterday's rain, so she took her newspaper out of her handbag, unfolded it, placed it on the seat and sat down. By her feet was a puddle that had frozen over; she cracked its surface with the toe of her shoe, breaking up the crust of ice until its fragments bobbed on the surface of the water below it. A crow strutted past, picking disconsolately at the grass.

The air in Green Park was still and thick, and stung Violet's lips and cheeks. It had a deadening effect on the world around it: although only a few metres away, she could barely hear anything of the crowds in Piccadilly, and the contrast was so great that it made her ears ring.

Afraid of what the back of the bench would do to her coat if she leant against it, she hunched forward, her elbows on her knees and her chin in her hands. Her face was numb with the cold, but it suited her to make believe that she was entirely frozen, that she didn't have to move or be animated in any way. Often, when she arrived home at night, the thing that she relished the most was the opportunity to wash off her make-up, and to imagine that all the fixed expressions of the day washed off with it, leaving a perfectly blank face. This was how she felt now, in the park. The mist offered a veil of anonymity, under which she could surrender, if only for a few moments, her public façade.

Every now and then, a figure would emerge from the mist and follow the path past her, black, ghostly. It seemed to Violet that they materialised from nowhere, that they stepped into her field of vision from behind a white curtain, and then simply faded away once they had passed her. She scrutinised their faces, trying to make out who they were, where they might have come from, where they might be going, but they all looked the same: smart, drab, genderless but for the shape of their shoes, wrapped up in hats and scarves that covered their faces; they bent their heads towards the pavement as they marched past her.

Violet pulled her own scarf tighter around her face. She wasn't dressed for the cold weather; she was used to the temperate climate of the office. Sitting here, utterly still in the freezing air, she felt colder than she had felt for a long time. She shuddered rather than shivered: big, hungry jolts seized her body, trying to cast out the cold that was creeping into her core. It made her smile to feel like this, to surrender to her body's impulses. The winter had seemed so far away from her until today, yet now, here she was, so cold that she was shaking.

She got up, stamped her feet on the hardened grass, let her lips chatter together. She forced her breath out through them so that she could hear how cold she was: *brrrrrrr*, she said, and felt the icy air deaden it.

And then, quite suddenly, there was a rush to her head, and then a bigger one, as if all the blood in her body had suddenly charged into her skull and was hanging there, making her ears boom and her eyes cloud with colour. For a few seconds, she was somewhere else – a classroom, watching a teacher draw equations on a whiteboard. She could see her own hands in front of her, laid across the table, a black biro resting between two of her fingers; but more than that, she could smell the musty school air, feel the ache of her elbows against a hard table, taste the obliterating cleanness of gum; she could feel what it was like to breathe there, in that room…

It was as if someone had kicked her knees from under her. She realised that she was falling and grabbed for the bench, holding on to its slatted back as she steadied herself. She inhaled deeply, trying to dispel the misshapen dots that floated before her eyes, and slowly they settled back into the space beyond her vision, like snow.

SEVEN

The hot chocolate, she told herself, was to warm up, and the chicken club sandwich was to get her blood sugar levels back to normal as soon as possible.

Even with this justification, she felt guilty eating it, and even worse for enjoying it. Her tongue seemed to buzz with pleasure at every taste: the oily, lemony mayonnaise, the salty bacon, the juicy chicken. It was gone so quickly; she rounded up a dollop of mayonnaise onto her finger and licked it off. She should, she supposed, have gone for a camomile tea and box of sushi, but then she couldn't be held accountable for what she chose when she was still woozy from her faint.

She crushed the box that the sandwich had come in, blew her nose on the paper napkin and took a slug of the hot chocolate. It was colder that it should have been, and there was little to it once she had got past the foamed milk on the top, but it was deeply soothing.

The café was hot and damp with the breath of too many customers; the windows were clouded with condensation. The man on the table next to her was doodling in it, stamping out baby's footprints with the side of his fist and the tips of his fingers, and drawing little smiley faces whose features drooled away horrifically within seconds of their creation.

Violet traced her finger around the rim of her paper cup, and gazed about her. What had happened back then? Was it simply the case that she had got too cold, that she wasn't used to being out in the weather? That a poor night's sleep and an empty stomach had caught up with her?

It made perfect sense that this would be the case. She was relentlessly, obsessively careful about her diet, and she had broken her own rules that day, rejecting the food that she knew was scientifically designed to do her good. She always took comfort in the efficient paternalism of *relish!*, the thought of placing her dietary needs into the hands of people more expert than she. There was an edge of discipline to her *relish!* subscription; they couldn't be held responsible if she didn't eat exactly what they told her to, in the order stipulated. Now, she felt like a guilty teenager who had disobeyed her parents despite their having her best wishes at heart.

And yet, and yet. Was that all there was to it? Was her body really so weak, so maladjusted, that her delaying lunch by half an hour would have such an impact on it? Was it really the case that a disrupted night's sleep could throw her into such turmoil? It seemed to Violet that this would have been quite commonplace behaviour for her as a teenager; could it really be that now, a couple of years short of thirty, she was unable to cope with even the smallest breach of her routine?

It was more than this; she knew it. Since seeing the girl...

But there was no girl. This was the trick that her mind was playing on her. People don't have doubles wandering around their hometown. The girl was a symptom of a deeper problem; she was Scrooge's undigested bit of beef, an Old Marley waving his chains, a ghost of winters past.

And the vision she'd had, back then in the park, was so real. She had felt utterly present in that room; it was as though she had experienced it rather than imagined it. Was this what mental illness feels like, when it arrives? This sudden blurring of the real and the imagined? These little states of fugue during which you are pulled into your internal world without a hint of warning?

But perhaps madness was too grand an explanation and besides, Violet was inclined to think that if she was really mad, she wouldn't be wondering about it, or even aware of the contrast between normality and the realm of her imagination.

No, she was tired, that was all. She had been tired for a long, long time. The diet, the vitamins, the nightly trips to the gym – none of them ever seemed to tackle it, that ache at the edges of her flesh, the heaviness in her legs, the endless longing for rest and comfort. She sometimes felt pursued by her own weariness, as if her days were filled with a series of strategies to stay awake, to keep going. She dreamed, sometimes, of a dark figure that chased her through the old East London streets, past the derelict warehouses and the monstrous wharves, getting closer and closer until it caught her and smothered her in its black cloak. On those mornings, when she awoke, she would have to struggle awake from under a thick blanket of sleep, as if she were swimming to the surface from deep, deep under the sea.

But what choice did she have? Everyone else seemed to cope. She swallowed the powdery dregs of her hot chocolate, picked up her bag and made her way back to the office.

EIGHT

She caught a taxi home that night. Walking up the steps of her apartment block, she paused for a few moments, one hand on the polished stair rail, looking into the marble lobby. It was all so sparse, so empty, so pristine; it seemed impossible that any human being had ever walked across it before. She could feel icy drops of rain pricking at her bare hands, but she had no desire to go inside. Until now, she had always simply marched through the lobby and into the lift without a second thought, but tonight it seemed to repel her with its coldness, its grandeur.

She remembered being impressed by this when she bought the flat. The estate agent, a woman of about forty, whose immaculate red court shoes and bobbing red hair made her look like an air hostess, had insisted on meeting her here, so that she could gaze about the room in mock awe and say, 'Impressive, isn't it?'

When Violet had nodded, her eyes so drawn to the enormous chandelier that dominated the space that she feared she might become entangled in it, the woman had added, in a conspiratorial whisper that was concealed from no-one behind her clip-board, 'The people who live here tend to receive guests down here, and then go straight to one of the local bars. Gives an excellent impression. There's even a concierge.'

The concierge. He would of course be watching her now from the bank of screens by his desk, as she stood and dithered on the front steps. Moments from now, he would be racing officiously to the door to let her in, assuming she had forgotten her key-card, or worse, seeing this momentary loss of nerve for exactly what it was, and offering moral support. Violet couldn't afford for that to happen. She fumbled in her bag, pressed her card up against the sensor, and the doors glided open. She was met by a rush of warm air, the heavy scent of the stargazer lilies that flared in a vase by the door, and the concierge, a soft-faced man of about sixty whose job, as far as Violet could make out, was to greet all the residents as they came home from work. A different man was employed to smile to them on their way to work in the mornings. For this service, for this tiny spark of human contact twice a day, Violet paid an exorbitant fee to the landlord, and was happy to do so.

"Good evening, Ms Andersen," he said, touching the shiny visor of his cap in a pastiche of deference. Like most nights of her life, Violet wished that she had never corrected him when he'd called her *Miss*, a month after she moved in. Back then, he had looked startled and confused by it, befuddled that his mannerly greeting could be somehow offensive. He was still awkward with it now, pronouncing it slowly and deliberately, elongating the 'z' sound at the end so that it became *Muzz*. He always looked pleased after he'd said it, as if he'd conquered some linguistic obstacle, but to Violet it now seemed to emphasise her marital status, rather than to render it inscrutable. She would happily have returned to *Miss* if she didn't think she would be stuck with it for the rest of her life. *Ms*, she told herself, would be much more suitable when she was fifty. It wouldn't sound so much like a maiden aunt.

She nodded to him, and said good evening. She wondered if she should say more, whether she was expected to extend the conversation. He had, after all, just watched her standing in the rain rather than entering the building.

"I thought I'd left something in the taxi a moment ago," she said, and laughed. "But then I realised I hadn't."

The concierge nodded, smiled awkwardly. "Happens to the best of us," he said.

"Must be getting old!" said Violet, and then felt embarrassed that she'd said this to a man who was clearly at least double her age. She laughed a little too much, and then turned cheerfully on her heels, calling, "Goodnight!" over her shoulder. Crossing the great expanse of the lobby, her shoes clip-clopping on the marble tiles, she felt intensely self-conscious, knowing that the concierge would be watching her.

It often seemed to Violet that she had left one life behind in which men like the concierge were uncles, neighbours and family friends, and had found herself in another life in which she was suddenly supposed to act as their superior. Surely they could see through it? There had been a time when she had gone to great lengths to befriend these people on the margins of her life: the lady that cleaned her office in the evening, the company receptionist, the man at the newspaper kiosk that she stopped at every morning. After a while, though, it became clear that they did not want her attentions; try as she might to be breezily friendly, her actions were interpreted as a condescension, an invasion into the time and space of people who simply were not interested in her type.

Nowadays, she had developed a mantra to get herself through the one hundred minor interactions of her day: *you can't be friends with everyone.* She was never certain that she quite believed this, but still she repeated it as she made her way to the lift. As the doors drew together, she caught sight of the concierge through their narrowing gap, watching her from his desk with a look of benign curiosity, much as one would examine an exhibit in a museum.

She was delivered into a corridor, her own corridor, which never seemed to become quite familiar to her, with its pervading smell of stale air and over-zealous cleaning. It was long, straight and uniform, broken only by heavy fire doors at regular intervals and lined with cream front doors. Each one was identical, save its number, which was nevertheless fashioned from the same brass characters as all the other doors, and was coated in a smooth laminate, rather than painted. Her front door, she had been informed in a list of regulations that was in her mailbox when she first arrived, did not belong to her, but to the landlord. She was therefore forbidden to customise it in any way; nor was she to inflict her character on the corridor by adding a welcome mat, a pot plant, or any other object. This, she was informed, would not only disrupt the building's corporate image, but would also represent a substantial hazard for the cleaning staff. Violet, and clearly every other resident, had obeyed.

Once inside, she swallowed two Nurofen. She had begun to take these regularly now for the headache that was continually boiling under the surface of her neck and her temples; she had given up waiting for the pain to break out, and now instead took them as a preventative measure, like vitamins. It seemed to her now that headaches were simply caused by ibuprofen deficiency, and that it was therefore her responsibility to keep topped up. Lately, she had begun to get headaches despite the Nurofen; she wondered if she should change brand.

Then she swallowed her real vitamins and supplements: five tablets before supper, six after. She mentally rehearsed their benefits, one by one like a catechism, as they went down: B-complex for nervous functioning, ginseng for concentration, ester-C and zinc to ward off colds, echinacea for the immune system, omega oils for brain health. She tried to visualise the effect of each as she took them; every one represented a fear of hers: sickness, ageing, stupidity.

She prised the lid off this evening's plastic tray of food and surveyed the contents. A fillet of salmon on a bed of spinach, a bowl of brown rice and a plate of sliced mango and papaya, with a wedge of lime for her to squeeze over it. The salmon and the rice both had labels on them asking her to reheat them, so she put them in the microwave, one by one and watched the seconds count down. It was a slow, hypnotic process; each beat of the timer was long enough for her to feel as though the clock had stopped altogether. It amazed her just how many thoughts she could have between two seconds, so much so that she felt as though she were inhabiting the spaces between them. Why am I always so tired? Why am I always so hungry?

She began to pick at the thin slices of mango. They were slippery between her fingers, so she had to tip her head back to drop them into her mouth like wriggling fish. They were sweet, cold from the fridge, and tasted of the summer, but they did nothing to sate her hunger. Her stomach felt so intensely empty that she could imagine these fine shards of fruit fizzing into nothingness as soon as she swallowed them. She gazed around the room. Her life, in the rare times that she was home, consisted of little more than a set of infinitives, the building blocks of survival: to sleep, to sit, to wash, to eat. This pristine flat, maintained by paid labourers whom she never met, offered up little true comfort at moments like this.

As it always was when she laid out her cutlery and napkin that the delivery boy provided every day, her head was teeming with thoughts, only tonight they were different from the bullying to-do list that usually presided over her consciousness. They were heavier, slower somehow; they flung out like a web over her mind so that she couldn't peep past them, and each strand spiralled back to a one, central thought: the girl.

Yesterday, back in Stonehithe, it had all seemed possible. It was a changed world down there, with the snow shrouding the gardens and the unmediated light of the sea sparkling through the windows. She had been able to conceive of a world in which an imprint of herself could exist down there, a carbon copy that had peeled away from her when she moved to London, and who was continuing to live her old life, unchanged. In the spare, rational capital, she could see that it had all been an illusion.

Perhaps this was the burn-out, or at least a warning sign. She stretched her fingers out over the polished wood of her table and stared at the network of tiny lines that were already printing themselves over the backs of her hands. I'll try get more fresh air, see more daylight; maybe join a yoga class.

She went to the bathroom cabinet, found her box of Melatonin and swallowed two of them, fighting back the minute lurch of guilt by telling herself that these weren't sleeping pills in the traditional sense, seeing as they replicated a chemical that already occurred in her body, they were practically a natural remedy. They were not like the bad old sleeping pills that formed addictions and knocked you unconscious. She was certainly not an addict; she would simply stop taking them as soon as she got through this difficult period in her life.

She brushed her teeth, changed into her pyjamas, and turned on her computer to check the day's emails, just while she waited for them to set in.

Ladies and Gentlemen: the inheritors of the free world!

Marvel at these chosen ones, these golden boys and girls who hold our beloved planet in the palms of their lily-white hands! These, my friends, are the famed one per cent, who divide between them the other ninety-nine per cent's share. These are the wealthy, the powerful, our feted Ruling Class.

Gather round, gather round (no pushing at the back!) to see this specimen, a case-study if you will, who illustrates the magnificence of the twenty-first century human, for your delectation and pleasure. Take a good look: observe her habitats, her rituals, her choices, tastes and preferences.

No drudge, she! The alpha of the species no longer has to concern herself with the mechanics of living. See how she glides through her life in an attitude of calm control, knowing that her each and every need is met! Imagine the ease, the grace of an existence in which one could get on with the finer things in life, safe in the knowledge that money does indeed buy you comfort and happiness! My friends, you may forgive yourselves for feeling a little envy; better men have turned green with it. For here, laid out before your very eyes, is the sum total of human endeavour; here, is the apex, yes, the very pinnacle of our existence!

Is there anyone reading this who believes that? Is there anyone who feels the most remote twinge of longing for the life we have just seen? It's perfect, isn't it – the aspirational job and the aspirational flat and the aspirational wage packet, but then, perfection is what we always think we want.

But – oh! – when we get it, how empty it is! How bland! How lonely! There's so far to fall from that little pedestal that Violet's put herself on that she hardly dares to shuffle two inches for fear of looking into the void.

We all dream of a life without chores, a life in which all your cleaning is done for you, your washing returns miraculously folded and ironed from the laundry basket, and your cupboards are magically replenished with loo roll and soap and all the other nasty little things that are no fun. Who would choose to cook, if someone else would do a better job for them; in fact, who wants to do all that nasty thinking about it either, the tiresome regulation of one's diet and the dull scanning of ones taste buds each night to decide what one might fancy?

Not Violet, that's for sure! She pays good money for the entitlement to have her mind clear of such matters. She knows that she can return home each night to a hoovered flat, fresh flowers, a meal, and a stock of expensive bubble bath to ease her aching limbs. The smallest need, the slightest whim, and she can pick up her phone (sanitised weekly by her cleaner) and dial one of a number companies around London who are only too happy to relieve her of her money. Were it not for brutal, tiresome work, she would not have to leave her flat at all. Think of it! Grand and luxurious seclusion, right bang in the centre of one of the greatest capitals of the world!

But there is something that niggles about this. Hard to put one's finger on it, quite. Is it the sense of preciousness, of reliance, that somehow leaves us squirming? There's more than a hint of infantilism in it: the quick and discreet cleaning-up of even our most intimate waste, the passivity of the diet, the patronising tolerance of our little moods and ways. Put aside for a moment the economics of it all, the exploitation of a growing underclass to pander to those with more money than sense; ignore the covert colonialism, the use of migrant workers from the less illustrious parts of the globe to service the Western rich; staunch, even, your ethical qualms about using other people to do the jobs you could very well do yourself, the sense of snobbery embedded in it. All of this is water off a duck's back to a generation who turned a blind eye to their trainers being stitched by child labourers and the run-offs from their shower gel changing the sex of the fish in our rivers. No, it's the ugly uselessness of it, the vile sense of learned helplessness. We are remarkably unconcerned about the fact that some of the most powerful members of our society could not even fry an egg, let alone work out which day to put the bins out.

Hope to God that you never suffer a medical emergency in the vicinity of these people! They would step neatly over your convulsing body, and then pay a boy to clean your spit off their shoes. This is a generation crippled by its own helplessness, reliant on mummy-substitutes to get them through the day. You only have to see them – tucked up in the safe womb-music of their MP3 players, suckling on bottles of water like someone whispered 'weaning' – to know that they're a potty-trained dependency culture. Boo-hoo. I can't cope without someone to wipe my arse.

But whenever I say this, in my speeches and pamphlets, I start to hear nervous shuffling from the back. As feminists, these buff-nailed squirmers say, we defend the right of women to compete with men on an even platform. We must be allowed to make the choices we want! We don't need you to throw us back into domestic servitude!

And there's the rub. The biggest puddle of false-consciousness you're likely to dunk your feet in. For this has nothing to do with choice. If I thought that people like Violet were making active, thought-out choices, then I may not like it, but I would certainly have to lump it.

But this is the death of choice. This is a generation in thrall, a group of youngsters whose pain threshold has got so low that cutting their own toenails makes them wince with discomfort. This is a generation so deadened by the doctrines of capitalism that it can't find its own way home; so helplessly materialistic that it cannot imagine a life in which it doesn't have the money (or the credit) for this week's mobile phone. This is the fruit of a society in which the choices are superficial as the conversations in cocktail bars; of industry that has cranked up the cycles of fashion and obsolescence so that they are all but impossible to keep up with; of a government that tolerates it. These people have never made a choice in their lives. They are drones, drugged by the opiate of the people that has superseded even religion: money.

And it's not the waste or the morality or the exploitation that really bothers me, although they're all appalling. It's the knowledge that we've bred a generation, maybe two or three, who are utterly divorced from the basic processes of living, from eating and drinking and sleeping. These are people who have replaced hunger and thirst with routine, pain with constant analgesia, sexuality with Viagra. I have heard more apocalyptic versions of this argument, that go on to say that, come the floods and earthquakes, the overload power cuts or the terrorist assaults, these would be the first to die, flailing around in their own dirt until their feeble immune systems surrendered.

But it is not that.

Friends, have pity on these people, for they are subject to the deepest, the saddest, the most abject enslavement the world has ever seen. Those in bondages past were held by violence, and so at least retained the power to love, to laugh, to cry. These men and women have not even that. They have only the empty blankness of their subjugated souls for company. They deserve our pity more than our anger. And we must work to free them, one by one.

This is the new revolution: the battle not for our bodies, but for our souls. Everything depends on it. Everything.

NINE

I have my first cup in the morning, as soon as I get up.
The woman's face looked slightly green in the recording, reflecting the damp afternoon light that streamed through the window from her garden.

That goes down pretty quickly, so I have a second one straight away. Once the kids have left for school, I tend to make another one before I start the hoovering. As if to demonstrate her dependence on tea, the woman on the screen raised her cup to her lips and took a deep sip.

"I bet she got those cups out specially for you," said Andrew, leaning back in his chair, "there's no way she drinks from Denbyware cups and saucers every day of the week." He turned to Naomi, the resident researcher, and smirked.

"No, I asked her that later, actually. It's on the interview schedule; yes, here it is: 'What do you tend to drink your tea out of?' She went out to the kitchen and brought her normal mug back to show me."

"Did it have kittens on it?"

"Close. Ducklings. Bone china. Scalloped edges."

"Jesus. Sounds delightful."

"Minimalism hasn't reached Stonehithe yet," said Violet, keen to cash in on her martyred authority on the place, if nothing else to join in the laughter. "Or, indeed, good taste. Look at those fucking dolls."

The assembled cast of researchers and account executives shifted in their seats and strained their eyes into the dark screen to see a cabinet of china dolls lurking in the background, all pale faces and wide eyes.

"Terrifying," said Annie with an exaggerated shudder. "It's a wonder she doesn't have nightmares."

"That's nothing. I used her loo at the end of the interview, and there was this host of stuffed animals lined up on the windowsill, staring at me." Naomi was already rising to meet the mood of the room, as she always did, casting off her researcher's objectivity as soon as she considered it safe to sell her subjects down the river. Violet was always secretly appalled at this, although she was also falling in with the growing sense of hilarity, despite her sympathy for this quiet, helpful woman. She had to watch her back.

"Oh, this is classic," Andrew was saying, stretching his hands across the desk and leaning in to capture his audience. "It's like the land of the dead. Did she have one of those signs on the door that tells you not to piss on the floor? 'I aim to please; you aim too, please'? My childminder used to have one of those." Violet remembered the same sign on her aunt's door, but laughed along anyway. This was fine. She was coping.

"No," said Naomi, "but she did make me take my shoes off at the front door to protect the new carpet."

"Oh, the smallness of it all!" Andrew was almost shouting now. Violet knew from experience that he was probably angrier than he was letting on. "I didn't think they even sold carpet anymore."

I have lunch at about twelve, the woman was saying, *and I have another one before I start off again. How many's that already? Six? Golly, I didn't realise I was such an addict!*

"How precious! Perhaps we should consider calling social services. Can't ignore an addiction like that, not with the children to consider." He affected the quivering voice of a Dickensian vagrant. "I'm sorry yer honour, I didn't mean

54

to squander the 'ousekeeping. It's just the tea, you see. Makes me act like a wild woman!"

"Don't laugh," said Annie, "You need something to keep you going when you've got kids. I was up three times in the night for various things." Silence fell around the table as everyone tried to avoid her gaze. The woman's voice filled the room. *I try not to drink it after nine at night. I had a bit of... well, I was having trouble sleeping a few years back, so I cut down on the caffeine. I tried the decaf once, but I found they had a funny taste, and I couldn't get on with the herbal ones either. Camomile I tried, but it tasted peculiar to me. Nowadays I have a cup of cocoa before bed. Gets me nice and sleepy. It's a devil to keep washing the pan for the milk, though.*

"MICROWAVE," boomed Andrew. "Has she never heard of a microwave? I expect she's still boiling the kettle over a bloody fire." It was getting tiring to find enough mockery to fire against this woman. Violet could see that she had turned herself out neatly for the interview, with an ironed blouse and a dab of lipstick, and that she was nervous of the camera, choosing her words with great care, and not so much shaking as discreetly vibrating, her movements betraying a whipped-up mobility.

Naomi reached to the centre of the table to pour coffee from the white plastic flask and bit into a chocolate biscuit. Violet tried to repress the thought that ran: *This is why you are out doing interviews and I'm commissioning them. I have more restraint.* "She likes the product, though. Watch this."

They watched in fast-forward as Naomi passed the woman a paper packet. The film jolted and lurched into real time, as the wrapper was torn off and placed neatly on the table, and the woman turned something in her hands, a small, baggy sachet. *Oh*, she said, *oh yes, I do like this. How sweet!*

"The maquettes look good," said Violet, "that's that first time I saw them."

"Obviously they're a fucking nightmare to manufacture," said Andrew, "but we can go for a premium price here."

The idea behind the heart-shaped teabag, Naomi was saying on the film, *is that it allows the water to circulate more freely, giving you a richer, fuller-flavoured brew.* The word 'brew' sounded artificial coming from her mouth, her clipped diction straining around it. Violet watched the woman studying the diagram that had been propped in front of her, her eyes following the arrows that described eddies inside the two arches at the top of the heart.

"You've swallowed that tagline whole, Omi. Well done. Violet, did we check up on the legality of our spurious scientific claims there?"

"Oh, yes," said Violet, who had checked nothing. "Legal will basically have to vet any claim individually, but the idea is to use language that isn't specifically scientific. Face creams have been getting away with it for years,"

"Of course."

"I wonder if the scientific claims are really the thing anyway."

"Meaning what?"

"Well, I think our brand appeal lies in the feelings of warmth and cosiness, rather than technical delivery. Our core customer's the kind of person – like this woman – who goes for cuteness over all else. Our profile is female, middle-aged, lower middle class, kids, pets, and time on her hands to care what shape a teabag is. She might also buy other products like aloe vera loo roll or scented bin bags; she represents the group that are susceptible to limited editions and novelties – Christmas pudding scented bleach or whatever. She's not going to care about the science."

"I don't know," said Andrew, "she's clearly responding to the diagram in the video."

"She'd respond to anything. She's trying to please us."

"Well," said Naomi, "perhaps we should test that at the next round of research. Once we have a name."

"I've given that some thought, actually," said Violet. This was a lie; she had entirely forgotten the ridiculous teabags until the film started playing, but plucking the first thought from her head at this moment seemed to be a reasonable defence against the blunt-headed idiocy of the previous day. "I was thinking we should just call them 'home'. Small 'h': keep the old biddies thinking they're trendy. But totally responding to their cosy values. Teaser advertising campaign, posters with 'heart is where the home is'. Browns, oranges, maroons, dark turquoise. If we can get them to find a way of making a decaf that isn't actively disgusting, that could be a selling point. Free sample on the front of Take a Break. Maybe some sort of built-in donation to a charity with every purchase: dogs, children, nothing international. No-brainer."

"Violet," said Andrew after a moment's silence, "my faith in you is restored."

TEN

Violet was still slightly reeling from this comment by the time she left the meetings room. The fact that Andrew had noticed her being off-colour was bad enough, but it infuriated her that he had felt the need to make this fact so plain to her. She worried about Andrew, his easy cockiness and sense of unquestioning entitlement. He had only joined the company last year as a graduate, but lately, he had dropped the act of respect and reverence that he used to roll out in her presence, and had instead begun talking to her as an equal; within each chummy interaction was hidden a bullying, challenging imperative, an ill-concealed desire to knock her from her pedestal, and take his place beside, or even above, her. She wondered, realistically, how long she could hold him back. He was like a force of pure ambition, pure will to power, and she mostly doubted that she had the energy to continually suppress it.

She found Marcus hovering over her desk, scribbling a note in his ratty handwriting on the back of a letter.

"Unlike you to leave notes, Marcus."

"Oh, um, Violet, good. I was hoping to catch you."

"Anything important?"

"Um, well, maybe we can have a quick word in my office?"

It was the sort of request that might be calculated to make anyone anxious, but which made Violet light-headed today. Marcus straightened and hitched up his trousers, an action he repeated at least a hundred times a day. He seemed nervous about making this request; he watched Violet unsteadily, shifting his weight from foot to foot, as if there was any possibility that she could say, *No, I refuse to have a word with you in your office. Go away.*

Instead, she nodded and walked past him to his glass-walled room, with its obscuring clumps of high ferns at the perimeter. These never offered the privacy that Marcus clearly craved, and instead acted as a frame though which Violet and the other employees watched his red face every day, working its way through various states of anxiety, fear and desperation. Even as she followed him now, he was raking his fingers over his pink, bald scalp, in case there was any hair left to rearrange. He always had a hunted look about him, as if, at any point in time, his whole career could end if he stopped pushing himself on just for a few moments. He seemed to feel every fluctuation in the life of their company more intensely than everyone else. Violet had seen him, a number of times, victoriously punch the air over the slightest of successes; on the other hand, he spent most of his time acting as though he was physically threatened by the tiniest problems. 'Shafted' was his favourite word; he used it almost continuously. There were very few situations in which Marcus did not feel – at least potentially – shafted, and he had a way of spitting the word out in pain and disgust, as if he was actually experiencing the sensation of some malevolent force bending him over the desk right then and there, and entering him.

He courteously shut the office door behind them, gestured to a seat where Violet should sit, and eased himself into his own leather chair. Violet waited while he tidied the papers before him, and peered discreetly at his phone to check for messages. He made a tense arch with his fingers in font of his mouth and said, "Um, Violet, now…how are you?"

"Very well thanks. Yourself?"

"Yes very well, but, um, that's not what I meant. How can I put this? I've, er, noticed you looking a little, um, off-form the last couple of days."

"Right."

"I just wondered if there was anything the matter. I ask, of course, not because I'm concerned about your work. Far from it. I just, er…"

"It's fine," said Violet. "It's all over. No longer an issue."

"Ah, I see, well, good. May I enquire?"

"Not really."

"As a friend, you understand, rather than a manager. A colleague."

"I'd rather not discuss it. It won't cause any more problems."

"Only, well, it has rather affected your work in the last day or so." He whispered 'affected your work' in the fearful tone that other people whisper cancer.

"Yes, I apologise for that. It won't happen again."

"No need, no need. It's just that, if I had an idea what it was all about, I could, um, put it into context a little more. For my own peace of mind. I have a duty of care towards you, Violet, as part of the company's HR strategy. As I'm sure you're aware."

Put it into context; more like decide whether it merited a formal warning. Violet was conscious that she could no longer avoid explaining herself to Marcus without sounding shifty. Telling the truth was unthinkable. She scanned her brain for a reasonable excuse, but felt as though the answer that emerged from her mouth had somehow escaped her vetting.

"My Gran died; I didn't want to bother you with it."

"When?" said Marcus, leaning against his desk and furrowing his brow in an attempt to convey sympathy. "You can always confide in me, you know."

"A few days ago," said Violet, staring past him out of the window, hoping that he wouldn't push her for details, and that she would therefore not have to construct an even more elaborate lie.

"When's the funeral? Do you need some time off? There's provision for compassionate leave, you know."

"It's fine. It's at the weekend. It won't affect my work."

"The weekend? You were lucky. When my mother died, they said that they couldn't do weekends."

Violet sniffed, amazed at the ease of her own confabulation. She wondered how long ago it was that Marcus had lost his mother. Was he very young, she wondered? Was this the source of his anxiety, that he was orphaned at a young age, dependent on only his wits to keep himself afloat?

"She was a very devoted churchgoer. The vicar was happy to help."

"I see," he said, and Violet realised that she had probably just slighted him somehow, by implying that his mother wasn't pious enough for a weekend burial, or by insinuating that there were favours that could be drawn upon by those 'in the know', a society to which Marcus had no access.

"It's only right they reward the faithful, I suppose." His voice trailed off, and he fixed his gaze on the same unspecific spot beyond the window that Violet had her eye trained on. Then, with obvious effort, he recovered himself. "Well, if there's anything I can do, just shout, okay? This must be a very distressing time."

"Thanks," said Violet, and got up to leave.

"No wonder you've seemed a bit distant. I thought you might have, er, had enough of us."

"No, nothing that serious." She left the office while Marcus was still in visible conflict as to whether he should laugh off this joke, or defend himself against such a terrible allegation.

When she reached her desk, she dropped down into her chair, and took a deep, long slug of water. She knew that, already, Marcus would be typing a discreet email to warn everyone of her bereavement, asking them to be sensitive. As much as it pained her to be handled with kid gloves in this way, Violet was relieved that this would buy her back some of her dignity. She was determined that she must not slip up again like this.

She straightened her back, smoothed her hair and immediately began to type up her proposals for the home brand strategy. All the while, she felt a bit of the huntedness that she had so often seen in Marcus.

ELEVEN

Violet checked her watch, her alarm clock, and even turned on the television to see the time on breakfast news. He was definitely late. He usually knocked fifteen minutes before now. There was no way she could get to work on time.

She took out her *relish!* customer card and dialled the customer services number. She stared at her watch some more while she waited for someone to answer.

"This is Violet Andersen *again*," she said before the girl at the other end of the line had time to complete her greeting. "I'm still waiting for my food. I need to leave for work in two minutes."

There was a pause as the operative tapped at her keyboard. "Right, Ms. Andersen, I'll just check your details." The thunder of fingers on a keyboard. "It says here that our delivery agent should have been with you at six o'clock this morning."

"I *know* that. That's why I'm calling. He hasn't arrived." Violet paced around the perimeter of the living room, speaking through gritted teeth. Did this woman, this moron, not understand how important this was? She pushed back the blind at her one window, a small oblong about the size of a cereal packet, and glared out at the street below. It was still dark outside, but the pavement bloomed white with frost. "Look, can you call him? And call me back? I can't waste any more time."

She heard the girl say, "Certainly, Ms Andersen," in her mechanical way as she cut off the line. The fact that the girl was clearly reading from a script, that she was some jobbing student who couldn't care less whether or not Violet got her breakfast, was infuriating. The fact that Violet herself advised all her clients to do this, and the fact that she often wrote these chillingly polite scripts herself, was something that she tried not to think about.

At times like this, what she wanted was someone to soothe her, to tell her that it would all be sorted out, to be concerned. What she usually got instead was something that only resembled a conversation; the prompts from which these operatives read never seemed to quite fit the questions that Violet was asking, and the whole experience was profoundly irritating, like some peculiarly modern delay on the line.

Violet slumped down onto the sofa, deciding that she could probably improve herself by watching the news for a few minutes. She flicked onto one of the many news channels that lined up in her cable package, and watched a bombed car burning in a street somewhere far away. She tried to register horror or concern, but she couldn't. The image seemed generic to her, with its billowing fire and crowed of awed onlookers, their faces washed orange by the flames.

She looked at her watch again. Another two minutes had passed. Surely the girl would be calling her back soon. Perhaps she should just leave without breakfast? But that would mean having no lunch, either, and probably no dinner, as she wouldn't be able to put it in the fridge. She would have to wait. It was nearly half past six. She could probably afford another five minutes and still be in the office before eight.

There was no point in panicking. She took a deep, full breath, blowing it slowly out of her nose. This only served to quicken her pulse. "When's he coming?" she growled to herself, aloud. She could feel the tension seeping through her whole body now: her jaw was set and her fingers tingled. She got up to pour herself a glass of water.

There was a clean glass in the dishwasher, and she lifted it out and set it on the top of the microwave. As she turned to get the water out of the fridge, she knocked it with her elbow. The glass teetered, fell onto its side, and then rolled slowly, in an arc, towards the edge; Violet grabbed for it, but she was too late. It fell off the side of the microwave and smashed on the slate tiles.

"Fuck it!" she shouted at the top of her voice, and slammed her hand, flat-palmed, into the door of the fridge, a kind of impotent, painful slap. She kicked out at the shattered glass, sending a shard scuttling under the table, and then leant back against the wall, frustration seeping into her limbs. She could have cried - there were tears ready to come at the backs of her eyes, and her throat was tight in anticipation – but, even alone, she realised that this would be ridiculous. She straightened. This wasn't so bad. She could deal with it. She was an adult; she was too old to cry over broken glass.

She would sweep it up, wrap it in newspaper; that's what you were supposed to do. But with what? She had no cleaning equipment: no dustpan and brush, no broom, no vacuum cleaner. These were all locked away in a cupboard in one of the interminable corridors. There was no newspaper, either; she always left hers on the tube, and her bins were changed every day so there were no empty bags or boxes that she could wrap it in. She scanned the living room for something that she could use, but all she saw were blank, tidy surfaces: a cream sofa with the same mauve scatter cushions that had lain artfully on it when she viewed the flat; her desk with her laptop sitting open on it; her dining table and its solitary chair.

It was as if anyone could live here, that this place was not hers. She had seen this décor - the mushroom walls, the polished wood floor, the curtains that pleated starchily into their valence – in hotel rooms all across the world.

She had pitied Marcus when, a year ago, he told her that he was living in a hotel because his wife had left him. At this moment it seemed that she, too, had submitted to the rigours and routines of hotel life, with the people who silently serviced her room every day while she was out, the concierge greeting her and doffing his cap, the rows and rows of identical doors in the halls. She had even submitted her diet to the whims of a commercial chef, somewhere on an industrial estate south of the M25. And now that this had let her down, she was strangely pathetic in the face of it, strangely unable to imagine how she would achieve three meals today without the neat little package delivered to her door.

She looked at her watch: it was seven o'clock. She shunted the glass into a neat pile with the side of her foot, and dialled *relish!* again. As she leant against the back of the sofa waiting for the girl to pick up, she glanced down and saw a trickle of blood running from a cut on the front of her shin, framed by a large, ragged hole in her tights.

"Good morning, *relish!* customer services."

Violet limped into the bathroom and pressed a piece of toilet paper against the wound. "Hello, it's Violet Andersen again. Have you heard from my courier?"

"He hasn't arrived?" The girl sounded genuinely surprised.

"Why would I call if he had?"

A pause. "I'm afraid we haven't been able to contact him. We think perhaps his mobile's out of batteries. I'm very sorry about your delivery. It's the courier's first day."

"My *breakfast*," said Violet, running the tissue under the tap and trying to rub the drying blood off her leg. "It's not just a delivery, it's my breakfast. I'm hungry."

"I can only apologise, madam." That facetious use of the word madam. Violet knew she was being put in her place. The girl was probably smirking now to her colleagues: *I've got a right one here.* "*Relish!* will refund you your day's food bill as a gesture of goodwill and an expression of our sincere apologies."

"But what am I supposed to do for breakfast?" Violet could hear her voice rising now. She was obliquely aware of how brattish she sounded, but she felt at the same time unable to control it. "I rely on your company," she said, hearing her angry breath rebound against the microphone in the handset. "I pay hundreds of pounds a month for this! What are you going to do?"

There was a silence at the end of the line, and when the girl finally spoke, Violet was sure that she was stifling laughter. "Don't you have anything in your cupboards? Some bread or cereal or something?"

"That's the whole bloody point, isn't it? I haven't got anything! I don't need to — you're supposed to supply me with all the food I need." Her face was hot, and her hand was slippery and white-knuckled as it gripped the phone. "I've got no food at all! What am I supposed to do?"

"You haven't anything?" The incredulity in the girl's voice was raw. "No, nothing! I don't need to — I've got a proper fucking job that pays me enough money that I don't have to cook my own fucking meals! "

"Please don't take that abusive tone with me," said the girl, coldly, "I'm only trying to help."

"All you have to do is deliver my food; how hard can that be? What's wrong with your driver? Don't you give him a map?"

"Let's hope, for your sake, that he's only lost. You're going to feel pretty bad if he's had an accident or something."

Her voice was clipped, furious. It had lost its sing-song cheeriness and had taken on a spiteful tone. Violet knew that she was losing this battle, but she couldn't back down now. She needed to defeat this girl, whoever she was; she needed to win.

"When your manager hears about this," she began to say when there was a loud pounding on her door. "Halle-*luja*," she exhaled in a drawn-out, sarcastic sigh, and cut the girl off.

She nearly ran to answer it, but despite her haste, her visitor repeated the heavy knocking before she could open the door.

"Alright!" she shouted as she fumbled to unhook the chain, and under her breath, because she didn't want the delivery boy to hear her and to take her food away again, she muttered, "It's too late to be in a bloody rush now."

Already, her fury was ebbing away. She felt oddly euphoric, emotional even. She had been rescued, finally; her faith had been restored. She knew that she would have to act cross with him to prove her point, but really she just wanted to shake his hand and thank him for turning up at all. She knew that she was hopelessly, childishly dependent on these people that fed her and cleaned up after her, but then she was very, very hungry and very, very late.

The chain finally freed, she pulled back the top and bottom bolts, and pressed the button to release the locking mechanism. She waited impatiently, with her fingers on the handle, for the lock to click, and pulled the door open as soon as it did.

TWELVE

Later, as she rolled what happened next over and over in her head, the thing that would haunt her the most about it would be the expression on her face when she saw him.

She gazed out onto the landing with her features soft, enquiring, unprepared. This was her morning face, her private face, the face that existed outside of her office, not her stern, hard London face, the impenetrable expression that set onto her features each morning with the first hit of diesel fumes and city dirt. That face was ready for anything; the face that she presented instead was ready for nothing, except perhaps a polite hello and the signing of a delivery form.

As she opened the door, she caught the eye of the delivery boy, and was puzzled by the huge, proud smile that was spread all the way across his face. He's overcompensating, she thought, and smiled back, mildly, disinterestedly.

Then, she saw his hand moving and thought, she supposed later, that he was handing her the bag that contained her food; she looked down, and that unprepared face did its stupid, humiliating thing.

Her jaw dropped.

It hung open for a few seconds, like some particularly stupid cartoon character, she would think later, as it waits for an anvil to drop on its head.

Standing less than an arm's length away was the new delivery boy, with his flagging penis in his right hand and a long drool of semen falling into her food, which was arrayed at his feet, its contents split open.

She would feel stupid later, too, for screaming as she clumsily tried to slam the door. Granted, it was complicated: she had to move herself out of the way of it before it could be closed, and she did this in such a rush that the hem of her skirt got stuck in it, so she had to open it again, a little, in order to free herself.

Perhaps she should have laughed and pointed at it, made a cheap joke about his manhood and then withdrawn in triumph; perhaps she should have been tougher, made use of those self-defence techniques she'd been taught at a workshop whilst at university: pushed his nose into his face with the heel of her hand, or simply kicked out at that most vulnerable part of him, as it bobbed there in front of her.

Perhaps if she had done either of these things, he wouldn't then have pushed his muddy white trainer into the crack she had made in the doorway, and tried to force his way into her apartment, the full bulk of his stocky body weighing against the door. Perhaps, she thought, and she said as much to the patronising WPC they sent round to comfort her, he would have just walked away and left her alone if she hadn't shown him that she was afraid. The scream, the panicked attempt to close the door, the way that her face turned whiter than the corridor walls and her hands shook so that she could barely grip the handle, were an unbearable humiliation, a betrayal of her capability, her toughness, her independence.

She opened the door again, wide, so that the delivery boy stumbled forward, and then swung it back again, hard against the crown of his head.

He must have reeled backwards, because the door then slammed shut. Violet leant against it with all her weight, hearing the reassuring electronic click of the lock falling into place, and reached up to pull the bolts across. As she did this, the man recovered and began to pound on the door so hard that it shuddered inwards with each new blow; she imagined him charging against it with his shoulder, taking short run-ups across the width of the corridor.

She picked up the intercom handset, and waited for the concierge to answer; when she finally spoke, she was taken aback by the smallness, the thinness of her voice, as if it was being flooded by the boom of her own heartbeat.

"There's an intruder," she said, "He's trying to get in."

The door continued to shake under the blows of the delivery boy, the bolts straining dangerously with each attack.

"It's just a different courier," said the concierge, his voice calm and paternal; "He showed me ID."

"No," said Violet, "he's trying to break in. Can't you hear him? He…" She paused, wondering how you put the events of the last few minutes into words. "He… he tried to attack me." She began to cry a little as she said this. There were implications to this word; it was imbued with euphemistic meaning, a dead weight of victimhood and predation. It felt absurd that she was saying this; it felt like a lie. But as the door shook once more under the force of the delivery boy's assault, she realised that this was the moment that she had feared all her life. She was powerless. "Please come," she said, and her voice sounded even smaller.

There was a pause at the end of the line. "I'll call the police," said the concierge.

The door jolted so hard that Violet thought it would be torn from its hinges.

"No," she said, "come *now*. He's going to get in." She began to sob.

"I've activated the alarm. The police will be here quickly." His voice was quiet; Violet thought how his calmness was a luxury.

"I can't wait for the police. He's here now. I need someone to come."

"The police are best placed to handle this. They're already on their way."

"But what if he gets in?"

"The doors are very strong. Just sit tight."

"Please come. Please help me."

There was a pause at the end of the line, the sound of a breath being drawn. "Look, Ms Andersen. I'm just not *qualified* to deal with this."

Violet searched for an answer, but found none, so she shoved the receiver back into its cradle, her hand shaking so much that the plastic rattled. This was what it came down to: this whole building was nothing more than a piece of theatre. The air of care and security, the fastidious politeness, the elaborate display of impenetrable technology were, all of them, nothing more than flimsy stage sets that quivered in the face of real life. A uniformed security guard on the door *implied* that she would be protected, but in reality it was all just a shallow reassurance, a man dressed up as a soldier who would nevertheless wave through anyone showing some form of ID, and would remain in his comfortable seat in front of his bank of screens while her life was threatened.

Violet leaned against the wall and listened to her fast breathing for a while, and felt the prickle in her arms and her legs of energy waiting to be released. The attacks on her door had been getting less and less frequent, and now she found herself with a few moments of silence. Maybe the man had gone. She felt, not relief, but a sense of shame, that the police would come and find nobody. She doubted if they would even believe her.

There was another bang on the door, but a gentler one this time, clearly made with a fist instead of a shoulder-charge.

Rat-a-tat-tat-tat.

Was this the police? She stood up and pressed her eye to the spyglass, and saw, there in the corridor, the delivery boy clutching his shoulder disconsolately, glaring at her door.

"Go away!" she shouted. "The police are coming."

This was, of course, another mistake. She watched as the boy made a rush at her door, forcing his eye up close to the lens in an attempt to see her. His face stretched grotesquely in the fish-eye of the spyglass, but Violet was nevertheless struck by how young he was. She had not really registered what he looked like when she was trying to stop him from getting into her flat, but in her mind's eye, he had been hulking and dirty, with unruly hair and a convict's swagger.

Now, as she stared at his distorted face up close, she could see that his features were fresh and unmarked, and his chin wisped with the beginnings of a beard. But for his incessant knocking on her door, and the fact that his jeans were still unzipped, he could have been anyone. Had she passed him in the street she would have thought him perfectly normal.

"You fucking whore!" he shouted, never letting up his urgent tapping, "You bitch! Open the fucking door!" His voice was high with hysteria, drenched with rage and desperation.

He was still shouting when the police came. By then, Violet had stopped watching him through the spyglass, and had sat down on the floor again, with her back to the door to make certain that he couldn't get in.

She heard heavy feet running up the corridor, and the delivery boy began to cry; she could almost feel the convulsions of his sobs vibrating through the door. He went easily enough, it seemed. There was no struggle.

There was silence for few minutes after that, while Violet imagined them handcuffing him and packing him into the police car, protecting his head as he stooped to get in like they did on TV. Then, the knocking on her door started again, but this time gentler, more solicitous.

"Miss Andersen," called a female voice that whispered with concern, "are you in there Miss Andersen? It's the police. It's safe to come out now."

They were all very kind, even though it took Violet ten minutes to get the courage to open the door. They sat her down on her sofa, tried not to look phased when she said she had no tea, sugar or milk, expressed concern about the cut on her leg.

"I have to ask you this," said the WPC, leaning in towards Violet and furrowing her brow in an attempt to remember her victim support training, "Were you sexually assaulted?"

It took a long time for them to go.

THIRTEEN

It was strange, this weekday London, this face of the city that existed only when the commuters were in their offices. Violet found herself rushing through a series of streets that were rendered utterly unfamiliar by their life and colour, their clutteredness, their languor.

In the mornings and evenings, when she made this journey to the tube station, these same streets were empty and lifeless, washed in sooty blacks and steely greys. The only people she ever saw at these hours were people dressed soberly like her, in dark coats and suits, scuttling towards the tube station with their heads down. Until now, she had imagined all the shuttered shops to be permanently closed, and the dirty-bricked warehouses to be condemned and awaiting the magic wand of urban renewal to revive them.

Everything was different in broad daylight. At this time of year, bitter February, she rarely saw the sun at all, leaving her flat and returning to it in utter darkness. Even in the summer, the sun was low in the sky whenever she came in contact with it, casting the golden light over the streets in the morning and sinking behind the Victorian factory buildings in the evening. At this time of year she would often be surprised by the heat in the air and the warm dusty smell that seeped from the pavements as she left work after a day in the air-conditioned chill. It was as if summer happened without her nowadays.

Today, the sun was already high, shining white against the crisp winter-blue sky, and it seemed to be drenching the streets in movement and colour. Only a few streets from her apartment block, she discovered a road lined with bustling shops and teeming with people who were buying, selling, or just taking in the view. The shuttered windows had emerged from their casings like butterflies, bright and tempting. Violet passed half a dozen smart grocers, with their wares stacked tantalisingly outside: neat piles of oranges and melons, lush bunches of fresh mint and coriander, rude purple aubergines and courgettes that still held the yellow frill of their flower on one end.

Violet, trailing a hastily-stuffed flight-case in her wake, found the streets so transformed that she had to keep checking for landmarks to find her way. For a few moments, she almost forgot the horrors of the morning. She slowed her pace and dawdled a little, gazing into the open doors of shops and the steamy windows of cafés. The glowing piles of fruit made hunger bite into her again, so she stopped, cradled a mango in her hand and breathed its heavy scent. The shop-keeper, standing in his doorway with his hands clasped over his round belly, smiled and nodded a greeting. She rooted for a coin in her purse, handed it to him, and slipped the fruit into her bag.

The midday sun was almost warm on her face. She imagined the new life she would have now that she knew about this place, the elegant meals she could make for herself out of the contents of these shops, sat at home at her dining table. Things weren't so bad; she could find a different life, a life with more control, with more feeling. She could be happy there, at her dining table. But then, in her daydream, the door began to pound, the monotonous, heavy thud of a man ramming his shoulder against it...

She couldn't go back. She couldn't face all that. She had to get out of this stinking city, just for a few days. The sun seemed to catch in her eyes, making them stream. She put her head down, quickened her pace. A woman walked too close, so that Violet's suitcase skipped over her toes and fell sideways. Somebody nearly ran into her as she stopped to set it back on its wheels.

A man on the corner of the street was frying burgers and onions, and Violet winced at the sickly odour, feeling it cling to her like a net. Ahead of her, a gang of lads in caps and tracksuits were lounging against a shop front, smoking and throwing back cans of lager; as she tried to pass them, one of them lunged out and blocked her way, laughing as she shuffled from side to side to try to get around him. "Y'awright, darlin'?" he said, turning to his mates to check their approval and spreading his arms wide to obstruct her further.

Violet felt the fury bubble to the surface again. "Get the fuck out of my way," she spat, and charged into him, knocking him sideways. She broke into a trot, not wanting to run, but afraid the boy might pursue her now that she'd raised the stakes; she was almost relieved to hear the whole gang laughing at her and singing camp 'oooohs' in her direction. "You feeling a bit frustrated, love?" shouted one of them after her, but by then Violet was already around the corner of the next street, where the people had thinned out.

She fumbled in her handbag, pulled out her mobile phone and called Marcus's office. He answered within a couple of rings.

"Y'hello."

"It's Violet."

"Violet! Where have you been? There's nothing in your diary to say that you're out of the office today."

"Yes. I know." She paused by a lamppost trying to decide what she should tell him. She hadn't thought this through, and stopping made her suddenly out of breath. "I've had a few problems at home this morning."

"Oh, Violet, your grandmother? We wondered as much." *Who*, thought Violet. *Who wondered?* Had she been the subject of general speculation in the office? She imagined how Marcus would have signalled that she was on the line through the glass walls of his office, and that they were all crowding in now, their faces fixed in expressions of profound sympathy. Violet could hear Marcus adjusting his voice so that it oozed gentleness and pity. "This is a difficult time for you," he said. "You must be kind to yourself."

"Yes," said Violet, "you're right. I think I need to go home, sort a few things out." As much as she loathed the condescension and false concern that her lie had elicited, she was beginning to feel grateful to it. It was the perfect screen for her to hide behind, a short-cut to being given the space she needed without the horror and mess of having to tell the truth.

"Well," said Marcus, "it's Friday anyway. Take a long weekend and see how you feel on Monday. Take care of yourself, yes?"

"I will. I'll be back bright and early on Monday morning."

"Okay. Good. And while you're down there mixing with our target client group, keep your eyes open for leads. Only joking, obviously."

Violet switched off her phone, knowing full well that he was not.

Only when she eventually ascended into the bitterly cold air of Victoria station did she begin to wonder if she was doing the right thing. She gazed around at the array of shops, the concessions selling baguettes and sushi, the newsagents stuffed with an impossible quantity of magazines, the ersatz market stalls selling chocolate and flowers, and began to feel guilty at this stolen leisure time. What on earth was she thinking, running away like this, to a place that she hardly had the right to call home anymore? What would she do there? Where would she stay?

Three girls were standing in the centre of the concourse, handing out a bright yellow umbrella with every copy of the Evening Standard they sold. Violet set her suitcase down and glanced at her watch: one o'clock. She could be in the office in twenty minutes. She could put all this behind her, get back into the swing of things.

But then the glowing boards at the entrance to the platforms flickered, and a list of destinations scrolled down them. Platform 5 for the coastal service, with Stonehithe glinting at the end of the line. Violet was too deliberately sensible to see this as a sign, but she let the jolt of it compel her anyway, towards the ticket machines and then, in a loose jog, through the gates and onto her train.

She took off her coat and propped it onto the overhead shelf, and then sat down on a bristly seat and felt the blood whirring in her veins. Through the window, the yellow umbrellas were increasing their circulation, spreading bright, buttery patches all over the station. She breathed the stale air of the carriage, tried to find a comfortable place to put her feet. *I just have to stay here until the train starts*, she thought, *and then it won't be my responsibility any more.*

The knot in her stomach, which had hung there all week, seemed as though it had grown; it was almost painful. She imagined it throwing out tendrils to her ribs, her neck, her collarbone, making them ache and stiffen.

The sirens went off to signal that the doors were closing, locking her in.

No escape now. The train jolted as it started, and Violet jolted with it, surrendering herself to the roll of the wheels on the track and the shriek of the gears as it gathered speed. The eternal twilight of the station broke into a bright, clear day, and she passively watched the last few sights of London passing her window: the dour high flats around Victoria, gaunt, hulking Battersea power station, the wailing dogs' home, teeming Brixton market...

After fifteen minutes, she found herself amongst a world of back gardens, with washing lines, rockeries, swings and ponds. She unzipped her bag and pulled out the mango. It carried its perfume in a thick cloud that drifted about her hands as she broke its waxy skin with a fingernail, and then peeled back a strip of it to reveal the bright orange fibres of its flesh inside.

She bit into it deeply into it, feeling the juice trickle across her hands.

Don't feel sorry for Violet.

She had everything she ever wanted.

I know how you think the story goes; I've told it myself, many times over the years. The poor, sensitive soul is condemned to a life of misery because she's sold her soul to The Man.

Is this how you picture it in your head?

Violet, a fresh-faced innocent, skips happily away from her graduation ball after bidding a fond farewell to her cheery chums. As she sets out upon the golden road that leads to her future, she is accosted by a smiling man in a morning suit. He is tall, grey-haired and benevolent; the waistcoat that stretches across his enormous stomach is buttoned together by straining dollar-signs. His eyes shine like new pennies, and when he speaks, he crowns his sentences with exclamation marks. My dear, he says, you must come and work for me! You will travel the world, drive the finest of vehicles, sample the delights of London town, and for all of this you will be handsomely remunerated!

Violet demurs; despite the man's kindly features, she is afraid that she is being lured into a trap. I have heard bad things, she says, about London town. The folk round here whisper that it is a place of wickedness.

The old man chuckles. Oh my dear, dear child, he says regarding the girl's pure and maidenly countenance, surely you do not believe the gossip of such simple folk! London town is the place of your dreams!

As he says this, he raises his cane high in the air, and the diamond on top of it casts a sparkling beam of light across the path that leads to Violet's future. Violet gazes at it as if entranced, her eyes gradually taking on the glimmer of the gem. Then, slowly at first, she begins to follow the beam, her feet heavy below her. The man jolts his cane, and Violet begins to dance, a halting, jerky dance like a puppet being shaken on a string. A sickly smile is plastered across her face. She dances on and on, until, quite suddenly, she finds herself at the edge of a cliff. Below is arrayed the city of London, its lights shining brightly.

Just one thing, calls the fat man from behind her, if you come and work for me, you have to hand over your soul!

Violet turns her glazed eyes to him. No problem, she says, and she smiles.

Excellent, says the man, and he jerks his cane again. Violet springs elegantly upwards from the cliff edge, arcs her body like a leaping fish and then dives head-first into the city below her. And as she does this, the man is laughing and wringing his hands together in triumph: mwah-ha-ha-ha-ha, mwah-ha-ha-ha-ha…

Is this how you imagine it? Really? Of course you don't. But you're happy, aren't you, with your model of things that says that Violet's life so far has been someone else's fault, someone dark, sinister, rapacious. Isn't it just so much easier to like her if you think that she was somehow forced into this against her will?

Perhaps that's where the soul gets dragged into it. Even in this secular age, how we love to talk about the commodity of souls, the buying, the selling, the theft and the redemption of them! How we love to imagine that we have one in the first place, a little woolly bundle that holds the sum total of our goodness and our integrity, that can be extracted from our bodies to leave us empty and diminished.

What do you think they do with them, these men who steal our souls? Do they file them neatly, awaiting reissue on our retirement? Do they distil them into a liquor for their own rejuvenation? Do they award them their own buff cubicle somewhere deep in the bowels of the office? Or is the soul an unwanted by-product of creating tame workers? Are our souls abandoned somewhere in stacks of specimen jars, where they buzz dumbly against their glass walls like bluebottles?

These people have no use for our souls. And the workers in our offices have not given them away, for they barely know that they exist. And even if they were in touch with their souls, with the essence of what they really are, who's to say that they would choose anything different? Perhaps they don't want to be strolling the highlands with a herd of Aberdeen Angus, or crafting artisan earthenware. Perhaps they are fundamentally disinterested in unleashing their inner poet, or inner cellist, or inner firer-eater. Perhaps they're quite grateful to be given something to do, to have their choices made for them, for conformity to do the job that a personality would usually do. Or perhaps their soul is the flicker of a computer screen, the reassuring spring of an anatomically-correct ergonomic chair against your weary behind, or the taste of vending machine mochaccino. Maybe they like it. Maybe they are it.

Because it pays its way, doesn't it? It brings home the bacon. It buys that lifestyle that's pedalled in Elle Deco in which your blouse tones with your sofa and holidays take place in luxury spas in the Far East. It pays for the sort of food that you don't have to cook for yourself and the gym machines that fool you into believing you're running along genuine terrain. It pays for moisturisers that make outlandish claims and television screens to rival your local cinema. It pays for meals in restaurants that make you feel anxious, and cocktails in bars that make you feel ugly. It pays for cleaners, reflexologists, therapists, and elective caesareans in private hospitals. It pays off your partner and your children when they snivel that they never get to see you anymore.

Don't tell me that the people populating every office, talking into telephones in stagy professional voices and mopping expensive coffee from their pressed shirts, are there under duress. They came running towards this with their arms wide open. They want it. They like it. It gives them self-esteem, purpose, a personality. Just what would they find to do without it?

So let's start again:

After university, Violet started working in an office because she wanted to.

Because it sounded interesting.

Because she wanted the salary.

Because she coveted the lifestyle.

Because she had an enormous credit card bill to pay off.

Because she didn't have any better ideas.

Because she couldn't think of success in any other terms than a hundred grand a year plus benefits, a big car and a serviced flat with a minimalist interior.

Because, frankly, it was the done thing, and she didn't really give it much thought.

And that's it. Nobody took her hostage and beat a hardened businesswoman out of her. She chose it. She got the life she wanted.

So don't feel sorry for Violet. Until now, she's been perfectly happy in her own way. It's just that, now she's starting to question that life, she gets a little more interesting.

Part Two

ONE

The seagulls were out in force, diving and reeling against the freezing air, despite the constant sideways shunt of the wind. Keeping her head down, her eyes streaming, Violet fought her way up the high street, against the oncoming wind, clasping a gloved hand in front of her to hold her scarf and the lapels of her coat together. She barely noticed the shops she passed, but she could see their lights and colours out of the corner of her eye, the fluorescent posters that still advertised the sales weeks after Christmas and the pastel yellows and blues of the early Easter displays. A man brushed past her, eating furtively from an open wrap of chips, and Violet's stomach rumbled into life at their savoury, vinegar-soaked scent.

Their smell lingered as the man continued on his way, and Violet knew that she must be approaching the shop that sold them. She found it a few doors down, a black and white painted frontage, windows thick with streaming condensation and a neon sign that peered through it saying, Now Frying. She remembered going into this place in giggling gangs after school, and coming out with one rustling bag of chips between five of them, ketchup on one side only so that everyone's tastes were catered for. They would eat them sauntering down the high street and calling out to any boy they recognised, cackling with nervous bravado, and being as vulgar as they dared. The first boy she kissed, an arrangement made between her mates and his, had a bag of his own chips which he offered to her before courteously laying them aside and approaching her open-mouthed. He had tasted salty, sharp, damp.

The wind disappeared as the door shut behind her. There, working behind the counter, she recognised the same couple that had run the place ten years before. He was a little greyer, and she a little fatter, but there was no mistaking them, her hair bundled into the same yellowing hairnet, and his right arm showing the scars of the fierce vats of bubbling oil that they tended each day. Violet's ears were ringing in the absence of the wind, and she felt assaulted by the sudden heat of the room. They didn't recognise her; of course they didn't. They just continued to work behind the streamlined stainless steel of their counter, which may well have been in service for years before these two were a twinkle in a fishmonger's eye.

Violet felt as though she endured agonies of hunger as she shuffled forwards in the queue. She stood and observed the rhythm of fillets of cod dipped in batter the colour of fresh cream and then shuffled in their bath of boiling oil until they turned golden; of piles of chips thrown steaming and crisp-edged on to the metal grille to drain, and then scooped violently into polystyrene trays; of tall, wide jars that were routinely fished for evasive pickled onions with a slotted spoon; of the rustle of thin paper folded expertly around each order. Eventually she reached the front of the queue, and tapped the edge of her two pound coin on the chrome surface as she waited for her own portion of chips to be drained, shovelled, salted and wrapped. When she handed over her money the woman caught her eye to thank her, and Violet thought that, just for a moment, she saw a spark of recognition in her glance, an acknowledgement that Violet might once have belonged here. But then the woman smiled as politely as you would to an utter stranger, and turned her back on Violet as she closed the drawer of her till.

Violet crossed the wind-racked street and sat in one of the wrought iron shelters that overlooked the sea. The glass windows had all been replaced with flimsy plastic, which creaked and boomed as the wind hit it, and distorted the view into the a slightly inebriated blur. She unwrapped the chips and felt their hot steam warm her cheeks; then, she took off her gloves and began to eat greedily, breaking the crisp skins against her tongue and savouring the soft, light interiors. She picked them up in clusters of three, four, five at a time, and crammed them all in at once, letting their mealy richness fill her mouth. The texture, the smell, the warmth, even the sight of the grease-stained paper was deeply comforting.

It didn't take long for the chips to go cold in the winter air. She picked at the last few, feeling heavy with the bulk of the ones she had already eaten, and then sucked at each finger in turn to get the salt off.

It was drizzling now, the wind carrying a fine spray of rain in the air that stung Violet's cheeks and soaked her hair. She could feel the moisture collecting around her eyes and imagined the blurry mess that it would be making of her mascara. She thought about going for tea in one of the old cafes that lined the sea front, still clinging on to their Formica tables and rubbery banquette seats, but she couldn't face the steam and huff, and the smell that she remembered for her childhood of burnt toast and bacon, particularly as she was still labouring under the weight of a bag of chips. More than that, she needed to know that there would be somewhere for her to sleep tonight.

The road that swung up steeply from the front to overlook the sea had always been the place for hotels, and as she climbed it, she saw a row of stately Georgian townhouses, now all washed in undignified pastel colours, displaying a tangle of boards that advertised their names: The Red Rose, Journey's Rest, The Sea View. Some carried boards that detailed what they offered: Satellite TV; Most Rooms En-Suite; No DHSS. One had an overflowing basket of plastic flowers at the gate, the leaves faded to albino yellow, and the rose buds now a sickly lipstick orange.

There was a picture in Violet's mind that accompanied each of these signs, of chaotic floral bedspreads and a lingering smell of cigarette smoke despite the signs ordering you to the contrary. She could imagine herself constrained to the bounds of a tiny room, with nothing but a wicker chair and a fizzing portable television for company, in hiding from a monstrous landlady who wanted her out at nine, in by eight, and who made pointed enquires about her marital status. She walked past all of them.

A little further along the street, she spotted a building that was slightly larger than all the rest, and detached. It was set back from the road and had a set of illuminated plastic letters above the front porch that spelt out 'Hotel Napoli' in green. The plate by the door showed three stars, and there was a light in the hall. Violet looked up at the guttering that was peeling like sunburnt skin and promised herself that she would turn around and leave if it was too bad.

TWO

The lobby was showing its age. Paint chipped away from the dado rails to reveal layers of colour: magnolia over chocolate brown, mustard, burgundy. There was a bell on the front desk, but she thought she wouldn't need it, as she could clearly see into the office through a window of reinforced glass, and there a woman was draped across a swivel chair, talking passionately into a phone, her hands straying into her clouds of red hair to tug occasionally at the roots in theatrical despair.

Violet knew that the woman had seen her, as she had sighed and swung her chair around to offer Violet its broad back, so she waited patiently, observing the red and green carpet that swirled beneath her feet, and the paths of the wiring that trekked along the walls and up the stairs like an orderly parade of ants. After five minutes, the woman showed no signs of finishing her conversation, so Violet began to wonder if there was perhaps another receptionist lurking in the wings, unaware of her presence. She pushed the bell, and waited a while longer, but nobody came so she pushed it again, this time a little harder and a little sharper. In the office, the chair swung back round to face her, and the woman looked out angrily through the glass, her hand muffling the receiver.

"Yes, I see you," she said in a clipped Italian accent. "Please hold on."

Violet knew that she should probably walk out at this point, pick up her case and slam the door behind her, but her legs and arms felt heavy, and the driving, drizzling rain outside seemed an impossible thing, something that she had neither the energy nor the skill to negotiate. She unbuttoned her coat, and rested her elbows on the reception desk's high counter, gazing at the sign that boasted an indoor swimming pool and a full buffet breakfast. At least she would be able to eat and take some exercise while she was here.

The woman was leaning over the phone now as she spoke, as if to indicate that she would hang up if only the person on the other end would stop talking. Eventually, she said a final *ciao*, and replaced the receiver. Violet watched her stand, brush down her wide-legged trousers, straighten the line of beads that hung around her neck, and then lick both index fingers so that she could run them in arcs over her eyebrows, grooming them like a cat. She was a petite woman, thin and delicate, with a face constructed of fine bones that must once have made her beautiful; now, they peaked and dipped under loose skin that sagged into deep, rouged hollows on her cheeks. Her eyelids were painted sooty black from lash to socket-bone, so that each blink appeared to be forced by the weight of them. Nevertheless, there was a grace, an elegance about her. Each part of the assemblage of her clothes, makeup and jewellery was carefully judged and placed: the silver rings that crowded her thin fingers, the beads arranged around her neck, the green leather boots that jutted out from below her trouser legs in chic, violent points. She stalked out into the lobby.

"Can I help you?"

"I'd like a room."

"Today?" The woman's voice was heavy with weariness and incredulity. She raised those carefully-tidied brows and let out an exhausted puff of air, as if the lobby were filled with crowds of tourists demanding rooms. In fact, it was so quiet as she flicked through the empty pages of the guest register that Violet could hear the central heating timer ticking on each second as it warmed vacant rooms.

"I can let you have a double," she said, "but there's no singles."

"No problem."

"How many nights?"

"I don't know. Two? Three? No more than that."

The woman sighed again. "You'll have to pay the full price, of course. I can't afford to let you have a double for the price of a single."

"Fine." It seemed a point of pride, by now, to win a room from this woman despite her reluctance. Violet straightened her back and looked her in the eye.

"And we don't serve dinner at this time of the year. You'll have to get it in town."

"Would you like to take my credit card details now?"

The woman waved her hand as if clearing away smoke. "Later," she said. Her voice lingered like perfume in the air. "Just fill in this form for now. Your name and address; I'll do the rest." She watched Violet's hand intensely as she wrote, as if trying to detect some subtle fraud, and then stared at her neat capitals for far longer than was polite, her eyes widening a fraction.

Violet was treated to a desultory tour of the facilities (a dark breakfast room and an unstaffed bar, each of which was gestured at with those thin fingers, before having its door slammed closed), and was then taken upstairs (carrying her own case) to a room at the end of the corridor.

As the woman opened the door, Violet realised that she was actually bracing herself for what lay inside, expecting some horror of furniture-board and nylon; instead, she was gently surprised by the tidy bed with a polished wooden headboard, made up with crisp white sheets, fawn blankets and an old-fashioned quilt that was studded with roses. There were long damask curtains at the French windows, which opened onto a sea-view and a wrought-iron balcony with just enough space to stand on. At the foot of the bed was a mahogany wardrobe with a chest of drawers to match, and a spindly-legged writing desk and chair on the opposite wall.

"It's lovely," said Violet, quite sincerely, as she glanced into the clean, white, en-suite bathroom. The woman smiled just a fraction, and looked her in the eye for the first time.

"I decorate the rooms myself. Each one is different; I go to the auctions in London to buy the furniture." She paused, bent down to pick an invisible piece of lint off the carpet. "If I'd known you were coming, there would have been flowers."

Violet put her case on the bed. "It doesn't matter," she said, "it's only me. The woman nodded, walked out onto the landing, and then thrust her hand towards Violet. "Antonia," she said. "Call down if you need anything."

Violet shook that hand, which was dry and cold and insubstantial, and thanked her. Then, she closed the door behind her, took off her shoes and sat down on the bed. She ached through to her bones, and her limbs were stiff, immobile. She rubbed her hands over her face, and then, as a reflex, reached into her handbag for her Nurofen. It must have been hours since she took one; she was falling victim, again, to her own lack of organisation, letting a headache seep in.

The pills were not in their usual compartment, nor were they in the other pockets. Violet drew a swift breath. Methodically, she emptied out the bag, forming a pile on the bed of makeup, tissues, her purse, several pens, her phone; they were not there. She pulled her case towards her, and tore at the zip, spilling the contents on her bed; but there was no rattling blister pack in her toilet bag, nor anything folded amongst her clothes.

She began to pack everything back into her case and her handbag. It was not the painkillers; she could buy them anywhere. It was the absence of everything else that frightened her, the echinacea, the ester C, the Korean ginseng, and particularly the melatonin. She told herself that this last item was the least of it, just a prop to help her get to sleep that she could easily do without, especially when she was on a holiday like this, but a persistent undercurrent of thoughts were shooting panicked signals at her: *You won't sleep without them. You'll be awake all night.*

There was no hope of getting them down here; her best chance was the internet, but it was already Friday afternoon, and so the probability of them arriving before she returned home was vanishingly small. Perhaps she could get an emergency appointment with a doctor, get some prescribed. Or failing that, get something else prescribed, a short-term stop-gap. But this would be more than she needed, of course. She did not take sleeping pills.

She would have to go back to London; there was no choice. Without her melatonin, she would be at the mercy of sleep like she used to be. It would take her days to get back into the cycle, building up an immunity to tiredness again. She slipped on her shoes and stood up, pulling on her coat at the same time. She could be back in London within a couple of hours if the trains were right. She could pay off the room if necessary; it didn't matter.

But she was exhausted. She already felt vulnerable without them, as if sleep would know and would come for her. What if she fell asleep on the train? Had to be woken up in the terminal, with her case and handbag stolen? And then, when she got home, would it still be as she left it, with the man's footprints on the door and broken glass in the kitchen? She took off her coat and shoes. She would lie down, rest a while, and then go out for dinner. She could find some pills in the morning, she was certain. Surely she could cope without the melatonin for one weekend, and she could hunt down the rest of her supplements on the high street. Skipping one evening couldn't do her much harm.

The room felt chilly once her coat was off. She pulled the quilt around her and lay her head on the pillow. She was on holiday. She was allowed to rest. She would just lay here for a few minutes and then head out into town.

There was nothing in the room except the sound of the wind against the glass, pounding like a heartbeat. Violet closed her eyes and gave in to sleep.

THREE

At the table where Violet sat, a fly endlessly circled above her, a slow persistent buzzing that absorbed all of her attention, and gradually, gradually found a focus, cleared. The air was white, and then grey. The sound was deeper, throatier, not at all like a fly. A drill: a pneumatic drill in the street below. Not a London street, somewhere else…

…Violet opened her eyes and felt the heaviness that her body had taken on in its stillness. Her mouth was so dry that her tongue and palate rasped together like a pair of woolly gloves, and she found that she was still wearing her pinstripe office trousers and white cotton shirt, which were now twisted, crumpled and greasy-feeling.

She rolled onto her back and looked at her watch; its hands showed two o'clock. She sat up, feeling the shadows of sleep draining away with the shock of the information. It could only have been three in the afternoon when she lay down on the bed to rest; surely it couldn't be the middle of the night already? It took her a while to find the switch on the bedside lamp, but eventually the golden glow of the bulb confirmed what her eyes had originally reported; it was two o'clock.

No wonder her mouth was so dry. She had long ago trained herself to take incessant drags on a bottle of mineral water, and now her parched body had been forcibly withdrawn from its permanent supply of hydration. She got up from the bed, hoping to find a glass in the bathroom so that she could stand by the sink and drink until she felt human again, but as she did so she noticed the unmistakable glow of daylight seeping from behind the curtains. She drew them apart, and looked out at the rumbling grey sea, overhung by grey clouds. It was dark, certainly, but not middle-of-the-night dark: overcast afternoon dark. Oncoming storm dark.

Violet smiled, let out a private groan of laughter. Her watch had stopped. She could only have been sleeping for an hour or so. She hadn't been thinking straight, dreary from her afternoon nap. Why was it, she thought, as she rummaged in her handbag for her mobile phone, that napping for an hour or so leaves you feeling so riddled with sleep? It's never as refreshing as it should be; instead of sneaking in an extra shift of rest, a little something to tide you over until bedtime, you end up introducing slumber into your system, and it's more tenacious than you expect; it clings there, settling in your eyelids and your joints, trying to drag you back under.

She held her phone up to the window so that she could read its display. 14.09, it said. Saturday 5th February.

Violet gave the phone a sharp shake, as if this motion would jolt it back into sensible life, and then stared at the screen, her wristwatch, the daylight on the other side of the window. They all agreed. She had slept, at her best guess, for twenty-three hours solidly without once waking up. Her bladder, which had suddenly bulged into life and was aching with the need to urinate, told her so. Without the control of her battery of pills, without the discipline of London, her body was clawing back its sleep, and now, this afternoon, she felt light-headed with it, anxious at having skipped so much time.

After drinking four glasses of water, leaning over the sink and letting the cold liquid dribble down her chin in her breathless urgency, Violet washed her face, brushed her teeth and got dressed. Her stomach ached with hunger, and she was desperate to get out and make use of what little daylight was left. Opening her flight case, she regarded the fallout of yesterday morning's rushed packing: two pairs of knickers, jeans that didn't match her work shoes, a shirt and a jumper. Everything, she realised now, was navy blue, so she wound her way downstairs looking like a policeman, hoping that she would be able to make a discreet exit before anybody saw her.

Antonia was in the exact spot that Violet had found her the day before, draped over the executive chair in the office, speaking in Italian on the phone, but this time she put an end to her call as soon as she caught sight of Violet, waving her finger to signal that she should not leave. There was no chance of slipping away. Violet hung back in the lobby while Antonia went through her elaborate ritual of straightening clothes and grooming eyebrows. Today, her high pillow of red hair was being restrained by a paisley scarf, so that it billowed out at the back in defiance. She was wearing a draped brown dress with a wide belt and boots, and a pair of enormous hoop earrings that bobbed and danced as she moved. Violet wondered how few people must witness the enormous effort that she clearly made.

"Good morning, Sleeping Beauty," she growled in her ornamented accent, but smiling today, showing not a hint of the adolescent resentment that she had exuded yesterday.

Violet nodded, blushed, wondering how she might explain away her long sleep. Antonia put a maternal hand on her shoulder.

"I knocked on your door last night, and when nobody answered I thought you were out, so I came in to make up your room. You didn't even stir when I turned on the light!"

"Oh, I'm so sorry," Violet began to say, now feeling deep uneasiness that anyone might have seen her so surrendered to unconsciousness.

"Ah, don't worry, you were like a peaceful little baby. I pulled the curtains for you and left a glass of water by your bed. Did you drink it?"

"No. I didn't wake up."

"No! Not even this morning. The maids say I should call an ambulance, but I say no, she is sleeping like a child. Not to wake her. Let her see it through."

"Thank you," said Violet, unnerved by this unexpected burst of concern. "I still can't believe it's tomorrow already."

Antonia smiled, and placed a thin hand on Violet's back, guiding her towards the dining room. "Come, you missed your breakfast. I saved you some. I'll make some fresh coffee for you."

It would usually have been Violet's habit to say that she didn't drink coffee, and to ask for herbal tea, or failing that a cup of hot water instead. However, this morning, with everything so transformed, it would have seemed mean to turn it down, and besides, the thought of a cup of deep, milky coffee was warming and filling, something to sustain her body rather than to discipline it. She pulled out a chair at one of the crisply laid tables, but Antonia tapped her hand.

"No, no, you come and sit in the kitchen with me while I make your coffee. You'll be lonely out there. All on your own."

Here it was, then: she was now an object of sympathy, of pity, to be coddled and cared for like a child. She was no longer a threat to the order of the hotel, an inconvenient customer arriving off-season and expecting the works; she was instead a stowaway, a foundling, a lost little girl who would be absorbed into the domestic life of the building, handed friendship and kindnesses as if they were blankets and tiny tablets of soap – as necessities, given dutifully to one who needed them.

"It's fine," said Violet, "I'll get breakfast in town. I need to buy some clothes."

"You drink some coffee first. And eat a little something. Then you go to town. Plenty of time."

She followed Antonia out through the swing-door into the kitchens beyond, where ranks of stainless steel equipment – ovens, hobs, a sink with a sprung hose suspended over it, a serving canteen set under heat-lamps – gleamed redundantly. In the far corner, beside the back door, was a smaller assemblage of less industrial items: a toaster, a kettle, a microwave and a grand chrome coffee machine, smeared and fingerprinted through constant use, and humming quietly to itself, ready to be eased back into action by Antonia's expert hands. Next to it was a high wooden stool, which Antonia pulled towards Violet and begged her to sit on while she ground out a dose of beans, flattened the powder they produced and slotted them into the mouth of the machine.

"This may be a crappy three-star hotel, but we have bloody proper coffee," she said as she flicked the switch that forced the steam through the grouts, dribbling two unsteady ribbons of muddy espresso into a large, white cup. "I try to drink your bloody awful instant crap when I first came over, but it barely got me up in the morning. You got to do things properly, or not at all. I tell this to Robert, but of course he doesn't care. Lazy bastard."

Violet nodded and wondered if she should know who Robert was. She watched Antonia steaming the milk for her coffee, easing the jug up and down over the billowing spout, conjuring a perfect rhythm of hisses and gurgles until a crown of dense foam rose out of it. The cup was placed in front of her and the milk poured in, at first with the foam restrained by a teaspoon, and then, the spoon withdrawn, with the foam allowed to flop lightly into the cup, so that it formed a folded mound which was sprinkled with cocoa.

"There," said Antonia, pushing the saucer towards her, "it might even keep you awake for a while!" And then, opening the door of the fridge and leaning into it, "You like eggs? Poached, scrambled? A little bit of bacon?"

It was painless enough to be taken care of in this way, to be fed coffee, toast, eggs and bacon, and to be chatted at gently, inconsequentially, about the snow and the wind and the rain, and their effect on the crocuses that had just begun to show through in the garden. Antonia had busied around the coffee machine while Violet ate her breakfast, methodically stripping it to its component parts, dusting the coffee grouts off each piece, washing it, drying it and fitting it back into its place, before starting the whole cycle again to make two cups of strong black coffee. She carried one of the cups through to the conservatory, with Violet mutely in tow, and put it down for her on a sea-view table.

"You wait 'til the rain stops before you go out," she said before retreating back to her office. "Shops close at five-thirty. You got a while."

FOUR

Twenty-three hours. She had slept for a night and a day, like a girl in a fairytale. Sleep had always held an unnerving, supernatural quality for Violet, stealing several hours of each night only to fill them with submission, oblivion and blankness, or worse, in the grasp of the melatonin, with the rambling symbolism of her dreams and the teasing amnesia that hinted at them throughout the next day. She used the melatonin to reduce her hours of sleep to a bare minimum, to make them as productive as possible while she extended her day, but the dreams themselves, what snatches of them she remembered, always seemed too huge, too lengthy to have been created and played out in those few hours. Sometimes she had slept for only a few minutes and had woken to find that a whole night's dreaming had been placed into her brain, complete.

There were times when she thought she would be glad to be rid of her dreams, for they had bullied and bewildered her, creating worlds too elaborate for her to have imagined by herself and offering her glimpses of reasoning that she was sure were too clever for her. She would find herself appalled, when she woke in the night from a particularly vivid encounter, at her dreams' ability to drench her in a pure emotional hit of grief or fear or erotic longing.

Had she dreamed last night? Violet hadn't thought to question it before, but despite the heaviness she now felt, it was possible. She cast her mind back to the moment she woke up, to the dry mouth and the muggy confusion, and then to the fly that became a drill as her mind fell into focus, and then to the fly that was buzzing around a hot café in her dream. Within seconds it all surged back into place, the life that she had taken on while she slept. She remembered sitting in a pub, sprawling across a corner seat and laughing, counting out coins from her purse and pooling them with a girl (someone she had never seen before, but who felt familiar, an old friend) to buy drinks; talking to a man at the bar, and then going with him to meet his mates; playing pool and losing. She remembered following them to someone's flat, a drab little place with a brown velour sofa riddled with burn-holes; drinking their bottle of cheap, sweet liqueur, melon-flavour, maybe, or peach; smoking a joint, perhaps two. She remembered, strangely, sleeping in her dream, curling up on that brown sofa under a coat with cushions below her head, and dreaming those odd, drunken dreams that feel furtive and guilty and thirsty. And then, waking up the next morning to a quiet house, when the sun was glowing through thin curtains, hungry and sick, and trying to find some way of making tea and toast while everyone else slept; and the smell in the bathroom, the smell of piss in the carpet, that made her stomach lurch and her head ache even more; and leaving, closing the door behind her quietly, wondering which way was home.

Every detail was there, as if she'd lived it: getting on a bus for the town centre and calling her friend from there. Sitting in a café, with yellow walls and wooden chairs, the windows steamed with the breath of all the Saturday morning refugees, buying a hot chocolate with the last of her change and drinking it slowly until her friend came; going over the night before, with that feeling of excitement flooding back through her, of having had an adventure, of having triumphed over her own, staid life, of being new and shiny and adult and tired, of taking pride in her hair that smelt of fag-smoke and her clothes that were really more Friday night than Saturday morning. And then talking her friend through it, telling her every little detail – the walk home, the bottle of cheap liqueur; and laughing, and planning the next night, poring over a pocketful of flyers; conspiring to go home to get another tenner, another twenty, whatever she could scrounge.

And then, the fly buzzing in, drifting around her head until it was all that she could hear, and becoming louder, until it was everything, until the light changed and she realised her eyes were open…

It wasn't like her usual experience of dreaming. It was clear, specific, free of the cryptic signs or the filmic, third-person view of herself that her dreams used to bring. It was like a life lived, in real time, and played out in pubs and cafes and houses and streets that she didn't quite know, but that were certainly familiar, and certainly here, in Stonehithe. She had felt different to how she had felt for many years: her dream returned her to her younger, more daredevil self, the part of her that saw endless fascination and variety in the people she had yet to meet, the part that felt sure that there was a more interesting life somewhere out there.

It was all bringing back memories, being here. It was hard to imagine it now, but there was a time when life stretched before her, was full of plans and possibilities. What age was she in that dream: seventeen? Eighteen? Old enough to be out drunk on a Friday night, but still young enough to believe that she could somehow find a life that solved all her problems, made her rich and free and glamorous. It made her smart at her own cynicism. Eighteen wasn't that long ago, was it? Only a few weeks ago, she had fought a sincere impulse to say *fifteen* when someone asked her age. And yet there had been a great number of lessons learned between then and now, about what could be reasonably expected from an adult life. It was realism setting in, plain and simple; compromises had to be made. No-one can carry on living the dizzy life of a teenager forever. There was work to be done, bills to pay, a body to take care of into old age. She just had different dreams nowadays, that was all. She wanted a challenging, stimulating career and the financial rewards that came with it, maybe one day the freedom to leave work and to pursue other interests. She was sure those interests would suggest themselves to her one day.

Violet tried to feel grateful that her life had changed. She would go home tomorrow. Everything would seem normal again.

FIVE

There wasn't much to choose from, but then there never had been. A couple of discount stores, their garments sparkling with nylon as the shop lights caught them; a dark hippie emporium, with rails of tie-dyed, tiered and tasselled skirts; a ladies' boutique of the type that could only continue to exist by the seaside, guarded by mannequins with bubble-curl 'dos', fawn kilts and awkwardly-angled heads. Even the chain-stores laboured under the tired liveries of years past, and seemed to carry an entirely different range of clothes to their flagship counterparts on the King's Road and Oxford Street.

Violet thanked her lucky stars that Marks and Spencer still maintained a branch in every town, and amused herself for an hour, buying far more than she needed, telling herself that she should take care of this sort of thing while she had the time. In truth, it was a few years since she had bought her own clothes; she entrusted this task to a personal shopper, an immaculate woman who arrived at her flat once a quarter with a rail of clothes that Violet inevitably bought, and whose opinions on what Violet should be wearing was extensive enough to include even her underwear. Violet tried to conjure this woman's phantom as she made her selection, in the hope that she would be guided to the right items. Still, she felt slightly lost and incapable in the sea of clothes, no longer having any idea of what was in fashion and what she liked. She had surrendered her own taste years ago, in favour of appropriateness, correctness and expensiveness. She decided, on balance, that it would be best to avoid the dangerous array of prints and colours, and so to buy only black things, which at least could not clash or be garish. She piled the items she found over her arm and carried them to the till.

Passing the lingerie section on the way, she was enticed by the prettiness of all the lace and satin, and felt a twinge of rebellion against the strict regime of flesh-coloured cotton that was enforced by her dresser. It occurred to her for the first time that she could break this woman's laws without getting found out. She picked up a couple of the silliest, frilliest sets she could see, and casually ignored the shop assistant's surprised glance as she rang up the price, placing her credit card on the counter and looking the other way.

Leaving the store, she felt elated at having taken part in a small piece of life that she'd forgotten, or at least had deliberately rejected, deciding it was a pointless chore that consumed her time. She was giddy with the knowledge that she had made her own choices, no matter how insubstantial.

It was already dark outside. Violet's mouth was dry with the muted excitement of her spree, and her stomach felt strangely empty despite her recent breakfast; her body catching up with its day of missed meals, she supposed. The bags, too, were heavier than she thought clothes could be – they were weighing her elbows into uncomfortable rigidity and making her shoulders ache. She tried to steel herself, to push her body up the hill so that she could get changed and go out for an early dinner; but she was newly incapable of resisting her own hunger, after all the years of spending her days hungry in order to stick to her diets, and when she passed a café she found that she walked in without even thinking.

It was busy, steamy with dozens of mugs of tea and cluttered with shopping bags and discarded coats, but she found a table to herself under the slope of the stairs, and settled into it, stuffing her bags behind her. She read the cardboard menu that sat upright on the table, and chose a cup of camomile tea and some brown toast, but found herself asking for a hot chocolate and a toasted teacake when the waitress came.

She brushed her hair while she waited, breaking up the damp straggles that had formed at the ends, and then checked her face in her compact mirror, dabbing away the black stains under her eyes where her mascara had bled, and blotting the shine off her nose and cheeks. Nobody else in the café was alone: they were mostly women, chatting and laughing in pairs, pulling garments out of their carrier bags, and handling them reverently, holding them against their faces to check the colours, or running their fingers over the fabric as if it was rare and luxurious. One woman was picking over her buys like a cat through a carcass, checking every seam and hem for defects and holding the cloth up to the light in search of snags and flaws; her husband sat opposite, looking at his highly-polished shoes.

This place seemed familiar, washed as it was in the bright oranges and blues that had fallen out of fashion in London ten years ago. The café took up a corner plot, so that two sides of the room looked out onto the promenade through large windows, the fine Victorian woodwork of which was painted a shoddy indigo. Framed posters in sunny Mediterranean colours were scattered over the walls, placed in careful diagonals to suggest easy haphazardness. As if, Violet thought, they imagined that Spanish peasants would have been too stupid to hang their pictures straight.

There was something more, though. The décor may have been familiar from dozens of cafes she had been in before, but there was also this sense that she seemed increasingly susceptible to, the sense that she had been there before. It was more than déjà vu; she had a precise memory of sitting at the table by the doorway, in daylight. Her memory was bright, specific: she recalled the view of the sea from that angle, cut in half by the sea-front newsstand; the cold gust of the door as it opened to admit another customer, and the rough patch at the side of the tabletop where the laminate edging had peeled off, to which her fingers were repeatedly drawn. She could feel the rhythm of it, her fingers flicking the trimming, pushing it back until it resisted and then letting it ping into place again, and a remembered sense of excitement, of expectation, of newness.

Had this place been here years ago, before she left? She certainly hadn't remembered it, and she was sure that, walking in, she would have felt a spark of recognition. She tried to picture the cafe from the outside, and found that she remembered a different shop in its place when she lived here, a music shop that she had once visited with a friend to buy a clarinet reed. Perhaps it had changed hands shortly before she left, and she had visited it once, and so it hadn't replaced the music shop in her memory.

And yet the images that assailed her, of sitting at that table – no, of *being* at that table, with all the feeling and breathing and thinking that being implies – were so fresh, so recent, so immediate, that she could hardly believe that they could have occurred ten years ago, and that she wouldn't have remembered them before. She dipped a teaspoon into her hot chocolate and stirred, whipping the dark sediment up from the bottom of the glass cup, so that it swirled through the milky brown liquid and made the foam on the top spin; this, too, was familiar, was recent: the experience of being in here, stirring her drink, with the clink and clatter of the kitchen behind her, the humidity of the breaths of a room full of people against the cold outside, and the smell of cheese burning on the griddle.

The thought came and planted itself at the front of her mind as if it had always been there: this was the café where she had sat and waited for her friend to come, feeling tired and fragile and brilliant. Violet felt it like a blow that somehow stopped her lungs from taking in the next breath.

It was the place in her dream.

SIX

Sitting in her room an hour later, Violet wondered why it had seemed so shattering. A little bit of déjà vu, that was all, springing from an overspill of dreaming, the result of having slept too long. She picked up one of the carrier bags and began to sort through its contents, pulling the paper labels off each garment and folding them into her chest of drawers. It was hardly rocket science: cafes being pretty much the same the world over, of course the one in her dream resembled the one she sat in this afternoon. After her long sleep this afternoon, her dreams had seemed near the surface all day. The two had got tangled up, that was all: the café in her dreams and the café in the real world. She had muddled them. She was still tired.

She looked at the clothes in the drawer for a while, and felt satisfied by their unsullied order. She had certainly passed the café before this afternoon, on her way to find the hotel from the station; she may not have noticed it on a conscious level, but that didn't mean that her mind hadn't clocked its existence, somehow. It wouldn't take a genius to layer the experience of being in the café over what she'd seen; dreams are clever things, anyway. They conjure whole worlds every night. This small feat of trickery was nothing to them.

Violet sat on the edge of her bed. She would usually take her vitamins now, a handful of gleaming pills to see her through to the evening, but it seemed that health food stores didn't exist in Stonehithe, and she couldn't muster any faith in the gaudy generic multivitamins she had found in the local chemist. She began to empty her handbag onto the bed, just as she had the night before, methodically searching each corner and compartment until it was empty. There was no hidden blister pack, no dropped tablet lurking in the dust at the bottom of her bag. She packed everything back in again, giving each item – her phone, her mirror – one last shake and turn, to see if she could make a pill fall out.

She craved the optimism that the medication gave her, the sense of control. She longed to feel that wash of ginseng-wakefulness falling over her, so that she could feel sure and confident again, certain of herself. She was jittery lately, prone to flights of fancy that went against the grain of her careful, logical character. It was not that unusual things were happening to her; it was that she was reacting in an unusual way to things that would normally have barely registered on the screen of her attention. Perhaps tomorrow, when she got home, the melatonin would make her firm and sensible again.

Yet despite her desire to return to normal, Violet found that the idea of going back to town for her dinner made her uneasy. In the years since she left it, Stonehithe seemed to have taken on an air of the uncanny. It was emptier than when she had last been there, and the buildings on the outskirts were beginning to decay, as if the whole town was eroding from the outside in. It was the same town she had left, but with unfamiliar faces. In her absence, she had often indulged herself by imbuing the place with a naïve homeliness and friendliness, but now, she realised that it had only been friendly before because she knew people there. She was no different from the tourists that still arrived every summer: a stranger, albeit one who knows their way back to the hotel.

With its black doorways and clusters of young men in tracksuits drifting around the streets, Stonehithe now held in itself the merest suggestion of violence, a threat that was not overt, but which imprinted itself on the town's face like a raised eyebrow or a sneer. Violet felt uneasy at the thought of being out there alone at night; but more than that, she was afraid of the place's magic, at what she might see next that would unsettle her. And anyway, she had lost her appetite; she decided that she would stay in her room, get an early night, leave early the next morning for London. It appeared that this would be a weekend for sleeping.

She ran herself a warm glass of water from the tap in the bathroom, changed into her pyjamas, propped her pillows up against the bed-head and switched on the portable television in the corner of the room. The first three channels fizzed black and white, but the forth showed a Saturday night game show, presented by a man and a woman she didn't recognise. It was loud, stupid, untidy; the screen danced with blinking lights and the puce faces of the contestants. The next channel, the only other one that worked, was showing videos that viewers had made of their pets: a cat slipping into a bath full of water, a dog trying to savage its own shadow. She pressed the standby button and the screen blinked to black.

For a few moments, everything was quiet in the room. The TV was letting out a faint, high-pitched whine as if it were losing air; hot water pipes flared and died down in the wall behind her head. She could hear cars passing outside, their wheels rushing against the wet roads and their headlights illuminating the curtains for a few seconds. She strained to hear the sea beyond the road, but it was absent, a void in the background drone of the outside.

She got up off the bed, opened the curtains and then the French windows, and stepped out onto her tiny balcony that overlooked the shore. The wind buffeted her bare arms

114

and feet, and the fine rain prickled her cheeks, but once she could see the black rhythms of the waves, she found that she could hear them, too: a brooding swirl followed by a brackish snap against the sand, petulant, bad-tempered. She stood and watched it for a while, the sea no more than a shifting pattern in the dark, veiled by the orange coronas of the streetlamps; she could feel her temperature dropping, an imaginary line descending on a thermometer. It was thrilling: the sensation of heat ebbing away from her hands and her feet, and then reaching her thighs, her biceps, her shoulders. This was real. This was the truth: the cold claiming her body and the sea prowling beyond the town's lights. There would be no more of these visions of people and places, no more of this encroachment of dreams into her life. From now on, she would have this to remember, if she wanted to know what was real. She had been getting it wrong, and now she must learn to get it right.

She heard the first knock on the door as only a small shuffle at the edge of her perception, but the second one was louder and pierced her concentration. She crossed the room and opened the door. There, as she expected, was Antonia, clasping her ring-laden fingers together.

"You okay?" she said, eyeing Violet's ragged hair discreetly. "I thought you were asleep again."

"No," said Violet, and stepped aside so that Antonia could come into the room. "Not this time."

"You've got the windows open! In this weather! Is your room too hot?"

"No, no. I was looking at the sea."

"Nothing to see this time of night." Antonia pulled the windows closed and drew the curtains over them. "Now, I don't like to think of you up here on your own. Come downstairs for a glass of wine."

"Oh no, that's fine. Thanks, but I've settled in for the evening." Violet indicated to her damp pyjamas, which were clinging around her arms and legs as if the air was filled with static.

"They're wet."

"Oh, are they? Yes, I suppose they are."

"You can't sleep in those. Get dressed, and they can dry on the radiator while we have some wine."

"To be honest, I don't really drink."

"You ill? On tablets?"

"No."

"Well then, a glass of wine won't hurt you. Come on."

Violet already knew better than to resist. She pulled her jeans, underwear and a new, black roll-neck jumper out of the drawer, and retreated to the bathroom to put them on. Her resistance was only habitual. She liked Antonia, her maternal bossiness and her immunity to rejection, but she also felt lonely in her room in the Hotel Napoli, bereft of her laptop, her work and her routines. She longed for some company to see her through until she got back to London. It was harmless, a change as good as a rest.

She unbuttoned the shirt of her pyjamas and draped it over the heated towel rail, tucking the bottoms underneath it. Next to it, on the sink, she noticed the smart silver box of Nurofen she had bought earlier. Mechanically, she pushed two pills through their stiff foil, but paused before she threw them into her mouth, thinking about her empty stomach and the lack of probiotic pills to cushion their blow. Besides, she didn't have a headache; she hadn't had one all day. She pushed the pills back into their pack, and folded the box shut again.

As she hooked her bra together and eased the straps onto her shoulders, she heard Antonia calling through the door, "I saved you some supper, too."

SEVEN

Antonia's living room, situated just behind the front office, was small and surprisingly Victorian. Its walls were split horizontally by dado rails, with busily-patterned wallpaper on the bottom and mustard paint on the top. Pendulous tassels hung from the long, draped curtains, and a crystal chandelier crowned the centre of the high ceiling; comfortable sofas had been forsworn in favour of a selection of upright Queen Anne chairs, with varying shades of upholstery, and an elegant chaise longue with a green silk seat. Antonia was draped across this, her shoes kicked off, cradling a glass of red wine in her left hand and a cigarette in the other.

"You must be missing London." She flicked pile of ash into an onyx tray and took another deep drag, first on the cigarette and then on the glass of wine, filling the glass with smoke blown from her nose. "There's much more to do up there, right? Better than this place."

"I suppose so. I don't really get out much." Violet held her glass in a tense hand. It had been a long time since she drank, and this seemed to be the hardest of her old restrictions to break, carrying as it did so many fears. She sipped the wine, letting its bitter dryness spread over her tongue, and mentally rehearsed all the harms it was causing: dehydration, memory loss, skin ageing, liver damage. "A girl of your age? I'd be out on the town every night if I was you."

"I work hard. I rarely have time."

"Bollocks." Violet had to smile at the way her accent jarred against the word, cutting it into neat, percussive halves. Bol-locks. Antonia batted the smoke out of the air before her. "Listen, I've given up my life to this place, and look where it's got me. Bollocks to work. Get out there and enjoy yourself."

"I don't think I'd know what to do with myself any more." Violet could feel the wine buzzing in her ears; it was making her dreamily focused, but tired, lazy. She was finding it hard to keep her thoughts to herself, to resist confiding in this woman who seemed to demand intimacy.

"When I came over here, I was a little girl. Seventeen, eighteen. My mother begged me not to go, but I was in love. I thought Robert would take me over to England and that I would live like the Queen. In my mind, all of England was London. I thought I'd be in bars, nightclubs, theatres. Instead I find myself here." She shrugged, drained her wine, then refilled her glass, waving the bottle at Violet until she, too, finished hers so that it could be replenished.

"At first it was okay. I was young, full of energy. Stupid. I should have gone back home to my family. Instead, I worked here, and on my days off I took the train up to London. Two hours there, two hours back, but I didn't care. I was always in the most fashionable shoes, fantastic clothes. People used to stop me in the street to ask where I got them. I made some friends down here, and we'd get together, play a few records, get drunk. It didn't seem so bad."

Violet nodded. "You'd only have done the same thing in London."

"You think that? You think that's all there is to it? Why do you live there, then?"

It was a good question. Violet could remember a time when she couldn't wait to run away from Stonehithe and never come back. She remembered the allure of the city, its depths and breadths, its gloss, its sense of importance, the promise that she would be part of something just by being there. "It's near to work," she said. "It cuts down my journey time."

Antonia shook her head. "And the rest!" she said. "Nobody pays all that extra money to take ten minutes off their commute." Violet looked away. She would have liked to have thought that Antonia was right, and that she was lying, covering up some deeper connection to the town, a romance or an ambition that kept her within its fumy folds. Instead, she feared that she was telling the truth; once upon a time, she may have had greater expectations about living in the capital, but now her motivations were deadeningly prosaic. It was simply about the commute, the preservation of time. For her, it was the only resource that was limited; the only one she was ever likely to bang her head against, anyway. There may have been a little voice at the back of her head that told her that her life was wasteful, that she consumed endless fossil fuels in order to keep up with all the things she undertook to do and to maintain her bodily comfort, but nothing ever happened that made her feel the crunch of it. Time, on the other hand, was an ever-present restriction, regardless of the efficiencies she achieved, the cleaners, the concierges, the delivered meals, the pills. "You'd be surprised," she muttered into her glass.

Antonia shifted in her seat, took a final, hot gasp on her cigarette and ground it into the ashtray. "Don't give me that," she said. "You stay in London because it's special, it's different. Once you've lived there, you can't leave it. You're drawn to it. Even if you don't take part in all those things that are going on around you, you like the idea that they're happening, and you're not so far away. You're almost a part of it." She lit another cigarette, and shook out the match as if she was delivering a scolding. Violet noticed the way that the deep wrinkles around her mouth made sense when they contracted around the butt, falling into a neat, perfect aperture. She liked the idea that a body could modify itself to meet its needs; but then thought about how that mouth had been fooled into conspiring against itself, meticulously accommodating its own poison. "Maybe," she said. "I don't know any more."

Antonia was sitting up now, leaning into Violet to ensure her attention. "I was a bloody idiot; I was fooled. I stayed in this empty place because everything's exciting when you're twenty. I thought a few nights in the pub with friends would be enough. But where are they now? They've all had kids, settled down. We still see them, but they're boring, they're flat. And this place has just got emptier and emptier. There's even less to do now."

"You could still get out."

"Nah. It's over. It's too late. I'm stuck here now with Mr Grey-and-Balding in there." She jolted a thumb over her shoulder to indicate an unseen location on the other side of the wall. "Don't worry, he can't hear us. He'll be sitting in his chair with the headphones on and a book resting on his fat gut."

"He's into music?" Whether or not he could hear them, Violet was reluctant to get involved in a dissection of Robert's personality without having met him.

"He's into bloody Phil Collins. It's different to music."

"At least he's still listening to something."

"Bollocks. It's old man's music. That's why he has to use the headphones. I can't fucking stand it." Antonia's neck was flushing scarlet, taken over by the wine and her own fury. The thick stripes of eyeliner around each eye had bled over the course of the day, and had now formed a cloudy haze of grey in her sockets, making her look severe, weary, skeletal. "We used to listen to good stuff, stuff that our parents wouldn't approve of. Loud stuff, dangerous. The Kinks, The Stones, Hendrix. I hardly remember the names any more. We'd go up to the clubs and dance to it, have a good time, come home on the milk train the next morning." She smirked, and it seemed to calm her. "It all goes, over time. It just gets lost."

"Yeah," said Violet. "You lose your taste for it."

"You lose your nerve."

"And all your energy." Violet smiled, laughed. "Jesus, listen to me. I sound like my own fucking grandmother." She swigged at her wine, enjoying it now, its musty savour, the tickling thrills it gave her nose when she sniffed it, the way it made her mouth relax and the words come out. She laughed, and found that Antonia was laughing too, and they laughed together, wiping the tears from under their eyes with their knuckles. Antonia refilled Violet's glass.

The door at the back of the drawing room opened, and a man walked through, the sort of middle-aged, kindly-faced father that all Violet's friends had when they were at school, and it made Violet draw a breath and stop laughing out of politeness. "Hi," she said, and made a small wave at him.

He smiled, nodded at Violet, said, "What are you two girls cackling about, then? Something's tickled you both," and then he shook his head like a benevolent uncle, continuing through the room and out towards the kitchen.

Antonia burst back into laughter in that fraction before he left the room that school bullies use to such good effect, and Violet joined her, convulsing into cascades of hot giggles that reached the reddening back of his head in the seconds before the door slammed. She could feel, as he disappeared, the bewildered hurt that must have pricked him, but was afraid to break the spell that she and Antonia had woven between themselves. It was odd to see a man like this from the other side, no longer the necessarily-neutered father of a teenage girl, but a husband, a lover, a companion. Violet could see how utterly impossible it was to stay interested in a man like this, when he was so clearly hell-bent on removing every trace of his personality.

She raised her glass to her lips to take anther long gulp, but found that the wine sloshed upwards, and splashed down the front of her new jumper.

"Don't worry," she found herself saying, although the words were a struggle; they seemed to want to elongate themselves, and to catch around her teeth as she pronounced them. "I'm wearing black. It won't show. It's all black. Everything I own," and she stood to brush herself off, only to lurch under the weight of the dizziness that suddenly assailed her. "Oh dear," she said, and felt Antonia's hand at her elbow, steadying her, and heard her say, from somewhere that seemed a long way away, "We'd better get you to your room, I think."

It wasn't so bad when she was upright, when her brain had settled back into its rightful place and was no longer washing around her skull. She placed the glass of the side table carefully and withdrew her hand from it in slow motion, determined not to tip it. Her legs felt rubbery and boneless beneath her, but she made it to the door on her own, and stalked out through the front office, conscious of maintaining control over her every step, lifting her knees high to stop her feet from snagging against the ground and using her hands to ensure that she cleared each obstacle on the way: the desk, the filing cabinet, the printer. She only knocked into one thing, a chair which had failed to be tucked under its desk, and she told Antonia that this wasn't her fault, that chairs were a mobile thing, a fundamentally moveable item, and so she couldn't be expected to predict where each one was.

It would have been funny, anyway, emerging from the back office into the reception for the first time, it being a reversal of everything she had seen before, a mirror-image; but it was stranger still, because it was colder out there, and she hadn't realised until that point how hot she had been in Antonia's drawing room. She felt her face glow against the chill of the hallway, and her eyes watered.

But more than that, the lobby was full of bodies, milling kids filling out the space. They stood in an approximation of a line that crowded down the hallway and under the staircase, clumped in twos and threes, wearing outdoor coats and long striped scarves, knitted hats and gloves, the smell of damp fabric and hair rising from them like steam. Their cheeks were red from the cold outside, and they were talking, all of them; not one of them was silent. The hall was filled with voices that amplified in the stairwell and reflected back onto themselves, creating a general rumble of noise, amongst which it was impossible to pick out a single word that made sense. A boy at the front of the line was throwing his body into exaggerated shapes that must have re-enacted some amusing deed, as his mates were laughing and pushing him away; behind them, two girls groomed each other, rearranging hair and licking fingers to tidy eyeliner, before scanning their eyes around the queue and then drawing together to chatter frantically; further back, a boy and a girl were kissing untidily, only breaking off when someone tapped them on the shoulder to tell them that the line had moved on. They took up their new position and started kissing again.

Three lads passed close by, holding out their hands discreetly below waist level, while a fourth dropped a small white pill into each of their palms. They passed a half-bottle of vodka between them to wash them down, glancing over their shoulders as they did so, trying to look casual. Violet could smell the sickly-sour scent of digested spirits rising from them, mixed with the vegetal tang of aftershave. One of them pulled a pouch of tobacco from his pocket, and began to roll a thin cigarette, which he placed in the corner of his mouth and allowed to hang down as he searched his jacket for a lighter.

"You can't smoke in here anymore boys. You know that."

Antonia's voice pulled Violet from her reverie. The people were real; she had not slipped into dreams again.

"What's going on?" she asked, stepping back from the crowd now that she knew they actually existed.

"Ah, these are our little friends. They come here once a month to use the cellar for a disco. Isn't that right boys?"

"A club, yeah," said the boy who had handed out the pills, and then turned inwards to his group, repeated the word *disco*, and sniggered. Antonia shrugged. "It's about the only money we make in the winter."

They could have been a dream, though, another vision. They were just as vivid as the things she had seen before, the girl and the café and the classroom. Like before, she recognised it all, not individual faces, but the mood and atmosphere of that crowd, what it was like to be in it, waiting. She had been in ones like it, standing and talking to friends, excited by the prospect of a long evening, maybe some music, maybe a band.

Violet forced herself to drink three glasses of water before she lay down, but still sleep took her forcibly, immediately, blackly.

EIGHT

Somewhere, there was banging: low, steady, rhythmic. Violet opened her eyes and it didn't go away.

She sat up, and spent several moments trying to superimpose the features of her room in London over the scene that was now being revealed by the streetlight seeping between the curtains. She could not; for a few seconds the room seemed to roll as she pinned down its features, and then it all became familiar again as she remembered where she was.

Music. The banging was music, heard from a distance, rumbling through the floorboards. She could hear nothing but the rhythm of the drums and the dance of the bass, but she knew it was music. It reminded her of her college digs, when every night a different person would come back from the bar with a group of friends and switch on the stereo, forcing Violet to lie in bed and be prickled by the peaks and troughs of the muffled conversation and the beat of whatever music they played. If it were a room nearby, she would sometimes be able to make out the lyrics. She bought earplugs in the end, and inserted them religiously every night, whether or not any music was playing. She could probably do with them now.

They must still be dancing down there in the cellar. She drank the glass of water by her bed, turned onto her side. The tune was impossible to decipher, but the rhythm was there. It never stopped. She would just go to sleep again, pay no attention. She willed her ears to block out the sound, but they seemed to turn all the more curiously towards it, as if her brain could not move on to the next part of its duties until it had made sense of the sounds it could hear. There was a gap in the music, a few seconds of peace when Violet thought that it had all ended, that she was saved, but then it started up again, fractionally faster than before, with a bass line that climbed and then fell. She pictured it, a hawk, flying high before swooping down for its prey.

She rolled onto her other side. Perhaps it was pointless trying to resist the music. Perhaps she should let it be a part of the rhythms of her sleep, let its regularity soothe her, a heartbeat. She breathed, tried to surrender to it, but found her own heart speeding, racing with the beat. Her body was tense, her shoulders held rigidly high. She tried to force them down, to tense her whole body and then relax it. It stayed tense.

She lifted the top pillow and held it down over her ear, burying the other one into the bed beneath it. The noise was muffled for a few seconds, but then seemed to ooze back into her hearing, as if she had simply adjusted to the lower volume. Her breath was hot under the pillow, humid. She could not sleep like this.

She lifted the pillow again and pushed it under her head. She closed her eyes. She would lie still, and wait for sleep to come. In the meantime, she would daydream, like she did when she was a child. Then, she had an archive of fantasies that she could jump back into whenever she wanted to be transported away from her mundane thoughts: how she would live if she were the richest girl in the world, each night imagining a different room in her endless mansion; or being kidnapped and bravely enduring a succession of trials in order to escape. Tonight, she found she had nothing, no story that she wanted to tell about herself. The only fantasies she had to fall back on were the new-age clichés: a rainforest, a stream in a meadow, a walk on a crisp amber autumn morning. An image of herself, drunk, red-faced and slurring in Antonia's living room, shoved each image away in turn. Her stomach contracted. She would have to apologise in the morning.

She tried to push these thoughts to the back of her mind; no point in worrying about things that you can't change. She wished that this were true, and moreover that her brain was something that could be disciplined in this way, something that would obey when it was told not to think about a matter. Hers, instead, seemed to take spiteful pleasure in torturing her with the things she would rather forget, spitting them back out at her when she was least expecting it, or churning them over and over in her head like the beat of the music downstairs.

Violet sighed and sat up. It was useless trying to sleep; she was nearly shaking with the tension of it. Tomorrow, she would have to go back to London and put everything in order again before she went back to work on Monday. She couldn't afford to be losing sleep, let alone to be dragging a headache around behind her.

The light hurt her eyes when she turned it on, and for a moment everything was blue-edged and indistinct. She swallowed two Nurofen and stared at her face in the mirror. She had fallen asleep without taking her makeup off, and now her eyelashes had bonded together in odd, uncomfortable clumps. She massaged cleansing lotion into her face and began to wipe it off with cotton wool. The music seemed quieter and less imposing now that she was up, its rhythm a mere murmur, such a small thing. It was odd that she couldn't just sleep through it. Her eyes were heavy. Maybe another attempt at sleep, now that she had got it all into perspective. She pulled off two wisps of cotton wool, rolled them into balls and stuffed them in her ears, twisting them deep into her ear canals. The muffled world that they created seemed dizzy, disorienting; she could not hear her own footsteps on the carpet as she walked over to the bed and climbed in. She turned out the light.

At first there was silence, nothing but the ringing in her ears and the rush of her pulse. But then, inexplicably, the music found its way back in again, just a tiny, unassuming pattern working through the earplugs, but irresistible nonetheless, impossible to ignore. Violet growled, "Fuck it," tore the cotton wool out of her ears and threw herself out of bed. She put on her jeans, her shoes, a tee shirt, a jumper and marched out of her room, stuffing the key into her pocket. It was not *on*, it was not *right*, for them to be making *this much noise* when people were trying to *sleep*.

The hall lights were as bright as they were at any other time of day; the hotel had to always be open, always ready, regardless of the hours its inhabitants kept. It felt incongruous to be in such a flurry of irritation in this calm, bland space, but the noise was still there, louder out here in the cool air, and she stamped down the stairs without really thinking what she would do when she reached its source.

There were a few kids using the chairs in the lobby – a boy with glazed eyes, clutching a plastic glass of lager and staring at the carpet; a girl straddling an unseen figure, who was entirely concealed by her splay of hair – but they only registered to Violet as clutter and mess as she passed them. She followed the hallway to the back of the hotel, and then turned down the carpeted stairs marked Cellar Bar.

The music was louder now but still somehow intangible, impossible to pin down as one tune or another. Already, rising up from behind the fire door that led to the bar, was the ground-in smell of smoke and spilt beer, that dank, intoxicating odour. The stairway was dark, lit only by a red bulb in a cage at the side, its carpet tacky below her feet. Just before the door was an abandoned table and chair, with a sign that said, *Entry £4*, written in black marker pen and decorated with a flurry of stars. Through the porthole window in the door, Violet could see that the room was darker even than the stairwell, but there was movement in there, people dancing.

She pushed open the heavy door, and felt the rush of music hit her like a gust of wind, something invisible but physical, unsteadying. She was dazed at first by the darkness and the noise, an assault on her senses, but gradually the figures in the room began to define themselves: a knot of bodies at its centre, surging to the song that was playing, and other forms sitting on low banquettes at the edges of the room, leaning in together as they bellowed to be heard, or slumped silent and smiling, alone. It was hot, the air damp with the breath and sweat of the dancers, the atmosphere compressed by the low, vaulted brick ceiling. At the back of the room, the gloomy lights of the bar were silhouetting a throng of men, some swallowing down pints of glowing beer as if they were medicine; some leaning diagonally against it, nodding their heads in an unsteady attempt to keep time.

To the right was a small enclosure built from rugged rockery-brick, and behind it stood the man in a tucked-out tee shirt playing records, cocking a headphoned ear towards a pair of record decks and bobbing his head to an entirely different beat to the one being played out in the room. His fingers were poised on the centre label of a gleaming circle of vinyl, inching it fractionally clockwise, anti-clockwise, clockwise until he found the place he wanted. He removed his headphones and gazed out over the dance floor for a moment, and then, as the music began to fade, started up the deck that he had been listening to, and eased over a sliding switch. At first there was a benign sonic jumble as one tune faded into the other; but then, just as the dancers had stopped and were swaying in their places, listening intently for the next rhythm to drive them, the new song began, a blizzard of fuzzy guitar, the crack of a snare, and a brittle, booming female voice, pleading, imploring, *Before loneliness will break my heart, send me a postcard darling.*

The mass of bodies picked up in time to it again: a man windmilling his arms, a woman weaving hers before her face. It was like being wrapped up, lifted, transported.

The DJ set down his headphones and rushed onto the floor to join them, allowing his hand to be shaken and his back slapped as the crowd made room for him, and then absorbed him.

And Violet, standing in her place by the door, felt the pull of this song, too. It was a joyous, fundamental drag, an irresistible magnetism that made her muscles twitch to catch its highs and its lows. Heard from a distance, the music had been impenetrable, maddeningly elusive, and broken down into its component parts. She had imagined it as noise only, a sound that she couldn't fathom; fractured, industrial. Music must have changed since she was last listening to it; she had been afraid that she would have no means of understanding it, and had felt alienated by this, afraid, stupid. But here, on the dance floor, the volume so high that she felt the repercussions of every beat in her ribcage, every flutter of bass in her stomach, nothing had changed. She could have stood here, ten years ago, and known it in the same way, the jagged chime of a guitar, the fluid roll of bongos. It forced her to move, to rush towards the dancers and to join them, her feet remembering unbidden how to step in synch, her hips recalling their customary flick and wriggle.

Here I'm waiting for a little sign, waiting 'til the end of time. It wasn't a modern song; the vocals had a pleasing roughness to them that would now be edited out, and the instrumentation was imperfect, imprecise, punctuated by little moments of space that gave the whole thing air. Violet had never heard it before, but she was overcome by a sense that she loved it, that it belonged to her. At the beginning of the next verse, she found herself singing along with the words: *Now please don't let me down, ain't no lover like me in town.* She didn't stop to wonder how she knew them. She opened her eyes, and realised that she had been dancing with them closed. Two girls were dancing with her, and one of them, dark-haired with jeans slung low over her narrow hips to reveal a perfect, taut stomach, smiled at her. A man with an improbable beard for his age took her hand and spun her around, before kissing it and working his way to the next woman in sight. She was a part of something, a member of the crowd. The woman in the song let out a long, wailing entreaty and the music collapsed in around her, creating an odd kind of quiet in the room, a sudden tangle of voices as people continued to shout above a sound that was no longer there. Violet looked over to see the DJ turning off the record decks while the crowd cheered and whistled and called out for more. He looked up, grinned, shrugged, and made a cut-throat motion with his finger to signal that he could play no more. *Come on mate, one more,* someone shouted, and people began to put their fingers in the air: one more! One more!

Fluorescent lights flickered on above their heads, and the fire door was thrown open at the back of the room. Everyone stood blinking for a few moments. It was a signal that was understood; once the lights were on, no-one was willing to commit the same acts of abandon that they were willing to commit in the darkness. People milled shiftily, bereft of the camouflage of the dim lighting, before obediently making their way to the door. Many of the dancers were revealed to be significantly sweatier than they had looked in the dark: hair was damp on the backs of their necks and their faces were pink and shiny with exertion. The man who had danced with Violet had deep sweat rings on his lilac shirt; the woman with the midriff had a smudge of eyeliner across her cheek. Violet herself felt ridiculous, red from dancing, her hair scraggy from sleep, and dressed drably in jeans and a black tee shirt compared to the spectrum of carefully-chosen colours and styles that were on display before her: knee-high boots, sparkling vintage frocks, lurid shirts. They walked uncertainly, chattering, calling to one another about late drinks and back-to-mines, laughing and spilling into one another.

It didn't take long for the room to empty, after the bottle-neck at the door had cleared, and Violet was left standing in the middle of a damp parquet dance-floor, bewildered at the way the magic had drained from the room. With the lights on it was uglier, more tawdry, decorated in the browns and oranges of decades ago. There were a few bodies left on the chocolate-coloured velour seats that lined the room: a man passed-out, his pint glass emptied into his lap, a young blonde girl draped over a shaggy-haired man, oblivious to the new light. His hands were wedged down the back of her jeans, and Violet could see them creeping around in there lasciviously. They barely flinched when the barman passed by them, picked up their glasses from the floor and called, "Alright folks, thank you very much. Time to go home now," as near to them as he dared. He moved on to the next figure on the couch, the unconscious man, gingerly extracted the glass from his lap and began to tap and shake him, leaning into his face and saying, "Come on, mate, party's over. Let's get you on your feet."

Violet felt someone's hand on her elbow, and turned to find the DJ standing behind her. He was dark-haired, with the traces of a beard, and seemed older than the crowd he had just been playing music to; his eyes crinkled at the edges. "I don't think I've seen you here before?" he said, a question rather than a statement.

"No."

"Thought I'd give you a flyer. We've got something on next Friday at the World Underwater. Do you know it?"

Violet took the photocopied square of paper, jagged from having been cleaved from a larger sheet by hand, and pushed it into her pocket. She remembered the big old pub from her life here years ago, when it had been popular for its dark back room that was let out for free at weekends. She smiled up at the man, feeling a small pang of loss that she would only ever hear one song from him, and thanked him as he walked away.

The unconscious man was now being helped out of the door by the barman, who seemed happy to let him take his chances once he was outside. He pulled the fire door shut, and made his way over to the couple, who still hadn't moved from the sofa. "Come on, love," he said, and tapped the girl on the shoulder, "Just 'cos your mum won't let you do it under her roof, don't mean to say you can do it under mine." The boy pulled away and grinned, and then looked over his shoulder, seemingly startled at the brightness and emptiness of the room. His face dropped.

"Sorry, mate," he said, and leapt to his feet so fast that the girl's legs dropped heavily onto the seat. He pulled up his jeans, which were sagging low over his hips, and thrust out a hand to his companion. She sat up more slowly, stretching and smiling naughtily, and then eased to her feet like a sleepy cat.

"You'll have to go out through the main door; I've shut up the back one now," said the barman, already turning away towards the ranks of glasses on the bar. The couple wrapped their arms around each other's waists, and began to stalk towards the door. As they approached, the girl straightened and wiped her mouth with the back of her hand, and Violet got a good look at her face for the first time.

It was pale and fine-featured, with a narrow mouth and dark, almond eyes. Violet felt her heart weigh suddenly heavy in her chest, and for a beat, the girl seemed to pause and stare enquiringly at her, as one would do into a mirror, before picking up her pace again and walking out of the door.

It was that same face again, the same face that she had known all her life, and that had haunted her this last week.

It was her own.

NINE

There was no doubting it this time, no going back over the memory and picking it apart, pixel by pixel. This time it had happened; this time it was true. Violet had seen it with her own eyes, straight-on. Not through a car window, not mediated by speed or snow or a mesh of people. It was her own face looking back at her. It was as simple as that.

It was not her current face, either, although it was just as familiar. It was the face that had been hers some time ago, a different face, a more brave and optimistic one. Violet had barely realised that her own face had changed before she saw it, but there it was: softer, rounder, clearer. Looking at herself in the dressing-table mirror now, the morning after, with the curtains thrown open to let in the clean, sharp rays of February sunshine, Violet noticed for the first time how her eyes had become more hooded, her skin looser, her chin sharper over the last ten years. She wondered when it had left her; if there was a point, a moment, when she should have recognised its absence, or whether her ageing had been a gradual thing, a layering of grey veils, each one in itself unnoticeable but cumulative.

Violet shook her head at her reflection and stepped into the shower that had already been running, filling the bathroom with thick steam. She stood under the water for a few moments, feeling it pound heavily on her scalp and saturate her hair. She looked down over her body, decorated with runnels of water. It had changed, too: her stomach was softer, rounder, and her breasts fuller, as if they had given up waiting for her to produce a child, and had sagged to accommodate its ghost instead. The skin over her thighs was white and ghastly. The exercise, the dieting, the vitamins; the expensive creams and serums, scrubs and soaks: none of them could have prevented this. This was time, taking its toll. There was nothing she could ever have done.

She lifted her face up to take the full blast of the water, opening her mouth to let it run across her tongue. It tasted salty, bitter, like iron. She spat it out, creating a flat, split flow through her teeth. It was odd that this was the thing that had got her, the vanity. There were so many other things to think about. Perhaps it was preferable to contemplate one's own cellular decay over the unknown, the inexplicable. Perhaps it was easier to grasp that she was ageing than it was to grasp that somewhere out there was her exact double.

Because it was more than a passing resemblance; more, in fact, than looking exactly the same. But for the age-gap, this girl was identical to her in every way: it was the same face, not a similar one; the same eyes, nose and mouth; the same arms, legs, throat. And more, too: there was a whole life in common, a shared town, a shared school, shared haunts. Did she have the same mother, sitting somewhere in a house in Stonehithe? Was everyone just repeated down here, a double created for each person that left? Violet had not, she recalled, recognised any of the people that surrounded the girl as being replicas of her own group of friends; but then, wasn't it all the more unnerving somehow to be the only one that is repeated like this, singled out for the creation of a doppelganger?

She turned off the shower and reached for a towel on the rail, feeling the hit of the relatively cold air from the bathroom outside, and dried herself awkwardly in the confined space, her elbows repeatedly knocking against the glass of the cubicle. On one hand, it was too mind-boggling to contemplate, this idea of another version of you living the same life as you had before you left town. On the other, she was surprised at how easily she had accepted it, how untroubled her brain was by the information, as if it were so impossible to assimilate that it had just surrendered to the information, and had swallowed it whole. After she had seen the girl last night, she had simply walked back up to her room and got into bed; she had fallen asleep immediately, and had passed an untroubled night, waking at eight in a kind of serene daze. It was as if, on some level, the truth of the girl's existence was no surprise to her subconscious at all. She had known since she first saw her that there was more to this than a passing similarity. This confirmation was a comfort rather than a blow.

She dressed slowly, dithering over her sparse drawer of garments until she had to force herself to pick anything that matched, and then sat down again in front of the mirror, unwrapped her hair from its towel and began to brush out the straggling damp knots that dribbled onto her shoulders. She took the hair dryer out of the top drawer and began to work her way methodically through her hair, section by section, brushing it out straight and blasting it with warm air.

She could remember going on nights out like that, when she was still in that early, hot grip of her own sexuality. There had been a brief period of time, perhaps only a year or two, when she had become aware of the power of her young body, its ability to excite and entice. There had been an incredible curiosity that ached in the fabric of her flesh, to experience this new potential for pleasure that seemed to have taken possession of her, but, more importantly, there was a sense of daring, too, a gleeful fascination with the interest that others seemed to be taking in her. The craze of sexual longing that had fallen across her and her friends in their last year at school had been fundamentally social in quality, concerned more with the possibilities of interest and intrigue than with base urges. They left them to the men, whom they characterised in their giggly discussions as slaves to their own desires, governed by the biological necessity of sex. For she and her friends, the act of sex was often a necessary evil that made possible the main events: the anticipation beforehand, and the discussion afterwards, that strip-tease of revelation and concealment.

It could only have lasted for so long; it was innocent, really, naïve. But before the breathless encounters developed into sticky relationships and unrequited attachments, there had been a period when sex had bonded them all together, acting as a straightforward substitute for the ballet lessons and hockey matches that had enchanted them before.

Violet switched off the dryer and smoothed the static out of her hair. She could remember one night, in particular, she and Sasha had holed up in her room on a Saturday afternoon, with bagfuls of clothes and makeup, and had drunk a bottle of bright green crème de menthe as they tried to construct the perfect outfit from the jumble at their feet. She remembered how cooperative their bodies had been, how pliable, how willing to fit into any size or style. Stomachs could be pulled in, feet pinched into shoes a size too small, and angular hips could prop up baggy waistbands. She had chosen her own pair of jeans in the end, but had decided to wear with them a tight man's waistcoat that showed more than a glimpse of her bra, and a bowler hat. She had sprayed on Sasha's perfume – sweet, dusty Obsession – and had spent the evening catching exotic whiffs of it, feeling transformed by taking on the scent of someone else.

She remembered that night in particular because everything had worked somehow, and she had felt triumphant, glamorous, exciting. They had taken a table to themselves at the pub in town that everyone was going to at the time, although Violet didn't even remember its name any more, and had talked and laughed and shown off, until Sasha saw a man that she had met before, and he came over and brought his mates with him. One of them sat next to Violet, a dark-haired lad who was home from university for the weekend, and who bought her drinks and made her laugh by bragging about the things he got up to at uni: cream-cracker eating contests, rag week, sitting pissed in lectures. It had all seemed unbelievably exotic to Violet, although she would never have admitted to it. When she was at university herself, a year later, she had looked on the whole thing with sour disapproval.

They had all gone on to a club, a little night held in some underground room somewhere; she barely remembered getting there, she was so drunk, but once they arrived it was already full, and the DJ was playing music that she didn't know but wished she did. The man she was with – had she even known his name? – knew the words to one of the records that was played, and she asked him what it was. He laughed and told her it was James Brown, and she felt embarrassed that she didn't know, and she went out and bought a compilation CD of his, the next day she could get to the shops. She probably still had it, somewhere.

She danced with the lad for hours. He was wearing jeans that were so loose that she gave him her belt to keep them up. After a while, they sat down, and he leant over and kissed her, and she remembered the smell of him, a sort of mossy smell of sweat and aftershave. She was drunk by then, but the kiss had seemed eternal, irresistible. He had stroked her left breast rhythmically with the edge of his thumb, and she had been emboldened by this, had wanted to prove that she was willing to go further, even here, and so had pushed her hand down the front of his jeans and had taken hold of his cock, pulling her fist up and down it awkwardly in the confined space. She remembered how he had looked startled at first and then had smiled; she remembered, too, how exciting it had been to be doing something so wild, so naughty.

They were stopped in the end by a barman, and she was terrified that he had seen what she was doing, but had decided to play it cool, to put on her best insouciant face and to stalk out as if she didn't care. Perhaps, she thought at the time, the barman would even envy them.

Violet had recalled this memory many times since: it still gave her a small erotic spark to think of it, an electric twitch low down in her stomach. She had found it hard to believe, the next morning, that she had done it; and even more so now, years after sex itself had began to feel too risky, too much of an emotional imposition. It was nothing, really, but it always made her smile, the idea of her giving some stranger a hand-job in a nightclub, purely for the thrill of the transgression. She could remember laughing hysterically with the lad after they had left the club, when the cold and the streetlights had hit them, and they both felt sheepish about catching one-another's eye.

Violet brushed mascara onto her eyelashes, playing the memory over in her mind. They were laughing at someone, she recalled, although she never had before, a woman in the club, who had clearly seen what they had been doing, and had addressed them with a look of utter horror and disgust as they had passed her to leave.

No, that couldn't be right. She saw, through her own young eyes, the woman that had stared at them. It was herself. Herself, last night. Standing on the dance-floor, staring in horror.

TEN

It was like having a twin, that was all, her own mirror-image. There was no reason for it to be a problem. She had a twin, and it was common knowledge that twins often had a link, that thread that ran between them to tug at their thoughts and emotions until they fell into line with each other. It was natural, miraculous, wonderful. So what if this was a displaced twinship, if one of them had been born sooner and the other later. So what if they happened to be twins by different mothers, different families. It was all within the realms of human experience, if you broke it down into its component parts. It was surely nothing that hadn't happened before. It was normal, nearly.

Violet stooped to pick up a shell, a tiny fan of pink stripes, half-buried. The wet sand peeled up around her fingers as she dug it out, and the hole it left immediately filled with frothy water. Brushing away the dark grey grains, she could see that it was still joined to its pair by a narrow hinge. She put her lips to it and blew the sand from between the two halves, and then tested their delicate spring, feeling them push back against her fingers. Pulled apart and flattened against her palm, they made a candy-coloured butterfly, the shell and her sister joined at the hip. It wasn't so odd to have a double, to be one half of a pair. There was no reason to be unnerved. She tried to fold the shells back together again, but the thin ligament that had attached them sheared away, and they came apart, two delicate arcs in the palm of her hand. She let them fall back down to the beach.

The sun was already disappearing from the watery sky, and the sea was beginning to take on its dark night-time tint, so that its currents appeared to boil just below the surface as the tide turned. Every seventh wave would lick at Violet's feet, as if it were gradually nudging her off the beach and onto solid ground. The wind, too, seemed to be expelling her, lashing out in blasts and gusts, so that her cheeks were numb and her ears ached. Within an hour, she knew, the sea would have marched across the sand and would be lapping up against the concrete barricades that restrained it from washing into the town. There was still time, she supposed, to pack everything up and go back to London.

But even she didn't believe this any more.

ELEVEN

"I thought you'd gone without paying."

Antonia had rushed for the reception desk as soon as she saw Violet come in, and was now leaning one elbow on it, dipping the other arm below the counter to conceal a cigarette from no-one in particular. Its smoke rose up in a blue ribbon between them.

"I'm sorry. I've been out on the beach."

"In this weather? You'll catch your death!"

"Listen, I thought I might stay. For a few more days."

"I know. I went to your room, and your stuff was still there."

"I hope it's okay."

"You're assuming the room is free. I might have a client waiting to book in."

"Have you?"

"Of course I bloody haven't. I've only got you and some other guy in the whole building." Antonia smiled, wrapped a strand of hair neatly behind her ear. "I cooked you dinner. Come."

TWELVE

"Oh no, not for me." Violet shrunk away from the glass that was held out towards her.

"You feeling fragile after last night?"

"Not fragile. Just embarrassed."

"There's nothing to be embarrassed about. We're just two girls having a good night in, huh? No, you must get back on the horse. Build up some resistance."

Violet took the glass and cradled its comfortable bulbousness in her hand. It felt right, the stem protruding between her fingers and the bowl resting against her palm. The scent of the wine was heavy, earthy and mysterious. She took a sip. "There. You're just not used to it. I bet you're a cheap date." A laugh like the grinding of gears.

Violet smiled, swigged her wine again. She could feel Antonia's good humour breaking through the solitary spell that had fallen over her today, and was glad of it, but wary, too, of being forced into unwanted confidences. Everything had changed now. She was party to something so fundamentally odd, so utterly unbelievable, that it would be dangerous to tell. And yet, at the same time, her every thought was possessed by the girl, so that it all seemed ready to burst out at the first moment she let down her guard.

"So you spend a little time down here, visit some family I suppose?" Antonia had kicked off her shoes and curled into a chair, showing off her long, thin, painted toes. "Catch up with old friends?"

Violet shook her head. A waft of tonight's dinner was snaking through from the kitchen, making her stomach gurgle. "There's no-one left down here." She might have added, *There's no-one anywhere else, either; I've got rid of them all.* But she didn't; there was no need to say it. It was probably written all over her face.

Antonia seemed oblivious. "They all got out of this shit-hole," she said, and sheared the cellophane off a fresh pack of cigarettes, crunching it in the palm of her hand. She pulled out one and lit it, waving the smoke away from Violet's face with her pristine fingers. "You hungry?"

"Starving."

Antonia smiled. "Osso bucco tonight. And I don't want to hear any of your English bollocks about eating veal, okay?" Violet thought of the list of things – the butter, the wine, the salt – that she'd raise an objection to before she even thought to engage her ethics.

The meal was right to the point of wonderment, and Violet was surprised at the sight of her own empty plate at the end of it. They ate it on their knees, chatting inconsequentially about a programme Antonia had watched on the television the night before, which showed women having babies using eggs bought from the third world. Violet was not sure if this was supposed to be instructional for her, somehow; if she was not supposed to see in it a shaft of light that illuminated the way out of her own childlessness.

Antonia said, "You did well," as she took the plates away, and returned from the kitchen after a few moments with two creamy-headed espressos. In their wake, the wine tasted strange and salty.

"I've got something to show you," she said, reaching behind the sofa and dragging out a cardboard box that was clearly too heavy for her to lift by herself. "I got Robert to bring them down from the loft this afternoon, when I realised you might be staying." Violet felt a slight sense of awe at the easy theatricality of this woman, who seemed to be able to predict her every move, and who could stage-manage Violet's evening so precisely that she could afford to bring the box out now, after an unplanned meal, wine and coffee.

She unfolded the flaps, saying, "You'll like this," and for a moment Violet had an unnerving sense that Antonia was even more omniscient than she suspected, and was about to reveal a collection similar to her own, a box of stones bundled up in white paper, awaiting the pleasure of their unwrapping. At first, when the box was opened and she saw them, she was so convinced of this that she couldn't make sense of the contents. She saw many colours of printed paper – books, leaflets? But then, as her eyes adjusted, she began to understand what they were: the box was full of records, singles in fact, small flat squares that crowded together in a jumble of faded colour.

It was years since Violet had seen a single – she remembered them, their lightness and their vinyl sheen, from her childhood, the first few records bought for her and played endlessly on the stacking system in the living room.

Antonia was already rifling through the contents of the box, leaning into it with her whole body as if she secretly longed to climb in and be packed back up in the attic with her precious relics. She was lifting out great handfuls of records and gazing at them one by one, before handing them to Violet with a comment or an exclamation.

"I remember this one – it was playing in a store when I first came to England, and I had to ask the man behind the counter what it was," she would say, or, "This one I bought when I split up with an old boyfriend. I cried over it for days. Don't even remember what he looked like any more."

Some of the records she would just look at and shake her head as if amazed at their continued existence, or would laugh or sigh, as if the stories they held were too large and too complex to even begin to tell. Others she would hum or sing, catching Violet's eyes in case she recognised them and could join in; for a couple, she even started to dance, still seated, clicking her fingers and shuffling her legs against the carpet.

It was enchanting to watch her, an infantile expression of pure joy breaking across her face as she savoured the memories that each song triggered. Violet felt like a child being shown around a family album, eager to absorb every little scrap of history that it offered. When Antonia passed records to her without saying a thing, she found herself demanding the story behind them, or asking for a rendition of how they sounded, and Antonia would grin broadly, showing off the gap between her two front teeth, and say, 'Ah, well, that one's a kind of Northern Soul, I suppose; a fast beat for dancing," or, "You must know that one! It's got the chorus that goes, *Gloooor-iah! Gloooor-iah!*"

At one of them, she just smiled and said, "I used to dance all night to that one. There was a little disco they used to run after-hours at the ballroom, a bit like those kids we had here last night," and for a moment Violet thought that she looked at her significantly, as if she knew everything; but then she turned to the next record on her pile and shrugged, saying, "Now this one I don't know at all. Perhaps it got mixed up with mine after a party one night. Ah yes, you see. It's got someone else's initials on it. *BA*. Can't think who that is." She cleared her throat and continued.

After that, Violet noticed that all the records had Antonia's initials on them, engraved deeply into the centre label in black ink. "We used to have parties," she told Violet, "where we'd all put our records together and hope that someone would bother to change them over when they finished. You had to sort all through them the next day to find the ones with your name on."

It struck Violet after a while that Antonia was getting the same pleasure from looking at these records as she would from her stones: the pleasure of handling, examining, considering and arranging, a combination of physical sensation and mental stimulation. The very feel of the 45s was faintly nostalgic for her, the bustle of brittle paper sleeves, the delicate pleasure of holding them correctly, the contrast between their individual lightness and their collective heaviness.

She noticed that, as she got nearer the bottom of the box, the records became more recent, as if the person who had packed them had journeyed back in time during the process, perhaps thoughtlessly relegating the more recent acquisitions to the attic at first, but then pausing as they held on to their old, more precious, specimens for just a little longer. There was a cluster of records from the 70s – Stevie Wonder, Pink Floyd and David Bowie – and a scattering of singles from the 80s, but little after that. Antonia's eyes lost a little of their fire as she reached these; she smiled and hummed the tune of Golden Brown, but it was half-hearted, lacking the conviction that she'd shown over the rest of her hoard.

Violet saw, too, how over the years Antonia's scrawled name had been replaced on the centre of each record by Robert's, and by the time they reached the 80s records, there were no names at all, as if the parties had ended and there was no longer any need to assert one's ownership over them.

As Antonia took the last few out of the box and gave them a cursory glance before putting them aside, Violet felt a quiet settle over the room, a mournfulness at the end of their hour of exploration, but also a sense of anti-climax, of the box having given up the best of its secrets too early on, and of the promise and excitement of the life represented by these records having somehow faded away, having somehow come to nothing.

"Well," said Antonia, "there," and Violet saw that when she did her next habitual sweep of her fingertips across the arcs of her eyebrows, she made a discreet dab in the corner of each eye, too. She began to tear at the foil on a fresh bottle of wine.

"You have a box of records like this somewhere I expect. At your Mother's house?"

Violet passed her the corkscrew. "No, my Mum threw them all away when I moved out. I've never given them a thought."

"But you loved them in just the same way at the time."

"I don't know," she said; "I mean, I had records that I loved, and that I played again and again, but that was never really the main thing for me. It was the stuff that came with it, the feeling of being part of a crowd. The clothes – looking different. Feeling like you're not a part of the mainstream."

Antonia scowled and filled Violet's glass. "You weren't always such a bloody serious old woman, then. Thank God."

It was a comment that should have stung, but it didn't. It was a statement of fact, an unmistakable truth. "No," she said, "I wasn't. Not at all. I used to be a bit of a handful, actually. I was always pushing it. I wanted to see how far I could go. I think my Mum was appalled most of the time. I think she wondered where she'd gone wrong."

"Your poor Mum."

"Yeah, poor Mum. It was nothing to do with her. I just thought that the bad kids were cooler. I felt like I was missing out. I was bored. I wanted to scare myself."

"You turned out alright in the end."

Violet rubbed the back of her neck; the conversation had made a small part of her stomach turn over. "It was a decision, in the end. A few things happened – all in a short space of time – that made me stop and think. In the end, I decided that I wanted my life to turn out right. I put my head down and worked hard for the last term of my A Levels. I knew I could get good grades either way, it was just a case of going that extra mile to make sure." She sighed, seeing her identical counterpart last night skipping across the dance floor as if she didn't care what she looked like, writhing around with that slack-jawed boy. She had a brief sense of how far away she had got from all that, how distant that feeling of liberation and daring and joy now was. She recalled it as a big whoop in the stomach, a bodily belief that you couldn't lose, that you were invincible. She could have choked on the remorse at having lost it.

"It all seems like a long, long time ago," she said, and couldn't quite manage to raise her head to look Antonia in the eye. Her lips were numb again from the wine, which she could no longer taste as she sipped it. Her mouth ached with thirst, but she felt an elation in her drunkenness, a sense that she had let herself go, even just a little. She smiled, making her muscles fight against the gloom that was resting on her. She would have hated to admit that this was all a mistake, that she was disappointed in the way her careful plans had turned out, even if it was the most obvious thing in the world.

"If you think it was a long time ago, think how it feels for me," said Antonia, and for a while they were both silent.

THIRTEEN

Later, in bed, Violet found it impossible to sleep for the thoughts rolling over and over in her head. The events of the last two nights kept colliding together, until they became one big, thunderous cloud.

Perhaps she was drunk, perhaps she would feel differently in the morning, but they all seemed to be winding together to spell something out to her. She felt heavy with coincidence and fate, superstitious at this odd configuration of events, despite her devout rationality.

It was all happening for a reason. It was a mirage, a sign, a path lit up to show her the way. If her life were wrong – if she had grown old before her time, was dull, constrained, miserable, lonely – then perhaps it was time for her to change. Perhaps she could grasp at the last few of her desires. Perhaps it wasn't too late.

Here was an opportunity to set it all straight, a second chance to get it right. The girl, she was sure, was her own exact replica, a carbon copy of her life imprinted on a different time. If last night had proved anything, it was that the events would be the same in this girl's life as they were in her own. They may be played against the backdrop of a different era, and may feature a different cast of characters, but with a little thought, a little remembering, they were entirely predictable.

Were they controllable, too? Could she change the course of this girl's life, effect some sort of influence to prevent her from making the same mistakes as she had? If psychology tells us that we're no more than the sum total of our experiences, then surely it would be possible to shape a life, to mould a character out of events and moments. Could this girl's life be bettered, corrected, perfected even, if only a few things were added and taken away?

At that moment, it all seemed possible, and Violet imagined herself as a kind of benign angel who could oversee this life and act to improve it.

As she drifted off to sleep, she was struck by another vision, that of the experience of lying in a different bed in a different room, hearing the noises of the street below, and smelling the musty weight of unchanged sheets.

She knew the girl was near.

There I am again.

You're too clever for this, aren't you? You've already guessed. I always say my readers are capable of divining seams of information I don't even realise I'm sharing, and you've done it again. I was trying to sneak it past you, but you've got me. Hands up. White flag. I'll go quietly.

It's me Violet's been obsessing over. I'm the girl. Now that we've all established that I actually exist, I can come clean. I'm the lovely little reprobate who clung so tenaciously to Violet's consciousness in the first few weeks of that year. I'm the drinker of crème de menthe (pretending desperately it was absinthe) and the seducer of nice young men with prospects. I may be a few years older and an awful lot wiser, but we are definitely one and the same.

Let me tell you a little bit about myself, seeing as we're (nearly) on first name terms. I was born into a family that Violet would have recognised well, if she'd have ever come across them. Not identical to hers, but similar enough to be a lesson to her if she'd have cared to seek them out. But then, that's obsession for you: can't see past the end of its own nose. Violet couldn't take her eyes off me for long enough to imagine that there might be another little mirror on her life, other than me. No matter; she learned enough, either way.

My mother was a teacher (Computer Sciences, if you can imagine the horror) and my father did some desk job in the local pharmaceuticals plant. Neither of us, my mother or I, really knew what he did, and I'm not sure if either of us really cared. She left him when I was fourteen, citing the sheer bloody boredom of their life together. I went to see him once or twice after that, in the thin-walled bedsit he had rented out near his mother's, the other side of London. He had turned grey: not just his hair, but his clothes and face, too. Grey cheeks, grey lips, grey fingernails, and speech that hung between us in thick grey clouds, so that we couldn't look one-another in the eye. He'd got into his books, he told me, and pointed to a bank of flatpack shelves stacked with those heroic WWII nonfiction titles with big, macho names and blockbuster lettering. The Serpent's Lair. Falling to Earth. Taking on the Gods. The Devil's Wrath.

I lost touch. We wrote a few times, but neither of us could really think of anything to say. It didn't take long for him to give up once I stopped replying. A year, eighteen months. It was kinder that way, really. Children understand the necessity of cruelty far better than adults, and teenagers have just about mastered the art.

It made me sad. It made me angry. I made friends with the kids who hung around the benches down the side of the station, and tried to be like them. I bought new clothes, dyed the old ones black, appropriated the kohl pencil from mum's make-up bag and made liberal use of it. I dropped my 't's and dropped a few grades; I rolled my eyes at my teachers and swore at my mother. No-one seemed to care. My auntie started calling me baby-goth or goth-lite. Put your arms in the air a moment, love. Oh look, it's a gothic arch! My mum joined in.

I learned that you have to make more of an effort if you're going to rebel against baby boomers. They've seen it, done it. Worse, it took me a month to realise that the kids who hung around the station were picked up at the end of each night by liberal mothers in Volvos.

It made me angrier still. I started getting drunker than everyone else. I tried pot, poppers, speed, mushrooms, E. I fucked two of the nice boys at the back of the station just to get the hang of it, and then moved on to their older brothers. I refused to go steady, to be anyone's girlfriend. I swore a lot, smoked all the roll-ups I could choke. No-one batted an eyelid. My mum, in the meantime, was developing A Life Of Her Own After All The Years Of Being Nothing But A Wife And A Mother. She had her hair cut, bought a wardrobe of short skirts and frilly knickers, and started dating dodgy-looking middle-aged men with hair that touched their collars. She announced that she would move to France as soon as I finished my A Levels. She didn't want to spend the rest of her life in this bloody place; she wanted to be in the sun, drinking wine. I didn't blame her. I wanted to get out, too, as soon as I could. I imagined that there was a non-specific sort of excitement to be had elsewhere, maybe London, maybe somewhere further away, Thailand or India. I could sing in a band, maybe. Something like that.

That's when I met Violet. Until that point, we'd lived exactly the same life (oh yes, Violet did all that too, not that you'd know it by looking at her), give or take a few names and faces. But that all changed. You'll see. Read on. There's lots to learn.

This is where it gets complicated. Up until now, I've shown you Violet's view, her own unique take on the world. Well, I'm not about to stop that, just because I've entered the picture, even if it does mean referring to myself in the third person and holding back from letting you know exactly what I was thinking at any given time. There's little that Violet didn't know, anyway. You will already have noticed – that extraordinary perception again! How do you do it? – that a sort of link formed between us as soon as we found out about each other. Violet's came earlier because she worked it out sooner, but mine caught up eventually. From the moment she first saw me, little bits of me found their way into Violet's consciousness, snatches of pure experience. They told her very little at first, except perhaps where I was and what I was feeling. It became more developed over the years, but now we're jumping ahead or ourselves. That's a while off yet.

For now, all you need to know is this: there came a point when we somehow got all mixed up together; my memories overwrote hers, and hers bullied and belittled mine. Sometimes I can't tell the difference, other times I can. It doesn't matter. We're a bit of a composite, the two of us – a chimera, if you will. Just lately, I've known more and more about her; her memories would just appear in my brain overnight, as if I had downloaded them. I understand why now. I doubt I'll be getting any more of them.

I won't tell you my name yet – you're going to discover it soon enough, and it wouldn't do for you to find out before Violet does.

In the meantime, I'll move the story on a little for you, as we're all just waiting for the next time I appear, just as Violet was all those years ago. She had a lot of nervous energy to spend that week. She woke up at five on Monday morning, knowing that she would have to call Marcus. She worried about it for so long that he called her in the end, at nine, on her mobile. I've watched her in my copies of her memories, the dry mouth and aching throat, the slight shake to her hands as she lied and said that they thought it was a virus, brought on by the stress of her Grandmother's death. Her GP had ordered her to take a week off. She even managed to make a joke of it, her fictional resistance to this edict, her trumped-up devotion to the cause of her work, and then her final, reluctant, capitulation when he suggested that she would be off work for much longer than a week if she didn't comply. She offered to take the time off as holiday, and Marcus said that of course he would never expect that. He must have known she was lying, even then, but I like to think that even a little worm like him refrained from calling HR straightaway. I suspect I'm wrong.

After the call, things didn't get any easier. Working on the hypothesis that I would turn up at the same club next Friday night, Violet had a lot of waiting to do. Can you imagine how the whole week stretched before her? A whole week of scheming and planning, of working out a way to rescue me from the horrors of my own future? She passed the time by buying things: a dozen alternative outfits for her Friday night out, a serious Russian novel to gaze at, a speculative packet of cigarettes to see if she could get the hang of them again, bottles of wine to appease Antonia and a bottle of cognac for her room, to drink in those gurgling moments when tension rose like acid from her gut as she tried to sleep. She even bought a reporter's notebook and packet of biros, and sat with them in cafes, drinking lattes and agonising over every detail of her teenage life: the names, the faces, the feelings, the events.

The notebooks stayed stubbornly blank. Instead, her brain chewed and choked over her adult life as if it was gristle. The question she kept asking herself was the old, familiar one: where did it all go wrong? She tried to think it through, to order her mind into a systematic enquiry of the facts, but every event she could recall, every choice and decision, every piece of good or bad luck, led her mind spiralling down a multitude of paths, living out all its past glories. It was irresistible, this orgy of reminiscence. She was amazed at how much she had forgotten. She was amazed at how fabulous she had been when she was 17, 18, fearless. Although the journey was her own, she couldn't imagine why she had ever let herself change so much. It made her wonder whether she couldn't change both of us, me and her.

She stayed out of my way all that week. She didn't want to meet me again until she was ready. She took long walks on the beach, her eyes fixed on the shingle, searching for trophies, until she suspected that she had exhausted the beach and its stones. She bought three newspapers every day, and read them until she was afraid of the world. On Wednesday, she rang her mother and cried down the phone, hearing the mystified voice on the other end try to feign concern. From what she could hear, her mother never stopped cooking dinner throughout the whole call. She said she was sure Violet would feel better in the morning.

And all this time she was catching little glimpses of me whenever she closed her eyes – the taste of toothpaste as I brushed my teeth, the view of the backs of my hands as I stared at them in assembly, the boom of the wind buffeting my ears as I walked home. I was less of a ghost to her than a possession, a series of sensory perceptions that took her over at her weakest moments. The sensation was exquisite to her.

There was one other thing that Violet learned to do that week, something that actually soothed her. Turn the page. I'll tell you all about it.

FOURTEEN

Antonia looked surprised when Violet asked about the pool, and then annoyed, and then embarrassed, but she went to the back office to take the key off its hook anyway. Even then, as she handed the key over, she held onto it for a little longer than she should have and said, "It's a bloody dungeon down there. It's ever so damp. You'd be better off going to the sports centre in town."

"It doesn't matter. I'll give it a go."

"Well at least wait an hour while I switch the heater on. I'll make you a coffee while you wait."

Despite the fact that she was already wearing her newly-bought swimming costume under her clothes, Violet felt that she had little choice but to comply with this. She had learned that she had to submit to Antonia's generosity in order to get the things she wanted, an inverted kind of trade-off. Antonia's soups, pastas and cappuccinos were stacking up in her body, and although her new self relished the abandon of eating and drinking for pleasure rather than discipline, a little of her old self was still managing to nag that she should at least fill all this empty time with some exercise.

Her hour spent, she took the same stairs that she had taken down to the basement bar, but turned left at the bottom through a door marked 'Health Suite'. Finding herself in a pitch black corridor, she groped for a light switch and had to wait for a few seconds as the fluorescent bulb blinked on to reveal a shabby, pine-lined corridor, and another door in front of her. She turned the key stiffly in its lock to unleash a cloud of warm, chlorinated air and the drone of an air-conditioning unit.

The pool was sunk into a room lit only by yellow light and walled by unpainted breeze-blocks. The bleachy smell of the water fought against a deeper, greener odour of damp, and black patches of speckled mildew grew in the corners of the room. The water was turquoise and perfectly flat, with stripes of light reflecting at regular intervals off its glossy surface. It was inviting enough for her to try it out, just once. She undressed in the wooden cubicle by the side of the pool, stretched on her goggles and eased herself into the water from the loop-handled ladder.

It was surprisingly warm, more like a tepid bath than a municipal pool, and she watched the presence of her body disrupt the mirror-stillness of the water until it was a chaos of unruly waves, peaked white by the strip-lights. The lingering odour of damp and chlorine had already been forgotten, and she was grateful to have the place to herself. She would take some exercise, make good use of her time here; she would fight away the obsessive, circular thoughts that were continually winding their way around her consciousness, snaking into every bone and joint to make her spine stiff, her shoulders sore and her ribcage resistant to each breath. She had already devised a programme for herself: forty minutes today, being eighty lengths. Twenty breast-stroke, twenty front crawl, twenty backstroke and twenty butterfly. Perhaps thirty crawl and ten butterfly. It had been a while since she'd done this.

She launched herself forwards into the water, pushing back against the uneven tiles with the soles of her feet. Her body was heavy and unwilling. She would try a few lengths of gentle breast-stroke to warm up; she stretched her arms before her and kicked back against the water with her legs. She tried four or five of these movements, but they somehow lacked the elegant flow that they had in her imagination, being instead ill-timed and jerky, her limbs feeling sprung like a mousetrap to snap back against her stroke.

She broke into a front crawl, feeling the painful stretch of her arm at the top of its arc. How was it you were supposed to breathe? She tried a short gasp at the end of each stroke, but this quickly made her dizzy; then she remembered that she was supposed to breathe on alternate strokes: an in-breath and then an underwater out-breath. Should she be evening out the pressure on her neck by taking one breath to the left, and the next to the right? She realised that she was forgetting to kick her legs.

Standing up, she stretched her shoulders backwards and rubbed her hands over her face. She should be able to do this; a week ago she was fit. Her goggles had already steamed up, and little pools of water sparkled below her eyes. She rinsed them, breathless, tightened the straps and then flipped onto her back, letting the buoyancy of the water carry her for a few moments before rotating her arms backwards, slicing at the water so that great splashes fell across her face. She inhaled some of it and coughed, feeling her stomach muscles twitch and retract. Her arms were already exhausted. She let them fall to her side and floated on her back for a while, half-heartedly kicking her legs to stay afloat. She had to whole pool to herself. There was no-one there to watch her, to judge whether she was exercising correctly, showing the right degree of drive, ambition, spirit. The sense of privacy was delicious. She closed her eyes and tilted her head back so that the water filled her ears and she could no longer hear the growl of the air conditioning and the faint hum of the lights. She was enclosed, alone, free.

Violet let her legs fall into the space around her, and then twisted her whole body into it, allowing her head to dip underneath the surface. She managed a strange, spiralling somersault first of all, and then a more controlled back-flip, guided by her paddling hands. It filled her nose with water so that the membranes at the top of her nostrils burned. She sneezed: once, twice. It made her smile. She took a deep breath, pinched her nose and picked up her feet so that she floated to the bottom of the pool.

Her bottom bumped on the floor, and she tried to fold her legs underneath herself to sit cross-legged, but it was impossible: her body seemed determined to find its way to the surface, and she floated uncontrollably upwards, as if the water was expelling her. The world rushed into her ears as she surfaced, and the outside air seemed colder than before. She took another deep breath and tried again, making a small jump before she let her body drop to the bottom of the pool this time, in the hope that it would lend her some momentum. She slipped down through the water to sit straight-legged on the rough tiles, but only for a few seconds; soon, her legs lifted away from the ground again and she drifted up, back-first, to the surface.

She still had a lungful of air, so she stayed there for a while, floating with her face under the water and her arms and legs dangling down beside her. She allowed the air to escape from between her lips slowly, bubble by bubble, feeling them roll across her cheeks. She could hear nothing with her ears submerged, but the water was far from silent, drawing out as it did the groaning undercurrents of her body, the bustle of platelets in capillaries, the minute seep of osmosis. It was a very loud kind of quietness.

Underwater, the world was a cloudy, mysterious blue, studded with hazy circles of light from the bulbs set into the side of the pool. The floor of the pool looked closer than it could possibly be, the grouted grid shifting with the movement of the water. Turning her head left and right, she realised that she could barely see the edges of her container, so that the water took on an infinite quality, offering her a sense of space that stretched much further than the known confines of the pool. Her chest ached emptily.

She surfaced, gasping in the cold air and trod water until her breathing calmed, before heaving in another breath and letting her body settle on top of the water again. She imagined its meniscus holding her up, a canopy, a hammock. The water, she thought, makes a cast of the pool, but a shifting, moving, dancing cast, a living thing inside its shell.

She turned her head to breathe again, and submerged it straight back under the water. By angling her face upwards, she could see the surface of the water stretching away from her, a curiously solid presence, a silvery barrier between the calm containment of the pool and the dangerous space of the outside world. She thought about all the times that day that she had breached it, without even imagining it as a thing in itself, a detectable layer on the top of the water that defined the border between water and air, wet and dry.

She had found a shortcut to total bodily surrender, giving herself over utterly to physical forces beyond her control. She imagined herself as a light, empty seed-case drifting on a tide, the heaviness of fear and anxiety borne away by the currents. It was like being perfectly, pristinely, wonderfully dead.

FIFTEEN

As Friday approached and her nervous expectation grew, Violet found that the pool was her only respite from the nauseous fears that washed around inside her.

On dry land, her thoughts circulated obsessively around the same questions. She needed to remember everything about her teenage life, but her mind was like a haughty archivist who judged her insufficiently qualified to be allowed access to the full scope of its records. She could recall the big details, but not the small; she could remember arguments, but not their cause, friendships, but not their beginnings. It astonished her to realise how little of the everyday she recalled, as if the imprint of her old routines, no matter how long-established, had vanished as soon as she created new ones to replace them. She could no longer remember what time she woke up in the morning and what time she went to bed; what she used to eat for breakfast; what she would do if she found herself home alone for a few hours, her homework finished and her friends all unavailable.

Yet gradually, as she pored endlessly over her memories, something did begin to emerge, the moment she had been hunting for, the moment everything changed. At first, it appeared to her only in the abstract, a black line drawn across her life story that signalled the change from her old insouciant self to a newer, more stunted one. She interrogated it and found herself repelled, as if the lights were off in this part of her brain. But then, one afternoon when she was tidying all the scattered newspapers in her room, the memory rolled into the front of her consciousness entirely unbidden, and she realised that she had been thinking about it all along, not just this week, but also in the countless other weeks that stretched between the present and the last time she had lived in this town. To look at it in the eye after all this time made fear gurgle up in her throat, like some arcane disease released from a sealed tomb. She had to throw open the balcony doors to let it out of the room.

All this time, the pool was her only escape. She found herself craving it bodily, her muscles itching for the release they gained from surrendering to the water. She smiled off Antonia's ill-concealed amazement that she would want to return to that dark, artificially-lit room on a daily basis; she just took the keys from her and descended the stairs, feeling the exactitudes of her day's investigations disperse with the first warm hit of chlorine. She even had a name for it that she was barely aware of: playing dead. I'm playing dead this afternoon. Only another hour, and I'll be able to play dead again.

One afternoon when she returned to her room, her fingers still bloated with water-wrinkles from her blue cocoon, she found a large, grey box sitting in the middle of her bed. It looked like an old-fashioned suitcase, a little like the vanity case her mother had left over from the sixties, with a rubbery handle and two big brassy clips to secure its lid. Resting on it was a note from Antonia, scrawled in green ink and surprisingly childish handwriting, that said, *I asked Robert to get this out of the loft for you on Sunday, and he has finally got round to it. I've put the records in your wardrobe. Listen to your heart's content!*

It was only Wednesday. Violet wondered if Robert was conscious of the weight of his wife's disapproval, or whether he was blissfully unaware of the way his name was trodden through the mud at every opportunity. She ran her fingers over the cross-hatched surface of the box, and then sprung open the two catches. The lid propped itself open to reveal a landscape of gleaming order: a black turntable framed by an array of ivory-white arms and switches, all moulded from the same sleek plastic.

Violet lifted the box onto her writing desk and plugged it into the wall. After she had turned it on, there was a pause for a few seconds and then a low buzz rose from somewhere deep within its machinery, and the front badge became backlit to reveal, in curly lettering, the word *Dansette*. She remembered seeing a record-player like this stacked on a shelf in her grandparents' wardrobe when she was a child. She had asked her Granddad what it was, and he had taken it out and showed her how it worked, telling her that it was left over from her mother's childhood. She had been fascinated, at the time, by the politeness of this object compared to the masculine flash of the stacking stereo they had at home, which was all black fascias and metallic switches; the Dansette, with its wallpapered exterior and tidy interior, seemed almost chintzy in comparison, as if its subcultural danger had been tamed.

Looking at it through adult eyes, Violet found it rather beautiful, a homely antidote to the minute exactitudes of the MP3 players that she had seen all her colleagues comparing at work. There was a reality to the Dansette, a sense that one could conceivably imagine how it worked, could somehow have an ongoing relationship with it. Its size, its square bulk, meant that you could hardly ignore it; it demanded a space in your room and therefore in your imagination. For all the careful domestication of its styling, it was far from discreet, even if it did try to announce itself as a hatbox or a piece of soft furnishing rather than a record player.

She pulled open the wardrobe door, and dragged the box of 45s out of it. Antonia couldn't possibly have carried these upstairs; she imagined Robert humping them about under his wife's hawk-eyed direction and then entering her room to deposit them here. It disturbed her slightly to think of these two people having such free access to her private space, not through any mistrust of their honesty, but due to a new sense of privacy and secrecy. It had never alarmed her in the slightest that a cleaner entered her London flat every day to perform far more intimate functions than Antonia ever did; she had rarely even met the woman that did it, and so felt not a single pang of embarrassment at the extent of this stranger's knowledge of her. Perhaps for the first time since she left home, she actually had some things she wanted to hide (the bottle of cognac, the cigarettes, the carrier bags of clothes that still hung on guiltily to their labels, the increasing tribes of shells and stones that rattled in the drawers) and so was wary of their discovery.

She pulled open the flaps of the box of records and began to examine its contents. Everything was there that she had seen a couple of evenings ago, except that they seemed tidier, as if they had been rearranged since she had left them. Perhaps she had returned them to the box in too haphazard a way to satisfy Antonia; or perhaps, as she suspected, Antonia could not bear to miss the opportunity to exercise another small piece of influence over her life, and to discreetly arrange the singles so that she would fall upon the ones intended for her.

She felt nervous at the idea of playing the records. She lifted a handful of discs out of the box and began to flick through them. She had forgotten how fraught an issue music was, with its weighty associations of identity and character, of coolness and insider knowledge. For years she had side-stepped the issue, she realised now, by telling herself that she simply wasn't interested, that music wasn't for her. She remembered conversations when she was a teenager in which a record collection was something that could be got right or wrong, a lazy marker for whether new people were 'one of us'. The sweaty-palmed pressure of this came back to her now as her fingers paused on the 45s and she fought the impulse to drop them all back in the box, put them in the wardrobe again and close the doors on them. They weren't even her records, but she feared them all the same, their ability to mark her out as stupid without her even realising it.

It was time to change. She had lived for years without music and during that time she had lived a shell of a life. By contrast, she remembered the excitement she found in music before she gave it up, the turning of the stomach at the sound of one track and the perceptible build-up of adrenaline in the muscles at another, the sheer power that invoked a purely physical response, the ability to change her mood and outlook. She remembered hunting down records that enthralled her, that shook her out of childhood and into a twilight period before adulthood, in which she felt closer to the scaffolding of life than she had ever done before or since, as if the music had pulled back its flesh like a curtain to reveal its white bones. When she lost this, she believed with increasing certainty, she lost everything of herself. She longed for that grasp of the core of things, that gut-wrench reaction to life rather than the considered, dimmed responses of adulthood. She wanted a taste of that joy that made you laugh and the sadness that made you cry, all over again.

It was easy; she didn't have to make a choice. The records had already been selected for her, whether it was by fate or Antonia; she was sure of that. All she had to do was pick one, put it one the turntable, play it, pick another. She could love each record or she could hate it; it didn't matter. The record at the top of the pile in her hands had a white paper cover, yellowed and brittle with age. She didn't even allow herself to look at the record before she played it, she didn't want to risk reading the centre label in case she rejected it for some spurious reason or other and then started the whole tense process of choice all over again. Instead, she slotted the single straight onto its pin, clicked the switched to select 45 rpm, lifted the arm, pulled it to the centre so that the turntable clicked into motion, and lowered the needle onto the spinning record.

There was a rush of white noise, pocked by crackles of dust, and then, suddenly, a grind of guitar, a snare, a cymbal, and a woman's voice over a galloping bassline, pleading, demanding, *Send me a postcard darling, send me a postcard now.*

She knew the song; the inevitable coincidence barely even surprised her anymore. It had been playing less than a week ago, two floors below her, just before she saw the girl again.

It hit her now as it had hit her then: the deeply physical passion of it, the irresistible hints of desire and transgression that her body seemed to respond to independently of her brain. She stood still in the middle of the room as she listened to it, drinking in every word and phrase, every instrumental nuance. It was a song that raced headlong towards a premature conclusion; she barely felt she had got to know it before it died on a minor chord, as if exhausted by the force of its own longing. The needle hit the centre of the record, and the arm lifted and returned to its cradle.

She picked up the single squinted at the label. The track was named after its entreating first line, *Send me a Postcard*, and the band that performed it were called Shocking Blue.

It was a little disappointment; she had hoped to recognise the name from somewhere, to add to the strange sense of circularity and synchronicity that seemed to cling to her at the moment. Instead, the name reminded her of the pool, the electric blue of artificial light under chlorine, of playing dead. It did nothing to allay her suspicion, though, that Antonia was somehow the orchestrator of all this, that she had some sort of a role in the bizarre configuration of events that seemed to be happening at present. Violet had begun to see her as possessing a subtle kind of magic, the same magic that imbued this whole town with the uncanny sense that anything could happen. Since she had been in Stonehithe, she had felt the superstitious potential of the place surging up inside her and she liked it, relished its abandon and sense of possibility. In the rare times she thought of London now, it was a grey place, weighed down by the dust of rationality that seemed to flake away from the grey concrete of its buildings to engulf its inhabitants.

She put the record back on the turntable and played it again. It was as if the very essence of her being was feeding on it, drinking in its nourishing surge of emotion. As she set it off on its third play, she rifled through her handbag for the packet of cigarettes she had bought in town that morning.

She took them and their accompanying box of matches out onto her tiny balcony and attempted to light one, shielding the flame with her cupped hand. She had smoked when she was a teenager – everyone had. She had wanted, desperately, the borrowed cachet of risk and rebellion, the easy belief that her life would end when she ceased to be cool.

The girl smoked now, of course. Violet couldn't remember if she had seen her doing it, had guessed it, or just knew. Even though she couldn't find it in herself to approve,

Violet nevertheless felt a desire for nicotine bubble up inside her too. She had attributed this to the girl passing on her addiction through the link between them, but she knew, too, that smoking was a part of her own need to measure the change that had come over her in quantifiable signs, in new behaviours and acquired objects.

She inhaled hard on the cigarette, and felt its smoke bloom out to fill her mouth. Her throat closed to resist it, but she stifled a cough and took another deep drag, which filled her lungs with hot air and dried her mouth. She already felt dizzy, but she liked it, to be standing on the balcony, staring out at the sea, and smoking. She imagined the picture of herself that this would present, a woman surveying the town and the coast, brooding over her memories. She hoped that someone would see her. She needed this at the moment, some kind of shortcut to authenticity.

The smoke was billowing a new mood into her. She should have been upset by all of this, but it was actually a comfort to find the source, the event that had occasioned the change in her life; even more so to know that it was not her fault, that something had happened to her, and that she could not be held responsible for its consequences. She recalled the night it all unravelled so clearly now that it was astonishing that she had ever forgotten it. New visions surged up within her almost hourly, adding ever more intricate layers of detail: the heat of ecstatic bodies pressed into a dark room; the bright glare of fluorescent light on tiles; the uncertain slip of feet on a wet metal fire escape; the taste of bare brick. She had lost so much between now and then; perhaps it was not too late to get it back.

The girl was, what, eighteen? It would happen soon. The time was right. Violet dived back into her room to start the record again, and then went outside to light another cigarette. She had been retuned to her other self's life at the exact moment she could make a change in it. It couldn't be a coincidence. This weekend she would hang back, watch the girl from afar, try to establish exactly where she was in the story before she acted.

If this one thing could be prevented from happening, the girl's whole life could be different. She would not make the same dreary decision towards success and conformity that Violet did. She could carry on in that glorious, brave life without the fear seeping in. She might mean something to someone, anyone. And perhaps if her life was mended, Violet's would be too.

SIXTEEN

Violet was not drunk.

In her room, she had taken a few deep sucks on the brandy bottle to steel herself for the evening ahead, but she was still totally in control. She could talk and walk as naturally as ever, and had certainly not lost sight of the evening's objectives. Maybe she was a little less nervous than she had been before, maybe a little more confident. This was no bad thing. She needed something to persuade her legs to carry her here, to risk the interrogating gaze of the girl.

The brandy tingled at her lips as she entered the World Underwater, and she felt the alcohol was a warm presence in her veins; it lent a kind of amber magic to the room, lifting it beyond her usual assessment of such places as unenlightened fleapits with ugly carpets and a depressing range of drinks. In fact, she seemed to have a greater than usual appreciation for the details, as if the spirit had offered her an alcoholic magnifying glass, so that she could notice the green Victorian tiles around the walls, the pewter tankards hanging from the ceiling and the elaborate etched lettering that still obscured the windows. This might have been a nice place, once.

She walked up to the bar and two men on barstools cleared a space for her with an exaggerated gentility that she knew would be the prelude to a conversation.

"You waiting for your boyfriend, love?" asked the one to her left, who was wearing a salmon-coloured silk shirt that could only have been bought by his wife. His friend turned his head away, shook it slowly and smiled, as if he had witnessed this performance many times before.

"No," said Violet.

"On your own, then?" Violet ignored him, and leaned over the bar to attract the barman's attention. She held up the flyer she had carefully conserved in her wallet all week, and said, "I'm here for this. Is it in the back room?"

"Good God," scoffed the man in the salmon shirt, "you don't want to be going to that, love. They make a terrible bloody racket in there." He tutted, and the barman raised in eyebrows in agreement as he addressed Violet without looking at her.

"They won't start for a good hour yet, love. You'll soon hear them when they come on."

"You're a bit early then, darling," said the man to her right, who appeared to have recovered sufficiently from his embarrassment at his friend's forwardness to join in. "You might has well have little drink with us while you wait."

"No thank you," said Violet, "I'm meeting friends." She surveyed the range of bottles hanging upside-down behind the bar: unbranded gins, vodkas and whiskies with their prices displayed on neon cards sellotaped to their optics. On the shelf below them was a spectrum of alcopops, the lurid colours of which were supposed to signal their flavours: lime was an acid green, blueberry was a piercing, plastic cobalt and a cloudy pink bottle appeared to be representing strawberry cheesecake flavour.

"I'll have a pint of Guinness," she said, hoping it wouldn't interfere too much with the brandy. It was, after all, what she would have ordered ten years ago.

The salmon-shirted man tapped his mate on the shoulder. "Better watch this one," he said, "it drinks pints."

Violet carried her beer carefully over to the other side of the bar, hoping that the men would forget her as soon as she was out of their sight. The thick cream at the top of the Guinness wobbled as she walked, occasionally escaping the confines of the glass to dribble down its sides and onto her fingers. She was about to sit at a small, round table in the corner, when she saw an incongruous little group sitting in one of the booths at the opposite side of the room, who were almost certainly here for the same reason that she was. There were three of them, all boys of around eighteen, and each of them was slumped against the chair with his back triangulating across its right angle. They couldn't have been comfortable, but that attitude of exaggerated indolence seemed to satisfy them, as they were giggling and pawing at each other with a measured sort of enthusiasm. One of them had his leg slung sideways across the seat, so that his trainered foot lolled over the side; another was resting his pint (cider, judging by its deep orange colour) on his near-horizontal sternum, presumably so that he wouldn't have to lift it too far when he took a sip.

Violet hovered by their table for a while before taking a breath and sliding onto the seat next to the third boy, an Asian lad who had matted his hair into a cluster of short dreadlocks that batted around his face as he moved. The three of them paused as she did this and stared at each other in a mixture of alarm and hilarity. The boy nearest to Violet shifted up a little, seemingly out of a childish impulse against close contact with a girl rather than any urge to make room for her.

"Do you mind if I join you?" asked Violet, flinching at the primary-school brightness she had forced into her voice. "The blokes at the bar won't leave me alone."

The boys were silent for a few moments as they threw glances at each other that were presumably considered subtle in the classroom, but which here made Violet's stomach turn.

"Sure," said the one nearest to her, mumbling into

his own chest and twiddling the cord that hung from his hoodie. The boy on the far side of the table straightened up, removing his foot from the seat, and began a stilted attempt at conversation.

"So, Jason, will you be exhibiting your paintings anywhere soon?"

The boy to his left blinked at him in astonishment for a few beats, before breaking into hales of laughter, flicking his mate on the ear and booming, "Ferret, you fucking idiot!"

As more boyish play-fighting ensued, Violet began to wonder if it hadn't been a mistake to invade this table; she had forgotten that boys of this age held onto their childhood more tenaciously than girls. Perhaps she had been fooled by the ranks of neatly presented young men that arrived to undertake internships in her office every summer, who were, after all, not much older than this, but who were worlds away in terms of their self-control and seriousness.

She picked up the glass in front of her, which was cold to the touch and beaded with condensation in the heat of the pub, and took a long, thirsty draw on its black liquid. The bitter, mineral taste transported her to another time in her life, when she might have managed several glasses of the stuff in one night; or was it in the present time, but just another life? She could no longer be sure. She took another mouthful, tasting its deep, treacly notes and feeling the density of the liquid as she swallowed.

The two lads were in their element now, competing to clamp each other in headlocks and guffawing loudly. Eventually, the one they called Ferret stood on his seat and crowed a victory, which appeared to mean that their tussle reached critical mass as far as the barman was concerned. He leant over the bar towards them, his face red and vicious, and growled, "Pipe down or get out!"

A hush fell over the room, broken only by a "hear, hear!" from the men at the bar. The two lads immediately fell silent and plonked back down on their seats, their faces white. As chatter gradually seeped back into the room again, the boy sitting next to Violet, who had watched the whole display in silence while peeling the label off his bottle of Newcastle Brown, turned to Violet and caught her in a pair of eyes that were black and searching. "I'm sorry about my friends," he said. "I promise we're not all like that." He smiled, a shy, self-conscious reflex that sat awkwardly with his features. "I'm Ravi."

There was a definite tightening of the chest, a flutter of the diaphragm that made it hard for Violet to breathe. She thrust out her hand and said, "Violet," feeling ashamed of the formality of her gesture even as she did it. "Are you here for the club?"

"What club?"

Violet pulled the flyer out of her bag again and unfolded it on the table. "This one. The White Room."

"Oh. Yeah. I wouldn't really call it a club. It's more of a…a thing. Yeah, I guess it is a club, really. Yeah. Mmm." He looked away from her as he drank from his bottle, and Violet felt that she had somehow fractionally embarrassed herself as an adult appropriating language that didn't belong to her, and misusing it.

"Ravi, you twat, of course it's a club. Don't be so fucking precious. I'm Stephen, by the way."

"I thought you were called Ferret." The boy blushed, as a child would when a teacher had invaded an in-joke. "Sometimes," he said.

"Why Ferret?" As Violet said this, Jason sniggered and then broke into high, red-faced giggles. "Was it something to do with rummaging in people's trousers," (here, Jason was laughing so loud that he alerted the attention of the barman again), "or did you just fancy a nickname and picked the silliest one?"

"The latter. Definitely."

"And does everyone call you Ferret?"

"Only Jason," said Ravi. "They keep trying to get it to catch on, but it doesn't."

He was the sort of boy that you would call beautiful rather than handsome. His nose and chin were delicate and his eyes were large and long-lashed; when he spoke, his teeth were white and straight, evidence of immaculate dentistry. He had a clean smell about him, the scent of fresh laundry. It was not at all what Violet would have expected from a boy of his age, and if she had thought about it, she would probably have detected the presence of his mother in all of it, the clean clothes and brushed teeth; instead, in her imagination, he carried with him the very essence of the sea. He was utterly enchanting, with his bird-like movements and his clear, quiet voice, so much so that for an hour she forgot the heavy burden of fate and responsibility that had weighed on her all week, and instead watched Ravi and his friends as they talked about a canon of hip films (*One Flew Over the Cuckoo's Nest*, *Withnail and I*, *Taxi Driver*) that seemed to have changed little since she was their age, and a canon of TV programmes that she didn't know at all, but that she felt she knew after they had been quoted extensively to her. All this time, she felt that there was an extra layer of refinement to him, a gentle intelligence and a subtle sensitivity that marked him out from his peers.

By the time The White Room signalled its opening via a loud wall of music that seemed to seep into the room from nowhere, Violet's glass was empty and ring-marked with white foam, as if it bore the scars of her every sip. The tension instantly returned to her limbs and her stomach as she remembered what she was here for, and she found herself unable to fight the impulse to stand up and lurch toward the door that led to the hall.

"What's the rush?" Ravi spun towards her as if she had woken him up.

"It's started."

"Yes, but it'll be empty until ten. I was just going to get another beer." Violet tried to sit back down next to him, but her legs seemed frantic with the desire to get into the club. She kept imagining scenarios in which the girl came and went before she had even got in there. It was all too important. After five minutes of waiting she stood up and said, "I'm going in, I'll see you later," and then, detecting the embarrassment that registered on their faces to indicate that she was transgressing yet another unspoken rule of adolescent etiquette, she added, "I just came for the music. I love it. I want to listen." She grinned desperately as Jason and Ferret exchanged more of their glances, and was relieved when Ravi gave her a slow, majestic nod and said, "Respect. We'll see you in there."

SEVENTEEN

The White Room was, as Ravi had predicted, utterly empty. Violet paid her money at the door, had her hand stamped and entered a room with the lights switched off and music bouncing harshly off the walls. Her teeth ached with the force of it. She took her empty glass over to the bar and waved it at the barman rather than attempting to communicate in words. He drew her a fresh pint of Guinness, and she carried it over to a seat at the side of the room, where she could keep an eye on the door as she waited.

For the first hour, very few people arrived. Violet drank steadily as she watched a young, silent couple come in and take a seat at the edge of the dance floor where they sat, wordlessly, for the rest of the night. Other lone customers turned out to know the DJ, slipping behind the decks to shake his hand and slap his back, as if congratulating him on the bleak abandonment of the room.

One man arrived and stood alone at the bar, nodding his head to the beat. He was older than Violet, and wore white trainers and a large Hawaiian shirt over jeans that looked freshly-pressed; he looked out of place even without the other punters to throw him into relief. Violet wondered if she, too, looked like this: drifting and desperate, jarringly out of context. Without the crowds of bodies to mop it up and soften it, Violet found it hard to comprehend the music at all. It distorted as it bounced unhindered between the walls, creating an abrasive cacophony of bass, voice and guitar. It was difficult to work out whether the rumble in Violet's gut was the result of nerves or the vibrations of the sound system.

As she waited, a mood of loneliness fell over her, a melancholy stillness that made her body so heavy and fixed that it felt as though she had put down roots that reached into the ground below her and anchored her body in place. She could leave, she supposed, and resist the humiliation of this solitude, this public display of being alone, but she knew that she couldn't allow herself to give in, that the violent level of her obsession would make that impossible. She spent an hour, maybe more, drinking steadily and watching the people who passed without noticing her. Several times, she had to fight the urge to slip outside for a nervous cigarette, fearing that everything would happen without her. By eleven, she realised that the room had half-filled without her noticing, and that a steady stream of people were now passing through the doors. The music seemed to make more sense than when she had last thought to pay attention to it, muted as it was by the bodies that were already swaying and dancing. She got up and went to the bar and found Ravi there, counting through the change he had salvaged from his pockets. She tapped him on the shoulder and waved a twenty at him.

"I'll buy these."

"Oh, er, no…"

"It's fine." She remembered how hard it had been to drink in pubs back then, how much of her week's allowance could be absorbed by a night out. She bought more Guinness for herself and bottles for Ravi and his friends, and then carried them over to the corner of the room where the other two had camped out on a pile of coats, oblivious to the chairs that still lay empty. She slumped down next to them and tried to follow a bellowed conversation for a while, but quickly gave up and reverted to staring out into the room. Soon, Ferret's head began to nod, and she watched Jason take the untouched cider from his drooping hand and exchange it for his own empty one. Ravi sat upright with his knees bent in front of him, twisting the label from his beer bottle around his agile fingers and watching his own feet, as if he was mulling over some complex and important problem. Occasionally, he would appear to remember where he was, and would turn to Violet and smile, before returning his eyes back to the ground again.

The throng of people was such that Violet couldn't see the door any more; from her ground level view, it was difficult to see anything more than a forest of legs that grew denser by the moment. It was hot now; her beer became lukewarm before she could finish it, and she began to feel as sleepy as the boys next to her. She could see Jason's eyelids flickering as he fought unconsciousness. The DJ was playing a song with waves of pulsing wah-wah and organ that seemed to flow into her head and wash around there like waves. Ravi had long since stopped breaking his contemplation to smile at her. The girl had most likely been and gone. She had missed her. Violet checked her watch; it was midnight. Too late for anyone new to arrive.

But then, in the corner of the room, there was a noticeable stir, a definite clearing of the crowd. Violet hauled herself to her feet and pushed her way through, snaking between figures who had paused, briefly, to stare. And, yes, there she was, making her entrance. She had dyed her hair pink for the occasion, and was wearing a red a-line dress whose demure white collar did nothing to detract from the daring shortness of its skirt, which skimmed just below her buttock cheeks. To emphasise this fact, she was wearing knee-high white socks and black patent Mary-Janes, a provocative juxtaposition of innocence and experience.

Violet felt the shudder of déjà-vu hitting her, as if there was a slight delay in her perception, an echo on the line. Three streams of memory were feeding into the front of her brain: her own recollections of a night like this, incomplete and fragmented by time and drunken amnesia; flashes of the girl's own current experiences: the confusion of the sudden darkness and people and noise, the flush of her cheeks against the heat of the room, and the lingering taste of ginger wine in her mouth; and her own, subjective view of it all, in which she saw a young girl, tender despite all her swagger, leering and out of control.

It was a shock to see her, an almost-physical blow. Violet watched her stagger to the bar and slur her order with great effort, as if it were a struggle to keep her head upright. She saw the barman shake his head, and the girl looked confused and then angry. She turned on her shiny heels to spit some remark of disgust to her friends, but seemed to be overwhelmed by the motion; her knees bent, briefly, beneath her and she reeled sideways. Violet felt a fierce, maternal kick inside her that made her lurch toward her to catch her, set her back on her feet, but she was relieved to find that she was not required. A friend ran to prop her up, and Violet recognised her immediately from her dream. She escorted her towards a banquette at the side of the room, where the other customers cleared a space for her, carefully pulling coats and bags out of her vicinity as they did so. The girl's head slumped against her chest as soon as she sat down, and her friend checked that she was propped upright before she retuned to the bar.

This had to be her chance. Violet wove her way through the bodies that had pressed back together again now the sideshow as over, and found the girl's friend leaning over the bar, in some intense discussion with the barman.

"I'm sorry, I can't serve you with your mate in a state like that. They shouldn't have let her in here."

"But I'm only getting her a glass of water."

"Who's the wine for, then?"

"Me, obviously."

"I can't give you any alcohol if I think you're going to give it to her, love. I don't make the rules."

"Fine! We'll have two glasses of water, then."

The barman rolled his eyes, filled two glasses from the tap and plonked them in front of her, saying, "If she's sick on the carpet, she's getting the bill for cleaning it," before walking away.

Violet reached over and touched her on the shoulder as she struggled to weave her way back from the bar.

"Your friend there, what's her name?"

The girl's eyes narrowed and she looked even angrier than she had before.

"Why's that any of your business?" She eyed Violet up and down, and Violet felt the assault of guarded suspicion that she would have radiated herself in the same circumstances. Was she the police, a social worker? Violet rushed to fill the icy gap that this girl's glare was leaving.

"Don't worry," she said, "nothing dodgy. I've just got a feeling I've met her before. Here? A few weeks ago? I was pretty pissed, but I get so embarrassed when I forget people's names. Don't you?"

The girl sighed and said, as if to imply that she didn't quite trust Violet but that she supposed the information wasn't confidential, "It's Daisy."

Daisy. Dai-sy. Daisy Daisy Daisy. Daisydaisydaisydaisy. The name settled into Violet's mind like a light switching on, like water filling a glass: elemental, inevitable, a perfect fit. A box had been opened that revealed something that she had always carried with her, inside her. Daisy. Of course.

"Listen, you take the water over and I'll get you your drink. What was it – wine?"

Suspicion flashed across the girl's face again, but it was tempered, this time, with a surreptitious look of greed, an ungracious surrender. She smiled "Yes, red wine. Thanks. I'm Ruth, by the way. I'm sorry. I didn't remember seeing you before."

"I'm not that noticeable." The girl laughed and Violet felt pleased that her joke had worked and stung by how convincing it had been. The barman looked as though he was going to question Violet when she ordered a glass of wine with her Guinness, but thought better of it.

Ruth had momentarily vanished from her line of sight, so she decided that she would take the glasses over to the table where Daisy was now sleeping, and watch her for a while, until her friend returned.

The drinks slopped over Violet's hands as she passed through the crowd. A couple were standing in the way of Daisy's table, primping each other's hair and clothing so intensely that Violet had to shout, "Excuse me!" to make them part.

Her heart jumped as she caught a glimpse of Daisy again; it was like falling in love. Her head was tipped sideways and her eyes were closed, all the vestiges of drunkenness erased from her face. But there was another presence to the side of her, a figure that merged with her in the darkness. It took a while for Violet to interpret what she was seeing, but then, when she finally understood, it froze her.

It was the man she had seen earlier, waiting alone in his Hawaiian shirt by the bar, but he was leaning over Daisy's unconscious form with one hand stroking her bare thigh and the other cupping her unguarded breast. Before Violet could act, she saw him lean over to kiss Daisy on the mouth; but this seemed to wake her and she opened her eyes in confusion for a few seconds before jerking the man's hands away in an untidy gesture of resistance.

Violet saw Ruth rushing toward them, and the man got up and walked quickly towards the door, brushing Violet's shoulder as he passed her. She turned to chase after him, spilling beer on her feet as she moved, and as she made it to the door, she turned back to see Daisy crying and being hugged by Ruth.

She passed through a brightly-lit corridor and out into the street. It was silent out there; the music from the pub only reached the outside as a dreamy murmur, and the air was opaque with cold. She couldn't see the man anywhere.

There was no point in going back in now. Inside, she knew from her own memory and from the muddy, intermittent signals she was receiving from her double, Daisy would be crying still, confused and humiliated, her flesh crawling with the lingering sensation of the man's touch. By the next day the memory would have become fixed, as nauseous as the morning's hangover; she would feel ashamed and exposed, newly-vulnerable and furious at her own inability to protect herself. Violet knew only too well that, given time, this would harden into a kernel of fear, a sense that her armour had been breached, a piece of grit in her shoe.

Still, at least now Violet knew exactly where she was in the story, as if a bookmark had been placed in the history of her own life.

She set the glasses down on the pavement and began to walk home.

EIGHTEEN

By the electric-blue railings on the promenade, an unruly crowd of seagulls were scrambling over a bag of chips that had been dumped, open, on the concrete. They pecked and stabbed and bustled, shouldering other grey-feathered bodies out of the way and fighting for the advantage with flailing wings and vicious yellow beaks. Several of the gulls gained their advantage by flying on top of the tangle of writhing white bodies and attacking the horde from above; others just snatched scraps from the triumphant mouths of other birds. Only a few took the time to stand back and swallow the chips, chugging them whole down their pulsing gullets in long, yellow streaks. Some birds flew away with nothing but a scrag of oily, translucent paper, which no doubt they would attempt to eat later.

They left as suddenly as they had descended, leaping into the air en masse, as if flight required a joint, concerted effort. The spot where Violet had queasily thrown down her chips five minutes before was now marked only by a few shreds of paper and one stupid seagull, who was attempting to eat the balsawood fork.

Eventually he flew off, too, carrying this fork with him for another attempt in private. Violet drew her knees up into her chest and retracted her hands into the sleeves of her jumper. The freezing, blue February sky dazzled her retinas. She had managed four, maybe five of the chips before her stomach had lurched and a rush of fever had swept up her spine again, leaving her skin clammy and her face hot. Even so, she was better off in the cold air than indoors; earlier, in a café in town, she had to leave her latte untouched on the table after the air of the café had pressed on her and the smell of hot milk and coffee grouts had sent the contents of her stomach surging up for fresh air.

Her stiff bones and the feeble flesh that surrounded them would have loved, deeply, needily, to have stayed in bed, wrapped in the blankets and quilt that promised to surround them in soft security, but she had felt conscious that a lie-in would advertise her hangover. This precaution had not saved her from ridicule; she had to endure Antonia's arch amusement at her lack of appetite and field sly enquiries about her late night as she stared palely at her boiled egg and toast. She had managed, as an act of sheer bravery and defiance, to crack its warm shell and lift off its white-lined crown; but the sight of the yolk oozing thickly down the eggcup had appalled her. She had to get out. She would probably have to apologise to Antonia later, and endure a skin-crawling admission of her own weakness. There was no avoiding it.

At least the Nurofen was working, so long as she didn't move her head too quickly. She swallowed down another fizzy gulp of Coke, and felt a sugary residue fur up her teeth in its sticky wake. Worse than all of this – the aching head, the sickness, the feeble desperation for stodge and sugar that she wasn't quite able to satisfy - were the little snatches of disgust and loathing that Daisy was, unknowingly, transmitting to her as she emerged from her own, more extreme, drunkenness into the morning blues. Violet knew that Daisy would remember very little of the night before, but would still hold some sense of a violation having taken place, an affront to her bodily integrity. She knew, too, that she would never, ever dream of clarifying these fragmented, foreboding memories with Ruth for fear of revealing the extent of her ignorance – and that Ruth would never raise the issue either, hoping that Daisy would not recall it.

For Violet it was all something of a relief, having never had the opportunity to understand this event before. She was quietly pleased that this had only been a discreet humiliation, a gentle assault. But she was plagued also by the sickening sensations of a hand placed on unconsenting flesh, of the man's purposefulness against Daisy's unwilling submission. Maybe this was the reason for her nausea.

The night's lows kept pulling at her, like the drag of the waves, the lethal temptation of the undertow. There were highs as well, brief glimpses of sunlight on the surface of the water. The name, *Daisy*, felt newly-minted on her tongue, and she longed to pronounce it, to lend it life by telling someone, anyone, about the wonderful creature it was attached to. Her mind, stupidly, giddily, had sung, *Daisy, Daisy, give me your answer do*, to itself for most of the night. *I'm half crazy…*

She marvelled, too, at how easily she had slipped into the society of the girls without any of them once showing a hint of recognition. They had been suspicious, granted, but only because they believed she was a stranger, and therefore potentially connected to that undefined cloud of harm that had pursued them throughout their childhoods and was now, finally, organising itself into focus. But they didn't know her, didn't suspect the far stranger, bleaker truth of the connection between herself and Daisy; she could only suspect that Daisy would be the same. Similarities are only retrospective things, which run backwards to imagine a time when two faces were identical. They could not be projected forwards, and therefore the features she shared with Daisy would attract nothing more than a passing remark. She was safe, for as long as she wanted to be.

Maybe Daisy should never know. Over the last week, Violet had endlessly run through scenarios in which she revealed her identity to Daisy, and none of them were particularly appealing. She could not imagine a scenario in which the girl was anything but utterly shocked and horrified. She knew that it would be unwise, ridiculous even, to introduce herself in this way from the outset, although the range of opening sentences were amusing: *hello, I'm your double. Hello I'm your future self. Check it out: this is how you'll look in ten years' time! Hello, my name's Violet and I can tap into your thoughts.*

It was obvious that this was no way to begin a relationship; it would sound even crazier to Daisy than it did to Violet herself. On the other hand, there was a real risk that getting to know each other first and then revealing the truth later would be all the more traumatising, making Violet appear sinister and deceitful, or most probably just as mad as she would have done if she had told her in the first place.

In weaker moments, Violet let herself believe that there would be no need for any grand revelations; Daisy would surely be feeling the same link as she did, and would eventually approach Violet off her own steam. They would laugh together, lament the time it took to find each other, vow that their psychic bond would be cemented by an unshakeable friendship. But if this were the case, Violet was sure that Daisy would already have made a move towards her, would have sought her out and shown at least some sign of interest or recognition. It was, after all, impossible to experience this odd link without encountering an accompanying curiosity about the other half of the pair, and Violet's life was likely to be all the more mysterious to Daisy for being in her future and therefore unknown.

Violet was increasingly convinced that she would have to take a more stealthy approach than this, and find a way to guide the course of Daisy's life in gentler, more subtle ways. She could see now that it would be impossible to do this from the shadows. Quite apart from the smallness of the scene in Stonehithe, which would make it impossible for her to observe Daisy unnoticed, Violet didn't think she could bear to watch her without getting closer to her. She was startlingly, magnetically fascinating, holding the kind of beauty that comes from familiarity, the known face of a mother or a sister. Watching her was like seeing one's own image step out of the mirror and take its part in the world; Violet was enthralled by observing her own tics and gestures from the outside, the animation of her own body, the way that expressions fell across her features like sudden changes in the weather. It was impossible to stay away from this astounding creature for much longer.

NINETEEN

When the nausea finally subsided enough for her to get onto her feet again, Violet thought she might as well go back to the hotel. The town's streets were filling with Saturday shoppers, and their deliberate bustle and their wilful expenditure of energy exhausted Violet. She had never noticed before the way that these people ate continually, grazing on pastries and chocolate bars, burgers and cakes as they walked along. The sight of it alone – the conversational spraying of crumbs and the filling of mouths past bursting point, as if the street were a private space in which manners could be disregarded – was enough to turn anyone's stomach, but the additional wafts of old cooking oil and over-seasoned meat that rose from the fast-food containers they carried were unbearable.

The new-season blue sky and still air failed to lend their desired lift today. Even the sea, which was nearly flat and was fighting off its grey hue for the first time in the year, couldn't elevate her depleted body to any level of enthusiasm. She must go home and sleep; her burning eyelids told her so. She turned her head away as she passed the caramel peanut man, whose wares were seeping a heavy, sticky odour into the surrounding air; still she smelt it, and felt a shift in her stomach that made her pick up her pace.

When she first heard her name, it barely registered; there was no-one around here that would call out to her anyway. But the second time, when it was pronounced slightly louder and more definitely, she turned and saw Ravi, Jason and Ferret huddled into one of the old wooden shelters that lined the promenade with their backs to the sea. Ravi was squatting on his part of the bench, as if resisting the urge to relax back on it, and it was obviously he who had called out to her, as the other two were now giggling, their jackets puffing up around their red cheeks, and whispering something behind their hands. Ravi had clearly embarrassed himself with this overt gesture of friendship towards a woman, so much so that even he restrained himself as Violet swung round, and only offered the smallest, most unenthusiastic wave, as if it were Violet who had called out to him.

In sober daylight, he was even smaller than she remembered, and ridiculously pretty for a boy of his age, with his huge liquid eyes and full mouth. His skin, she noticed today, had the translucent quality of a toddler's, so clear and fresh that might have been back-lit. Perched as he was in the shelter, his thin arms draped across his knees, he looked like a little bird, all delicate bones and gleaming eyes. There was a constant, twitchy cycle of movement about him, although he did not fidget but instead seemed to be driven by a teaming energy that boiled just beneath his skin. Seeing him avert his eyes as she greeted him, Violet was filled with an urge to rescue him from his two ungainly companions, to help him to throw off the childhood that he had already so clearly outgrown. She wanted to take him aside and welcome him into the adult world, a sort of fast-track induction, a lighting of the way. But then, she wondered what she could possibly offer him if she had not yet found the way herself."What are you up to today? Still recovering from last night?" As she spoke, she was again conscious that she sounded like a children's television presenter, her voice defaulting to an overly-bright, breathy bounce, full of patronising, primary-coloured questions.

She watched Ravi flinch, as if too much information were being demanded of him; Jason, as ever, took it upon himself to fill the gap in the conversation with his own booming voice. In the piercing spring light, his skin looked almost grey, brightened only by florid outcrops of ripe acne on his chin and cheeks. He was, she noticed today, actually rather well-spoken, with the kind of lumbering schoolboy self-confidence that always made her toes curl when she interviewed each year's new recruits. He pounded each brash comment into her ears by over-emphasising every pertinent word, so that Violet imagined his sentences to be peppered with italics:

"Well Ferret's *vomited* twice *already* and Ravi's *sulking* because you left without saying good-*bye* last night, so if you could call that a *recovery*, we're doing very *nicely* thank you."

Violet rotated her body even further around to emphasise the point that she was not speaking to him, and tried not to smile at the thought that Ravi might have felt her absence last night. Ferret said, "Fuck off, dickslap," and buried his chin even deeper into his jacket; Ravi just glared at him, a dangerous vulture warning.

"I'm sorry I left so suddenly last night. To be honest, I was a bit worse for wear and I must have had my homing-legs on. They just walked me home. Thank God. I've been suffering for it this morning."

"Oh *God*, a chick with a *hang*over. *Imagine* the *fuss.*" Ferret sniggered along to this, as if his face wasn't the nearest thing to green that Violet had even seen in her life.

"That's enough, Jason," said Ravi, who suddenly seemed to uncoil and be on his feet without any effort. His tone was definite, vicious, but not violent, the irritable finality of a teacher pushed too far rather than a teenager up for a fight. Jason noticeably receded, expelling a small, defeated, "Oooh," as he did so.

"We were on our way to see a friend of mine, The Bogman," he said. "But we had to stop for Jason to rest on the way." He glared at his two friends again. "But I think we can continue now. Come with us if you like." He paused, looked at tatty All-Stars on his skinny feet. "I assume you're comfortable with, um, narcotics." He whispered the last word.

"Blow," said Jason, as if he suspected Violet might need some help with this concept. "Weed."

"Amsterdam Gold," said Ferret, enlivening in the light of this prospect.

"Amsterdam Gold's a specific type, you moron."

"I'd love to," said Violet. "I mean, it's not like I've got much on."

TWENTY

The smell of stale urine first caught in Violet's throat as they all tramped up the echoing stairs of Havisham House. It was only after the door opened, though, and a thin man ushered them in, that Violet realised the stink was emanating from the flat itself, and not from loutish misdeeds on the stairwell.

The whole place reeked, the acrid must that sometimes billowed out of particularly bad public toilets. Violet covered her mouth and nose with her scarf – no hardship, given the freezing temperature in the room – and let her eyes wander over the stained green carpet, the peeling walls, the yellowed ceiling and the velour sofa, pocked with black burn-holes. In the kitchen, visible through a door at the other side of the living room, a limescaled tap dripped on a pile of filthy crockery.

None of this seemed to deter Ravi, who was hugging the man enthusiastically, his black dreadlocks mingling with his friend's blond set. This was Bogman, then. He seemed to Violet to be a hardened, more calloused version of Ravi, a representation of his future given a certain set of choices, a certain path pursued. His cheekbones jutted out below eyes that were ringed with grey, and which he rubbed repeatedly with his nicotine-stained fingers. His torso coiled like a whip above mean hips. His own odour of staleness fought for dominance against the ammonial stench that crept from the bathroom.

After returning the warmth of Ravi's greeting, he gave the two boys the briefest glance and a grim-faced nod, and ignored Violet altogether.

"I hope you don't mind me bringing Jason and Stephen," said Ravi, following his gaze, "and Violet, a friend of mine."

Bogman shrugged and said, "Long as they know the rules."

"Sure," said Jason, springing into deferential life, "Absolutely."

"Nothing on the premises," sniffed Bogman, clearly convinced that the rules ought nevertheless to be rehearsed, "and don't go recommending me to no-one."

Ravi placed a hand on his back. "They won't be any trouble," he said.

Bogman snorted, and shuffled out of the room past Jason, Ferret and Violet, followed closely by Ravi, who was chattering attentively to him, never glancing at his friends. Violet felt for the first time what it was like to be outside of Ravi's adulation, that chilly withdrawal that must have been so familiar to Jason and Ferret. It was odd to feel allied to them, one of the rejects, a potential embarrassment.

"Wanna know why they call him Bogman?" said Jason.

"*The* Bogman," said Stephen.

"*The* Bogman, then."

"I don't think that needs an explanation," said Violet, and then, seeing the confused expression on Ferret's face and realising that the smell probably had little impact on a teenage boy, she added, "No, sorry, why? Tell me."

"It's because he's all leathery. Like the people they dig up out of the bogs in Ireland. Ravi reckons he's in his fifties."

"Oh, *Ferret*, that's *bollocks*. He's like, *thirty* or something. He's getting on, but he's not *ancient*." Jason glanced at Violet. "Obviously," he mumbled, fixing his eyes on the carpet.

There was a silence between them for a while. Stephen picked up a trio of beanbags from the windowsill and tried to juggle with them, and then hastily put them back after one hit the ceiling, sending a cloud of paint flakes down onto his head. Jason flicked through the porn magazine that lay on the sofa, folded open on a colour spread of a glossy-haired blonde, her brown thighs parted to reveal the tiniest wisp of pubic hair. Violet watched him attempt, for a few seconds, to find a page that it would be acceptable to read in front of a woman, his face reddening all the time. He found nothing, and eventually threw it down as if its pages were alight.

After fifteen embarrassing minutes, during which Violet had repeatedly steeled herself to leave, Ravi reappeared and waved a small zip-lock bag of dry leaves and buds at the boys.

"There you go," he said, "A tenner's worth. You can pay me later."

"Great," said Jason, and snatched the bag into his pocket. "Ferret's mum's out today, so we can do it round his if you like."

"You take it," said Ravi, "I'm staying here. Got some stuff to discuss with The Bogman."

"Oh," said Jason, "okay," and Violet watched his shoulders fall. He turned immediately and went to the door, followed closely behind by Ferret, and Violet supposed that she was also supposed to just allow herself to be dismissed by Ravi once he'd found something better to do. She turned to leave all the same, promising herself that hers would be a haughty and permanent exit, in contrast to the boys' obedient one, but as she picked up her bag, she heard Ravi say, "I didn't mean you, Violet. I wanted you to meet the Bogman. You'll like him. He's, like, a philosopher. He understands things."

TWENTY-ONE

An hour later, Violet finally persuaded herself to relax against the wall of Bogman's smoking room. She was sitting on an old bread crate that he had thoughtfully topped with a folded towel, while he and Ravi were slumped across a bare mattress, sucking at the little pipes that each of them had produced, pausing occasionally to let the flame of their lighters lap against the crumbs of brown resin that they held. Violet wondered if Bogman actually slept here, as there was a duvet and two pillows crumpled up at the side of the room, none of them covered, and so all of them having a brownish tinge. Her mouth was dry and her head felt light. Gulping at the amber-coloured tea that Bogman had made for her seemed to make little difference, especially now it was cold. Ravi smiled at her and offered her a draw on his pipe, and she took it gladly.

The conversation between them was rambling and polemical, constructed of regular, rehearsed monologues from both parties, and accompanied by sighs of agreement from the other side. Although this display of rhetoric was clearly being carried out for her edification, Violet found herself zoning in and out of it, her attention wandering to the black spaces between the flowers on the wallpaper, the spider whose legs quivered from a crack in the coving, the blond hairs on the back of her own hands. Every now and then, Ravi would smile and catch her eye, as if only she could see the value in the point he had made, and Violet would wonder who on earth he thought she was.

"I feel this incredible pressure," he was saying, "and, like, I know I come from a fairly bourgeois background, so it's inevitable I guess, but," he shifted his body upright to emphasise his point, "but I still feel like, even at my age, I'm being shovelled towards this whole life of money and 'achievement'" – here he flexed two pairs of fingers to indicate speech marks – "and it's like, what am I getting out of this? Ultimately? In the end? Does anyone seriously think the money's worth it? Or am I just supposed to be after 'success'" – again, the mimed quotation marks – "some kind of grandeur or status?"

"It's all about amassing power, mate," said Bogman, who never seemed to take his eyes away from the glowing rock in his hash-pipe. "It's all about this big battle to have control over your fellow man. We might as well all be going at each other with fucking great sticks. It's all about power. Survival of the fittest. Subjugation of others."

"But then, all the power never actually comes, does it? Except for a very few people, the really big, vicious bastards. For everyone else, it's like this endless slog with a carrot dangled in front of your nose that says, one day you'll be rich, and being rich will make you happy. If you keep working and working like this, and don't complain, one day you'll get to the top of the pile."

"It's not even that, after a while," interjected Violet, whose thoughts had suddenly lurched into focus at the thought of work. "It's all got so competitive. Nowadays, you have to keep working like a dog just to stay at the bottom of the pile. " She said it almost involuntarily, and as she did, it was as if a light was cast on her whole working life, illuminating the layers of people above and below her, the feeble illusion of her own success, the tricks the company had played on her to squeeze out every last drop of her time.

Ravi and Bogman nodded wisely, puffed on their pipes, and Violet felt the dope glowing in her veins. She put out her hand to ask for one more.

"The modern office worker is the new proletarian," said Bogman, and Ravi nodded as if this was something meaningful.

"Working harder and harder," said Ravi.

"More than that, mate. They're alienated. They believe there's a point to what they're doing, a reward. But actually, their work is completely meaningless. Advertising, marketing, sales…teaching, medicine, even. They're all servicing a corrupt set of values, and handing over half their lives to make someone else a pile of money. They give their extra time for free, for fifty, sixty, seventy hours a week, and get spat out at the end of it. Their bodies, their time, are the capitalists' surplus value."

"They make a profit out of people giving their time for free." It was clear to Violet that this was a conversation that Bogman and Ravi had held many times before, and that this current exposition was entirely for her benefit. Ravi, in particular, seemed to have taken it upon himself to clarify any concepts he imagined she would find difficult.

"There's a whole false economy built around it. Money passing from hand to hand for things that don't exist. Futures-trading, branding: they're all these little puffs of air designed to make money."

"Did you know that Britain's workers have the least amount of holiday in Europe? Work the longest hours, too? There's people in the City working ten, twelve, fourteen hours a day."

"The bonuses are astronomical; millions of pounds being shared out between a tiny sect of traders every year.

They can afford to buy second, third homes while the rest of us are priced out of the market with higher and higher rents."

"But the point is, they sell their souls to get there. Hand themselves over to those companies wholesale – evenings, weekends, holidays spent working on a laptop."

"And in the meantime, this whole industry grows up, aimed at pressing every last minute out of people's days, so that they can see even less of their friends and families than they did before. They're all popping little pills, raiding the natural world for solutions to their addiction to money, taking up whatever fad diet or exercise regime that they think will keep them awake a little longer. Instead of giving in to their natural feelings of exhaustion, taking it as a sign that their bodies are fatigued, they spend all that money on ever more aggressive assaults on rest."

"Bogman doesn't believe in uppers. He only sells downers."

Bogman nodded majestically as if this was some kind of tribute to his wisdom. Violet cleared her throat.

"I've been there myself," she said, "getting up at five, in the office at seven, lunch at my desk, in the gym at ten; home by eleven, twelve, too strung out to get to sleep. Which was no surprise after I'd spent the day trying to keep awake. I tried everything: vitamins, herbs, sleeping pills, diet, exercise: nothing worked. And all around me people seemed to be coping so effortlessly, heading out to bars for a night out when all I could think about was crawling home."

"You've done all that? When?"

Last week, Violet wanted to say. "A while ago. Not so long. It's only after you break the cycle that you begin to realise how destructive it is. At the time, you're just caught up in it. It seems perfectly normal."

Ravi crawled across the floor to hug her, a boyish, innocent gesture of solidarity and for a moment she felt as if she had shared some important trial that she had endured, rather than an insight into the mundanity of her recent past.

"You're a hero," he said, "an example to us all. You've been there and escaped. You've rejected the materialistic life in favour of a better one. Do you miss it? There must be some sort of a come-down when you leave?"

"I hardly think about it," said Violet, and wanted to add: but then, my life's been so weird since then that I haven't had time to think about it.

Bogman took a long, significant drag on this pipe. "The new struggle," he said, blowing blue smoke of out his nose, "will be fought over sleep."

Violet laughed, choking on the dry smoke in her throat. "Sleep?"

"The right to sleep," said Bogman gnomically, "is the right to dream. Capitalist society is robbing the proletariat of its dreams. Its reach is more invasive then ever."

"I don't think it's like that at all," said Violet. "It's just a choice people take. They don't have to work in that sort of job, but if they do, they're choosing to compete. They can drop out any time they want."

"But they don't drop out, do they? They burn out." Bogman leaned back against the wall and caught Violet in his hard, blue eyes for the first time. "There's millions of people slaving away just to feed their filthy addiction to consumerism, the worship of the mighty checkout. They have to have new clothes, new cars, new gadgets; food that rots in this plastic carton in the fridge and is thrown away. And it's not just that; they have to make progress, too; they have to afford more and more every year to feel like they're keeping up. Bonuses, promotion, climbing the ladder: it's all we're supposed to care about. But it makes us miserable. We must fight to liberate people from this cycle, and from their own misery."

Bogman's voice grew louder as he settled into his lecture, booming out his practised monologue in a way that signalled discussion was not invited. Violet hadn't thought before how her unhappiness, her gut reflex to get out of London, could be anything more than her own, private reaction, a result of her somehow not getting life right; she was struck by the idea that all of those around her were all experiencing variations on the same theme.

"I don't know," she said, "I'm not sure it isn't patronising to suggest that everyone who's got a good job is miserable."

"Not a good job, a prestigious one. There's no good in them."

"A prestigious one, then. You know what I mean. You can't assume that they are all these wicked people that live sad, repressed little lives." She thought about her flat with its identical front door and the three plastic containers of food a day, and the little table she used to eat at, and felt sure that there must be some good in it all, somewhere; that the whole sum total of her life's achievement so far couldn't so easily be dismissed as a social evil.

"It's understandable. You've been brainwashed by the system and it's hard to shake it off." Bogman had tamed the zealous glint in his eye and had now taken on the calm superiority of a teacher who was assured of his own rectitude. His voice had a measured gentleness to it, as if it was calculated to demonstrate the right way of behaving, while conveying a deep sense of pity. "You should go home and think it all through. These are big ideas. They take a while to get your head round. But you could help us. You've seen the other side and come through. You just need to decide on where you stand."

TWENTY-TWO

All the way home, the afternoon now dark and brittle with cold, Ravi talked fast and excitedly about Bogman and his ideas, his breath dispersing whitely in the air.

"He's a genius," he said; "he sees right through to the core of things. He's like, from this really poor background, but he's so well read. He never went to university. He just followed his own path."

Violet stayed silent. Bogman's intensity seemed dangerous to her, his analyses so exaggerated that she doubted the truth of them. On the other hand, even though she searched her mind for evidence to the contrary, she found nothing that disproved what he said. More than that, there seemed to be a basic truth in it all, a seed of correctness that niggled at her. Her way of life had been bad, destructive, insidious. She had been mistaken in everything.

Despite this unsettling conclusion, she found it impossible to succumb to Ravi's outright idolatry of a man who had seemed hard, sly and weaselly to her, who used words as if they were fists. It was not just that she resented being harangued and lectured, instructed on what to think; it was also that there were things in her old life that she still aspired to, the clean, controlled legality of it all, the expensive cut of her clothes, the soft leather of her shoes, the cushioning layer of money that was breaking her fall, even at this very moment. Without it, where would she be right now? Unable to afford a hotel, a train journey away, a new wardrobe of clothes, endless cups of coffee to stare into while she figured it all out. The simple truth was that she saw no viable alternative in Bogman's life, no hint of aspiration in his disintegrating flat and lean face. On the other hand, she saw plenty to aspire to in Ravi's intelligent, critical bridge between his comfortable, professional parents and the fringe culture he so avidly sought. He was radiant, electric, charismatic, alive with the possibility of the life before him, the opportunities he saw for change and reform. It was crushing to think that he valued this so lightly, that he instead chased the more despotic magnetism of the likes of Bogman.

He was still talking, saying something about globalisation that Violet hadn't caught at the beginning and so didn't understand now. They turned onto the promenade, which was all but abandoned now that the shops had shut. The seagulls hung around, eyeing each person that approached them in case they carried food. Violet ran her bare hand along the cold, blue railing that ran along the sea front and then, without even thinking, let her footsteps divert from the path and down the concrete slope towards the sea. Ravi followed her, his persistent voice getting lost in each icy blast of wind that fired from the sea. The water was almost black under the darkening sky. Their pace slowed as their feet met the sand, sinking unsteadily in its damp softness. Violet reached out for Ravi's arm to steady her, and he took her hand, instinctively, without even appearing to notice. They crossed the beach as close to the sea wall as they could get, kicking at the glossy deposits of seaweed that hung around the high tide line, throwing up the smell of salt and muddy water.

"Listen," Ravi was saying, "Anyway. The point is that we're running a bit of an event tomorrow afternoon, and

I think you could really offer something to it. You could inform people, spread the word about how bad that world really was, before you escaped."

Violet wanted to laugh out loud at the idea that she was somehow held captive by her life in London; yet the earnestness with which Ravi spoke gave her a deeply satisfying sense of her own suffering, and she was unwilling to break that spell. She sensed, however, that pushing this image too far would have felt too fraudulent even for her to bear. "I'm not sure," she said. "Do you mean you want me to give a talk or something?"

Ravi laughed. "Nothing like that. It's grass-roots, non-hierarchical, a celebration of life, of sleep and dreaming. Everyone would be there to have fun; its not like a lecture or anything. You could talk to people, tell them what it's like."

"Okay," said Violet, imagining herself as the party bore who took the kids aside and told them what bad lives they were all living. The politics of all of this seemed unnecessarily complicated to her; the vision off all these serious-minded teenagers trying to change the world made her heart sink. She was sick and tired of seriousness, and held a profound, stony resistance to taking on a new set of anxieties just to please Ravi. But when he was talking politics, he was at his most beautiful; that stray electricity that wandered beneath his skin found a giddy focus, making him more enchanting than ever. He was wiser, grander without his entourage of idiot friends, impossibly charismatic for his years. Violet felt jealous of all the ideas that drove him, wanting his eyes to alight on her with such passion and fascination.

"Are you going home now?" she said.

"I suppose so."

"Anyone expecting you?"

"Not really. Why?"

   "I was thinking," she said, and then thought better of offering him the bottle of cognac back at her hotel room. Instead, she took his face in her cold hands and kissed him, watching his eyes widen like a child's before they met hers and closed.

TWENTY-THREE

The tray sat unsteadily on the bedclothes, its contents chiming together every time one of them moved. Or rather, every time Violet moved, as Antonia's body seemed to touch the bed so lightly that the quilt barely showed the impression of her weight. Violet poured the coffee in her saucer back into the cup and pulled the sheets up further around her waist, afraid that her bare thighs might be revealed.

"I hear you in the corridor, playing your Janis Joplin records – or should I say mine," she drawled, wriggling her bare, thin toes with their beige-painted nails, as if to signify their freedom outside of her shoes, "and I thought, maybe Violet is hungry and would like a little breakfast with her old friend, who she has abandoned lately."

Violet gulped her coffee and took a hurried bite of the toast that rested on her lap. "I didn't want to get under your feet," she said through a crumb-filled mouth, "I'm sorry if I've offended you."

"No matter. I am just the landlady here and you are entitled to your own life if that is what you want." Antonia pursed her lips and blew smoke out through her nose. She had lit a cigarette the second she set the tray down, and this after she had walked in through the door moments after knocking, finding Violet lounging in bed, listening to a pile of records she had stacked up on the Dansette. It appeared to Violet to be an imperious gesture, an outright statement of ownership, but one that a mother might make.

Violet had immediately pulled the covers up to conceal the fact that she was wearing nothing but a tee-shirt, and continued to feel self-conscious as Antonia leaned back on the pillows she had plumped up. She kept thinking how she was naked under the sheets, and how she would have to admit to this if she was for some reason required to get out of bed. Worse than this, she kept wondering if there was evidence of Ravi's presence here last night, a strand of black hair, an item of mislaid clothing or an unmistakable odour of sex rising from the bed linen that Violet herself wouldn't be able to detect. Not that any of these clues would matter; Antonia had seen Violet come in with Ravi yesterday afternoon, would have seen him leave a few hours later, and would have drawn her own conclusions. Whether or not Violet chose to acknowledge it, this fact existed between the two of them.

"You have plans for today?" Antonia had already finished her black coffee, and was pouring herself another dose from the silver pot she had carried up. She was leaving her toast, with its accompanying gold pat of butter, untouched, as if her abstention was a lesson to Violet.

"I'm going to a party-thing this afternoon."

"A party-*thing*? That sounds fun."

"And I thought I might have a swim first."

"Always in that pool. I can't imagine what you see in it."

"Just trying to keep fit." Antonia grunted, then flinched as the Dansette dropped the last record of Violet's stack on top of the rest and began to play it. "You shouldn't use that stacking arm," she said, "it scratches the vinyl."

Perhaps she hadn't seen Ravi leave after all. Perhaps it had occurred during one of her rare breaks from watchfulness, and she was therefore hoping to catch them at it this morning, with her hurried entry and the way her eyes were now roaming around the room. It appeared from her mood that she was disappointed, although given that her eyes kept darting to the bathroom door, maybe she had not given up hope that he was hiding in the en-suite, waiting nakedly for her to leave.

"You didn't tell me that."

"No. I didn't." She returned to her coffee, hunching over to sip it, and Violet watched her compose herself by gradually straightening her back. "Still," she said, "no matter. Not like I play them." Violet wondered if she ought to feel guilty at this point, should admit to taking Antonia for granted, apologise then and there and be done with it. But she felt strangely unable to speak this morning, her body heavy with its own thoughts. In particular, her attention was perpetually snapping back to the scent of Ravi's body last night, a clean smell like limes and sea-water, and the way their bodies moved together, the smooth hairlessness of his skin.

"No," said Antonia, "not to worry." She sucked on her cigarette, and Violet wondered if it would be alright to ask for one. "Anyway, I came to ask if you had made any plans yet."

"Plans?" Violet again fought back the excited fizzing behind her hips, the momentary flashbacks of Ravi's face, blank with blissful concentration.

"How long you'll stay. Now, I don't want you to feel like I'm pushing you out, but Easter is coming, and I can fill my rooms at the bank holiday. Most of my other customers tell me how long they're staying."

"Oh," said Violet, "I'm not sure. Another few days, I suppose. A week? Two weeks? I hadn't thought."

"You still got stuff to do here? Family, friends to see?"

"Yes, yes. Probably." Again, Ravi's face, the delicate passivity of his body, the shady trace of his ribcage.

"And I thought that maybe you're missing London by now. Or London is missing you. You not got to go back to your job?"

"Yes, I do have to go back. Soon."

"But you've been here a long time already. I'm beginning to wonder that maybe you're not on holiday any more." She looked at Violet sideways for a moment, before sipping at the dregs of her coffee. Despite its practised slyness, there was a kindness in it, an attempt at opening a pathway between them rather than an accusation.

"No," said Violet, "you're right. I'm on sick leave. It all got a bit much for me back there. I'm having a rest. "

Antonia stroked her cheek and leaned over to kiss her. "There," she said, "that wasn't so hard, was it? Poor thing. Too much stress. I read about it in the papers."

"It wasn't like that," said Violet, and then wondered what it *was* like. The routines and strictures of her London life seemed ridiculously distant now: the early mornings and late nights, the meals delivered to her door, the fear of caffeine and alcohol, of seemingly dangerous contact with others. It all seemed like an eccentricity, a bizarre obsessive impulse that she had fallen into for a period of time, and to which it would now be impossible to return. The thought of dragging her body into the tube every morning, of spending hours and hours awake, of pounding away on the gym machines every evening, made her feel heavy, exhausted. And yet, when she made her run for the coast, it had been an impulse, a reaction to extraordinary events. It was only in retrospect that she could pick up on her own dissatisfaction with the life she had been leading.

"There's no shame in it," said Antonia, who had now taken Violet's hand and was stroking it as if she was a distressed pensioner. "Better people than you have needed a break."

"Yes," said Violet, "thanks," but she couldn't help squirming at the notion that she couldn't cope.

She spent an hour in the pool after Antonia had gone, floating watchfully on the surface of the water until her lungs ached. The link with Daisy seemed weak today, offering her only tiny snatches of information that signified very little. From what Violet could tell, her counterpart had spent the morning watching TV, but it was hard to make out. She was giving very little away, and Violet's brain was occupied with other things that were pushing her out of focus.

Every thought, every action, seemed to lead back to Ravi. It felt as though her body was remembering their evening together, and was rehearsing each touch, each scent and taste, over and over again.

It was only afterwards that it occurred to her that it may have been his first time. He had got out of bed with a sort of odd punctuality, and had spent a long time in the bathroom. Violet heard the taps turned on and off, on and off, and the toilet flush. She lay there, drinking water, and felt a warm thrill at the thought that she might have played such a significant role in his life. She liked the idea that his sexual education might be in her hands: it was a sort of role reversal, a woman stripping a young man of his virginity and introducing him to a very adult world. It was quite a responsibility and ought to be done well. She made him some tea, and invited him back into bed when he finally emerged from the bathroom.

There was a reserve, a sort of ingrained politeness about him that never seemed to disappear, even when he could no longer hide behind the usual convention of behaviour that guided him. She wondered how he would behave towards her today, after the readjustments of the intervening night.

The thought of seeing him amongst people again, encased in the immaturity of Jason and Ferret, or fired by the vulgar politicking of Bogman, left her empty; it was alone that she desired him, free of the irritations that accompanied him. And yet, alone, he had been diminished, a nervous schoolboy, thin and gauche, uncertain. It was only in the company of his friends that he was thrown into relief, made remarkable for his delicacy and subtlety; perhaps, without his companions, she would never have noticed him at all.

CHAPTER TWENTY-FOUR

She could hear the party before she saw it. She had walked over to the far side of town, leaving the decomposing hotels and pound stores behind, passing the intimidating estate of tower blocks where Bogman lived, and finally finding herself in an industrial zone full of wood yards and truck depots, which reminded her with a pang of the warehouse in which her collection of stones were boxed and wrapped, silently waiting for her.

This was surely the wrong place. When Ravi had written the address for her on the back of a till receipt, she had imagined that he had hired a hall or the back room of a pub; there was certainly nothing like that around. In fact, as she got further along the road, the businesses seemed to thin out and were replaced by vacant lots and locked sheds, the gravelly ground that surrounded them straggled with thistles and old man's beard.

The whole place had a desolate, dangerous feel about it; it reminded her of the backdrop to hostage exchanges in gangster films, or the TV rapes of women who should know better, walking alone and unguarded at night. There was music, from somewhere, an indistinct thud at first that wafted in with each gust of wind and then drifted, tantalisingly, into silence again. Violet strained her hearing to try to catch it, and for a while found herself repeatedly fooled by the cawing of a seagull or the distant drone of a ship's horn. Eventually, something more rhythmic came into focus, a heavy, tribal drumbeat, and perhaps a melody played over the top on some unidentifiable instrument. The road curved, became nothing but two high walls of chicken-wire fence and bramble. At the peak of the bend, Violet thought she caught sight of something, a flutter of scarlet amongst the trees, and then the smell of dope and wood-smoke, the rattle of a tambourine against a hard routine of drums.

The glimpse of red turned out, on closer inspection, to be a pair of long silk pennants with tattered edges, flickering either side of a metal gate whose rusted chain and padlock lay in a heap at the kerb, presumably having been cut. Above it, strung over the black and yellow height restriction bar, was a wide banner, upon which someone had hand-painted, in rainbow letters: *Dream eScape.* It boomed surprisingly loudly in the blustering wind. Thick, brown-flowered buddleia billowed behind it.

Crossing this threshold, Violet followed a long drive, conscious now of the movement of bodies just beyond the trees. The tarmac had cracked through years of neglect, and was breached by wiry grasses and tender-looking saplings; but today, somebody had lined its verges with flares made of burning rags on sticks, and had propped scraps of wood against the brambles, adorned with slogans painted in dribbly black letters: *Fight for the right to sleep; Celebrate Dreaming; Don't get high, get low!*

She could see the drummers now, a semi-circle of men pounding on tribal-looking instruments at the front of the camp. They wore combat trousers and roughly-knitted sweaters, with their sleeves rolled up to reveal blue-black, thorny tattoos on their arms. Their faces glinted with an array of piercings – lips, eyebrows, noses; one man wore a bar that passed through the bridge between his nose and forehead. Violet felt her hand instinctively reach for that part of her own face, as if to soothe a pain.

Human activity flurried all around them. The site was dominated by a huge, open-sided shed, whose original use was revealed by the tangle of scrap metal piled in one corner. The rest of the space had been dotted with glowing braziers whose thick smoke rose to hang around the roof. People were hanging around them, doing their best to ignore the cold. Some drank from bottles; others passed joints. One woman in a long, beaded skirt, fingerless gloves and a parka was dancing expressively to the drumbeat, making her arms rise and fall like a ballerina's. A skinny man joined her, his ginger hair straggling around his face. He smiled as he danced, making big, awkward staged moves and grasping for the girl's hand to twirl her. She consented, smiled, and danced away. Behind her, a man stretched enormous bubbles out of a washing-up bowl, flicking them to release them into the air. A small crowd had gathered at his feet to watch them, glazed-eyed, as they wobbled unsteadily upwards, their undulating rainbow surface reflecting the fire of the braziers as a hundred piercing, orange eyes.

At the far end of the shed, a woman wearing a bowler hat over her clouds of grey hair had set up a table and chair, and had hung a bed sheet behind her, painted with the words, *What do your dreams mean?* She had replaced the dot of the question mark with an unblinking Egyptian eye. She smiled incitingly to anyone that passed. To her left was a whitewashed wall, upon which someone had painted *Wall of Dreams*, and had hung marker pens on strings so that people could record their dreams. A boy was writing on it, his nose pressed nearly against the breeze blocks, evidently detailing the minutiae of some unconscious experience. His tongue roamed across each lip in turn as his narrative continued in ever-smaller script.

There were a surprising number of people milling around the site, stamping their feet against the cold as the sunlight slowly drained away, sitting in little drunk clusters, looking embarrassed or enthralled by the drummers and the stilt-walkers. Many of them seemed to be following the path that led behind the shed, disappearing into the relative gloom of the scrubland. Violet followed them, and as she did so, she noticed Bogman, crouching alone under the Wall of Dreams, glaring soporifically at anyone who passed. Violet gave him a non-committal wave, and he nodded in return, his brow deeply furrowed.

The path was dark, but Violet could hear music coming from behind the shed, the soft burr of a man's voice and a guitar. As she rounded the corner, she could see that two tents had been pitched, each of them glowing from the inside. A couple of laughing women crawled from the flap of one of them, and with them came a waft of incense and a seep of orange light. Violet stooped to crawl in herself, and found that she was eye to eye with Jason and Ferret, who were sitting cross-legged outside, passing a large plastic bottle of cider between them.

"Don't mind us," slurred Jason, "We're not part of the inner circle so we've decided to sit outside."

"The incense was making me feel sick," said Ferret. Violet ignored them and passed through the opening of the tent. Inside, it shone with the light of dozens of candle lanterns, hanging from the ridgepole and resting on plates on the ground. Rugs had been laid over the floor, and cushions were scattered around, a clash of blues, pinks, greens and purples. In the centre of the room was a large, brass incense-burner with curls of loose smoke rising from it, and an odd bouquet of evergreen foliage in a vase beside it, a gesture of optimism for the spring. The air was heavy with the musty scent of sandalwood and at first Violet choked on its thickness, drunk with the fumes.

"Hey, Violet." At the far end of the tent, Ravi was kneeling attentively in front of a woman and a man, who were laid back against the cushions in each other's arms. He turned briefly to greet her, and then returned to the diatribe he was offering to the couple, the same fierce eulogy on the ills of capitalism that he had treated Violet to the day before.

"Ravi," she said, "come over here." He looked startled, said, "Oh, okay," apologised to the couple and crawled cat-like towards her across the patchwork of furry rugs. "Are you alright? It's good to see you."

Violet leaned over to kiss him, and he at first turned his face to offer her his cheek, before giggling ashamedly and kissing her lips. "Those people probably came in here to shag. They don't want you lecturing them."

"Oh," he said, "do you think so?" and they both turned to see the man and woman wriggling through the lacing at the back of the tent. "Oh," said Ravi again, and his face fell.

"I brought some booze," said Violet, pushing a carrier bag of clinking bottles towards Ravi in the hope that they would distract him. "Red wine. Screw top and everything. Here." The seal of the bottle cracked as she opened it, and she poured each of them a slug of the wine, using teacups that she had brought from her room.

"It all seems to be going well." She was surprisingly desperate for the wine, her mouth tingling at the first taste of it. She sucked down a couple of big mouthfuls. Ravi sipped his thoughtfully, gripping the cup by the tips of his delicate fingers. "Yeah," he said, "I mean, it's not been easy. One of the collective didn't like us using marker pens on the Wall of Dreams, because of the chemicals. And Bogman's taken a couple of Diazepam, so he's out of it. And not many people here really seem to care about the meaning behind it. It's just a free party."

"Come on," said Violet, "that's not the point. You're showing people a better way of life. Just try to relax and enjoy it." There was a flutter of eye contact between them, and she saw Ravi flinch a little and blush. "What's in the other tent?"

Ravi shrugged. "It's supposed to be the House of Sleep. But no-one's sleeping in there. They're just getting pissed." There was a blast of cold air on Violet's face, and the dancing girl climbed into the tent with one of the drummers. She immediately fell back upon the cushions and reached her arms out to the drummer, who eased his body on top of hers and smiled as she wrapped her legs around him.

"Shall we go?" said Violet.

CHAPTER TWENTY-FIVE

It was almost dark outside now, and the lights of the camp glowed warmly in the twilight. The air was crisp and still, and stepping out into it made Violet realise how humid the interior of the tent had been.

As they crossed the grass to the other tent, she took hold of Ravi's hand and squeezed it; he squeezed back. Then, just as she reached out to open the canvas door of the House of Sleep, she felt a dizzying lurch in her head, as if her brain had come loose from its moorings, and she was struck by the sensation of being simultaneously inside and outside the tent. Daisy must be in there. Her heart quickened and her breath stalled. She fell to her knees and scrambled in there as quickly as she could.

The House of Sleep was lit in a colder, bluer light than the previous tent, with storybook images of smiling, benevolent moons painted on the walls. It contained the same pile of rugs and cushions, but also offered a pile of blankets in the corner, ready for any visitor to defeat their capitalist urges by taking a nap. The planned tranquil effect, however, was being heartily subverted by the small group who had taken residence there. They lounged around the boundaries of the tent, draped in the blankets to keep them warm, and passed a bottle of vodka between them, laughing raucously.

Daisy was, of course, at the centre of the action, sitting upright with one blanket over her lap and another draped over her head, as if to underline the fact that the temperature had dropped rapidly now that the sun had gone down. Ruth lay beside her, wearing an aviator's hat with fleece-lined earflaps, and a pair of sheepskin mittens, and around them was an odd collection of hangers-on that Daisy had attracted, men who were universally older than her and united in their intense fascination. The one to whom she was paying the most attention was a high-cheekboned twenty-something with a carefully-dishevelled mop of curly hair. He was more handsome, more arrogant than the rest, and seemed to believe that his supplying of Daisy with vodka from his bottle was some kind of sexual triumph in itself, rather than a clever manipulation on her part. With every deep drag Daisy took on the bottle, he would turn to the friend who sat next to him and raise his eyebrows in the manner of a proud father at a school play.

As Violet crawled into the circle and laid down opposite them, she saw Daisy reach across to draw a cigarette from the man's pack, give him a wink and a salute, and then lean over to light it from one of the lanterns on the floor. The man laughed and caught his friend's eye. Violet laughed too, a kind of hot hilarity at Daisy's shameless use of him to make sure her own needs were met. She watched the man's hand creep under Daisy's blanket, only to be slapped heavily away. "Just because I smoke your fags, dick-boy, doesn't mean to say I want to fuck you."

The circle roared with laughter, particularly the men who hadn't quite managed to gain a ringside seat in Daisy's performance. One of them licked his finger and mimed pressing it against a hotplate in mid-air, hissing as he did so. Daisy shook her head. "Jesus, Christian, you're so fucking camp."

The man with the curly hair was rising to his feet beside her, untangling himself from his blanket and brushing down his jeans. "Going so soon?" said Daisy, and then cackled with Ruth.

"I've just realised," said the man, "that I ended up in the children's tent by mistake. Little girls who promise more than they can give aren't my style."

"Off you go, then. Go and grope girls half your age elsewhere." She was quite magnificently drunk, her voice strident and precisely-intoned as if it took a great deal of effort to control it; the flow of her words, their jaggedness and bullying humour, were undiminished, though. Violet felt grateful that she was able to laugh, anonymously, alongside her, rather than catch in the glare of her disapproval. The man brushed past her as he left the tent, coughing, "Children," as he disappeared through the door.

Daisy leaned back against her cushions and smiled. "Cunt," she said, and drew deeply on her fag.

Ruth leaned over and snaked an arm around her. "There, there, muffin," she said, "he didn't mean it. He did take his bloody vodka, though."

"And his fags," said Daisy, jutting out her bottom lip and gazing around the room for a fresh supply. Ravi looked away as her eyes passed over him.

"Hey," she said sleepily as her eyes alighted on Violet. "Don't I know you from somewhere?"

Violet felt the blood rush to her face as she encountered the high-beam of Daisy's attention. "Yes," she said, her voice wavering. She cleared her throat. "I've seen you around, here and there. The White Room and stuff." She went to drain her wine, found her cup empty, and so drained Ravi's instead. He was picking at his fingernails, looking intently at the floor.

"Oh god, yes, probably. I'm always so fucking pissed I don't remember. I hope I haven't been rude. I'm Daisy by the way."

"Violet."

"Well, hello, Violet. We'll be two flowers together. Let's shake hands." She got up onto her knees and stretched over, groaning with the effort, to touch Violet's fingertips. An electric shock passed between them, a minute explosion in the wrist that at first Violet thought was the imaginary product of her own excitement, until she saw Daisy shake her hand and laugh. "Jesus, these rugs much be woven from pure nylon by the Inuits, or wherever they come from. Fuck, my head's spinning. We were doing poppers in here before you came, Violet. You missed it. We're all a bit fucked, I'm afraid. Actually, now I come to think of it, they belonged to that gay-boy who just left. Figures." She let out her rough caw of a laugh, and Ruth joined her. Violet felt Ravi's body tighten beside her. He looked at his watch.

"I'm going out the front to hear the band," he said. "You coming?"

"No," said Violet, "I'll stay here I think. It's a bit cold out there." Ravi gave her a significant look, which she pretended she hadn't noticed, and then crept out of the tent. Daisy rolled her eyes and giggled.

"I've got a couple of bottles of wine here," said Violet, realising that she had already downed the majority of the first one without thinking. "Shall we open them?"

"Thank god," said Daisy, "a saviour! I think I'll need to be comatose if I'm expected to put up with all these fucking hippies," and she held out a plastic cup for Violet to fill.

Being with Daisy was like having a light cast on Violet's soul. She felt herself glow form the inside, illuminated by Daisy's reckless cleverness, her unedited barrage of words, her fearlessness. She laughed until she could feel her face grow hot and red, tried to join in by throwing back barbs of her own. It was surely impossible that she had ever been this enthralling, this lively and careless herself; she felt like the last ten years of her life had been a shrinking process, a diminution of her own well of interestingness, as if she had been steadily leaking some vital fluid. At the same time, she looked on Daisy with a sense of pride, for if she had once been a faction of this, then she had created and passed on something truly wonderful.

When Daisy finally drained the last drop of wine into her cup and gulped it down, she threw the blanket off her head and said, "Our booze has run out. Those blasted pixies must have taken it. Let us go on a quest for more alcohol." She kneeled up, and Violet saw that she was wearing a short denim skirt, knee-high boots and no tights. "Come on Ruthie-baby," she said, as she grabbed her friend's hand and tugged her upwards. Ruth groaned. "You can't lay here like a little dormouse all night." The two other lads were slumped back in the corner of the tent, having fallen asleep a long time ago. Violet eased unsteadily onto her knees, and then made her way out of the tent like this, moving so awkwardly that it made Daisy nearly collapse with giggles.

Contact with the cold air outside set everything spinning. Violet straightened onto her feet, and for a moment had to steady herself by holding onto the guy rope while the ground settled into an equilibrium. The camp had quietened down, with fewer people trailing between its tents; there was still some music seeping around from the shed, the sound of many voices singing together with a high lead straining to be heard over the top of it all.

Daisy stumbled out of the tent, falling immediately onto her knees. Violet rushed to help her up, but she batted her hand away, her face contorted into a grimace which could have been laughter or tears. It was the former: she knelt up, inspected her hands and said, "Jesus, that was so fucking funny," and then paused for a moment, said, "Oh god," and vomited copiously at Violet's feet.

Ruth's head emerged between the tent-flaps. "Was that Daisy?" she asked, and then seeing her friend standing now, retching up the remaining contents of her stomach, said, "Ah. I see. Plus ça change."

Violet found a bottle of water in her bag, which Daisy swilled around her mouth and spat out. "Rots your teeth, that fucking stuff," she said, wiping her face on the sleeve of her jumper. "Who's that bloody girl at school, the bulimic? Breath like a...a...an old donkey." More laughter, accompanied by an alarming amount of lurching and swaying.

"Time to go home, I think," said Violet, feeling suddenly guilty at the state Daisy was in. "I'll call a taxi."

"Would you? Have you got any money then? I'm skint."

"Sure. It's a long walk otherwise." Violet pulled her mobile out of her bag and dialled the number, the same as it had been years ago. As she was about to place it back in her bag, Daisy said, "No, no, no, no," and pulled at her arm so that she could take Violet's phone. "I'm beaming you my number so you can text me," she said, flicking through the menus on her own phone with her face crumpled in intense concentration. Once she had found what she wanted, she touched the two phones together like an electronic kiss, and Violet's screen lit up to show that a contact had been received.

They made their way to the main road, skirting the edges of the camp to keep Daisy out of everyone's way. "Ooh, spooky," she said, as she brushed past the overgrown foliage at the sides of the shed, now unidentifiable in the dark. As they neared the gates, they caught a glimpse of the remaining Dream eScapers sitting in a circle in the shed, which now glowed warmly against the dark. A woman was strumming on a guitar, and several of the drummers were joining in; all were singing. Violet could see Ravi amongst them, his back straight, looking as though he was taking his part in the song very seriously.

"Fuck me, the hippies are bloody singing now," said Daisy, "Fucking Kumbaya." The song was not, in fact, Kumbaya, but Daisy offered her own rendition of it anyway, putting on her best school assembly voice and holding her hand over her heart. Ruth accompanied her with an interpretive dance, her face an image of piety. *Someone's crying, Lord*, was illustrated by sobbing so loud that it made one of the singers look into the gloom towards them. The actions to *Someone's praying, Lord* were mercifully quieter.

Daisy had introduced *Someone's pissing, Lord*, by the time the taxi arrived, a verse that even Ruth seemed reluctant to act out. Violet hushed them both, and opened the passenger door to explain the three destinations to the driver.

"What are you doing all the way out here," he said; "I'd already radioed control to tell them it must be a prank."

"A party," said Violet. She opened the back door and ushered Ruth and Daisy in, reminding them to use their seatbelts, and then slid into the front of the car next to the driver. He was craning his neck to look down the drive at the amber lights of the braziers.

"Funny sort of a party," he said, and then, glancing into his rear-view mirror, watched Daisy struggle to muster the coordination to fit her seatbelt into its clip. "She'd better not be sick in my car."

"Don't worry," said Violet, "I think she's done throwing up for tonight."

TWENTY-SIX

Monday started late, after a night passed staggering to the bathroom to gulp down glasses of water that never seemed to sate Violet's arid throat. She felt sick and feverish when her phone began to ring at eight, as well as unspeakably grateful that the name of the caller flashed up on its screen. Marcus. She waited until it stopped ringing and then switched the thing onto silent. She was in no mood to invent excuses.

Sleep took her again, quickly and dreamlessly. She woke at eleven, feeling light-headed and empty, but definitely a little more ready to face the world. Her mouth was so dry that it felt wrinkled. She plodded into the bathroom and emptied five glasses of water into it. They were only small; she needed them. She climbed into the shower and stood, shivering, as the water washed away the feeling of greasiness that had slid over her skin. She didn't bother to dry herself, but wrapped a towel around her head and her body, and lay on the bed, chewing on one of the cellophane-wrapped biscuits that were left on her tray each day.

It all felt heavy on her this morning. The heady joy of her evening with Daisy seemed now to be a grave thing, as if the chemical high that accompanied the girl's presence had its own counterbalancing low, a long come-down from her dizzying sphere of influence. Being with Daisy was like being illuminated, physically lit-up from the inside so that you glowed with the same light that she did. Her lively capriciousness, her ability to be horrifically rude and utterly charming at the same time was an absolute revelation to Violet, who supposed that she too must have been like this, although she couldn't imagine it now.

Away from her company, Violet felt as though the tide had pulled out, leaving a scattering of debris on the shore, sharp-edged words and shimmering actions that Violet would stumble across and turn over in her mind for a while, smiling and enjoying the residual glow of their author. It was hard to believe that soon all this would be gone; soon, if Daisy's life followed Violet's, she would refashion herself into something more serious, more controlled and, as Violet believed, more dead, more crushed under the weight of her own regrets. Violet remembered only too well the deliberate process of change, the drawing in of all those dangerous qualities that made Daisy so entrancing. And then it would be like a winter for her: long, cold and dark, difficult to thaw.

She could stop it all, of course, and she must; it seemed to her that the purpose of this bizarre link between herself and her double must be that she should correct the mistake, offer redemption to her counterpart even if she couldn't find it for herself. The time was coming, and she was ready.

Laying still, she could feel Daisy's thoughts welling up inside her, like the much-anticipated kick of a baby. Stillness brought them close to the surface, and her tuning inwards to find them was by now a conscious act rather than an involuntary experience that sometimes took her by surprise. It was comforting to know that she was there, tugging at the invisible cord that linked them, but it was uncomfortable too, an invitation to voyeurism that Violet was only too keen to accept, but which she knew was an intrusion. On the other hand, most of Daisy's thoughts were so familiar to Violet that it barely seemed worth censoring herself. She remembered, for example, harbouring fantastical crushes on men with barely any link to her own life, and Daisy was indulging in this today, dreaming about travelling to India with the man who served behind the bar at the Green Man in town. Violet also recognised the complexity of planning that next Friday's outfit took, even as far in advance as Monday morning, with Sunday's hangover still lingering.

It appeared to Violet that her link to Daisy had stepped up a grade in terms of clarity over the weekend; offering her full concentration to the experience, she could almost believe that it was she who was sitting at a dining table, sipping weak coffee and trying to focus on a copy of *Emma*, one with notes pencilled in every margin. Except that every now and then, Violet's own face could crop up in Daisy's thoughts, a remnant of the previous day, and Violet would feel herself shrinking from her own mirror-image.

It would appear that she had made a reasonable impression, although Daisy was wondering how old she was and how she had ended up at the Dream eScape. Violet shuddered at the thought that she was so obviously other, and then laughed at her own vanity, the very idea that she expected to pass herself off as an eighteen year-old girl. Maybe it was best, after all, not to delve too far into Daisy's thoughts; she might come across something she didn't want to know. It was now almost impossible to disconnect the link between them, though; the more she tried to ignore the images that were flowing to her (waiting for toast to pop out of the toaster, staring at the glowing element within), the more they drew her in.

She needed to distract herself. Reaching for her phone on the bedside table, she scanned down the list of missed calls: Marcus, Marcus, Marcus, Marcus...He would have resolved, she knew, to make a fresh assault on her conscience after the weekend. It was best if she kept ignoring his calls;

she just wouldn't know what to say to him anymore. She tried to picture him sitting behind his desk in his glass-walled office, but all she could conjure up was a caricature, a stereotypical man in red braces, a slick yuppie braying into a telephone. Consciously, she was pretty sure she had never seen him in braces, but the image persisted. It was almost impossible to imagine herself in that context now; the rigours and disciplines of waking at five, the uncomfortable curse of her commute, the days spent preserving the immaculate appearance of her suit, and having to be aloof and formal and clever whenever she spoke. It was already unthinkably distant, and she knew that Marcus would baulk at the languid necessities of her current life whether or not she was on his payroll. Best to avoid the conversation until she had done what needed to be done; then she could consider how to operate her life in the absence of the money that had continued to flow into her account. No sooner. Not yet.

The final call on the list of those she had missed was from an unknown number; she dialled her answerphone in the hope that not all her messages were form Marcus. She found that he had not left any messages at all, clearly having decided to go all-out for talking to her in person. Instead, the message was a recording of a quiet voice, which at first she didn't recognise, but which gradually came into focus as Ravi's.

"I'm um…I'm sorry I didn't get to say goodbye last night. I was doing stuff with the camp and I didn't see you go…Listen, are you doing anything today? Only I haven't… I'm at home. We could go somewhere. I've got the car. Call me. She had almost forgotten he existed, so tied up were her thoughts with Daisy, but his voice sounded thin and vulnerable, and made a surge of desire rush up inside her.

She called back, taking a gulp of water as the phone rang to clear her voice of its morning thickness.

"Hello," she said as he answered, "so you're home alone are you? Would you like me to come round so we can spend a day in?"

There was a pause. "I had something in mind actually. For us to do. Somewhere I'd like you to see."

"Oh. Okay. Sure." Violet hoped he hadn't noticed the seductive tint she had put into her voice, which now sounded ridiculous, the kind of thing that counts as arousing in adverts for cheap coffee.

"I'll pick you up. Ten minutes?"

Violet pulled on some thick, black tights, a denim mini-skirt that she now thought was similar to Daisy's, a tee-shirt, a thick jumper and a pair of cowboy boots; she dragged the tangles out of her hair and divided it into two low bunches, which she fastened with a pair of orange plastic bobbles. The effect, she knew, was vaguely ridiculous, a wanton mish-mash of styles with a kitsch infantilism that she would once have found hideous, but she felt she had to do something to keep up with her new crop of friends, make some kind of offering to the god of youth and fashion.

She hurried through reception, hoping to breeze past Antonia without having to give any sort of explanation of her plans, but the elder woman was sitting behind the counter, her hair piled into an elegantly-disordered tangle of curls, smoking a thin, black cigarette.

"You look good," she drawled, standing to catch Violet's attention as she passed. Her sooty eye-sockets creased into a smile.

"Oh, um, thanks."

"New skirt?"

Violet gazed down at it in a pantomime of not knowing which skirt she was wearing, of having thrown something on haphazardly. "Yes."

"Suits you."

"Does it? Thanks. Anyway, must rush – someone's picking me up. See you later."

She heard Antonia say, "Always in such a rush," as the front door swung shut behind her, and registered the way her face dropped. It was made all the more embarrassing by the fact that it took fifteen minutes for Ravi to arrive, during which time she waited on the front steps, knowing that Antonia would be watching her on the security camera that monitored the hotel's entrance. She half-expected Antonia to come out and sit with her, bringing coffee and biscuits, but she didn't emerge. When Ravi finally arrived in a smart little car that must have been his mother's, she ran down the steps and climbed in as fast as she could. It was impossible to explain this light, cringing fear she had developed of Antonia's company, but it felt the same as her reaction to her mother when she was a teenager, that brittle bridge between privacy and familiarity, the urge to evade scrutiny.

TWENTY-SEVEN

Ravi was playing some wistful folk singer over the car stereo, a woman who croaked and whispered the lyrics over sparse guitar; every now and then, he would break their conversation to whisper along with a chorus or a phrase that pleased him, his soft voice mimicking the woman's almost exactly.

He did not kiss her when she got in; instead he passed his eyes over the flustered chaos she brought with her and nodded a hello. They sat very separately; Violet felt, not for the first time, that to touch him would be somehow to infect him. He drove slowly and carefully, giving it the same consideration that he gave to everything. He steered with great precision, adjusting his hands to maintain a ten-to-two position at all times; the gears were selected gently and meticulously.

"I didn't know you could drive," said Violet after a while, as Ravi navigated a roundabout and took a turning towards the south coast.

"I only passed a month ago."

"First time?"

"Of course." He smiled at this, aware of his own fastidiousness.

"Where are we going, then?"

"Dungeness."

"Dungeness? With the power station?"

"Yes, that Dungeness." He smelt of tangerines today, a musky citrus scent that wafted at Violet when he moved. His hair was still wet, which made his dreads blacker and put steam on the windows that he had to fight with the air conditioning.

"Why would we want to go there?" Violet remembered Dungeness from childhood daytrips, when she and her father would board the miniature train that ran along the coast and terminated there. They never even got out; it was, to her recollection, a bleak, shingly promontory, littered with low black huts, where the light was always muted somehow, as if the sun couldn't quite get around the looming power station to reach it. She only remembered the way the track looped round there to send them back home; nothing else. It seemed like a desperate place for Ravi to take her.

"It's ugly, I guess," said Ravi, "but it appeals to me when I'm in a certain mood. I go there to think."

"Great," said Violet, "we'll drive all the way to Dungeness so that you can get all brooding. Can't we go to Rye? I'll buy you lunch."

"No," said Ravi, laughing as if this might have been a joke. He reached across and put his hand on Violet's arm. "You'll be fine. We'll have a wander round." Violet let herself be soothed by this, placated by the very fact that he had touched her at all. His hands were light and papery, neither warm nor cold, as if he wasn't susceptible to the same fleshly weaknesses as anyone else. He soon returned both hands to the steering wheel, unwilling to extend the risk any longer than necessary.

The landscape flattened as they drove on, became low, bleak and marshy. Sheep grazed the fields now, their wool blackened and straggly. Some raised their heads to watch them as they passed, chewing on the thick grass. The houses they passed were low and broad-windowed, their gardens decorated with driftwood and shingle. Ravi turned onto a road that ran parallel to the coast, although the sea was invisible, hidden behind a bank of cafés and amusement arcades, their plastic colours looking faded and dirty in the grey light. These soon disappeared, as if the terrain were growing more and more inhospitable with each mile they travelled. The land became broken by patches of gravel and sand and the houses along the way looked battered by the weather, faded monuments of peeling paint and rotting woodwork. The road became a track, flanked with shingle, and the black huts that Violet remembered appeared, dotted across the land like monopoly counters, each one solitary and gardenless, icily proud of its isolation.

The yellow- and grey-flecked shingle was everywhere now, a resting place for tarpaulined boats and scraps of frayed rope that littered the roadside. It was broken only by a pair of lighthouses, one black, one white, but still no sighting of the sea, even though it was everywhere. Beyond them, looming like a clinical colossus over the whole scene, was the power station, an edifice of dull glass and blunt steel. It was unbeautiful, brick-like, an insult to the land around it.

Ravi parked the car behind the lighthouse, and they got out into the blustering damp wind. Violet wished she had brought her coat, and that she had chosen jeans over tights.

"Come on," said Ravi, stretching his hand towards her, "we'll have a look around." Violet unrolled the neck of her jumper so that it covered the lower part of her face. The gravel slipped backwards under their feet, so that it felt like walking uphill; they made their way onto the road and followed it round the end of the peninsular, past the station for the miniature train, with its picket fence and brave air of make-believe, and a low pub that promised fish and chips.

Ravi grew quiet and they walked, leaving Violet's imagination to flow across the cosy details of the place: the aluminium flue that emitted curls of smoke from a fisherman's hut, evidence of a warm fire inside; the thin, blue tin-roofed chapel that spoke of a dour religion flourishing, even in this outpost. She began to project herself into those little shacks, their small imagined rooms and their sense of comfortable sufficiency, of enough being enough. She would need a bed, a kitchen, a bathroom with an old enamel bath and somewhere to sit, nothing else. It would be utterly perfect to be alone like that with only the sea for company.

Ravi stepped off the road and across the gravely stretch towards the shore, so she followed him. They had been silent for a long time, each walking alone. Ravi had his hands in his pockets and the collar of his coat turned up; Violet had retracted her fists into her sleeves but she could still feel them numbing in the cold. They followed a wooden boardwalk across the shingle, and soon got their first glimpse of the sea, a grumbling, muted teal at the bottom of a steeply-sloping beach. Ravi broke into a trot as they approached it, and slid down the groynes on his heels, unpocketing his hands to steady himself as he let his body ease down so that he was sitting in one of the dips, his back against the bank of shingle. Violet followed him, too afraid to slide, and so stepped gingerly towards him, her arms held wide to balance her. Here, they were exposed to the wind's full blast, an eye-watering tirade that drowned their voices when they finally spoke.

"They give the residents tablets, you know, to take in case of a nuclear accident." Ravi didn't take his eyes off the waves as he spoke.

"Really?"

"Yeah. Bogman told me. Jesus, why would you live here anyway? Perhaps they're all suicidal."

"I dunno," said Violet, "I like it. It feels so far away."

"It's fucking awful."

"You're the one who wanted to come here!"

"I'm fascinated, I suppose. The people living out here, they're like limpets clinging to a rock. Someone's come and ruined their landscape and they're refusing to budge."

"Perhaps the power station becomes part of it after a while. It's a different kind of beauty. I can't explain it; it feels more like mood than place here."

"Yeah, it's like being depressed. You can see all the worst things about man here – the destruction of the environment, the putting of money before everything else, the urge to be alone, rather than to cooperate and form communities. It's a reminder of all the things I want to fight against."

"Fight against? You planning on running for government?" Violet smiled and leant in to nudge him, but Ravi's body was fixed and resistant. He dragged in a deep breath.

"I've decided to drop out of school, Violet. I'm not going back after half term. Leave home, too, join the camp, travel. I'm not learning anything there anymore. All the teachers care about is getting me to pass my exams; they can't see past their fucking league-tables.

"I've learned more from Bogman than I ever learned at school. What's the point in going to university when the world's caving in around us? I've got to go out into the real world, live a real life. Anything else is just kidding myself."

Violet struggled to find words to answer this, wary of entering into a discussion on Ravi's future. "What's the real world though? Do you actually think that all those people on Sunday were the real world?"

"They're more real than sticking your head in the sand and pretending none of it's happening."

"But where do they get their money? I bet most of them go home to rich mummies and daddies at the weekends to do their washing and get some cash."

"I had no idea you were such a fascist. At least they're trying out something alternative." Ravi sat up and pulled his knees in towards him, still keeping his eyes fixed steadily on the sea.

"I'm just saying," said Violet, "it's all very well from the outside, but how does it work? What are they changing? What difference does setting up a few tents and passing joints around a campfire make to the big boys out there?"

"You can't force other people to change; you can only show them the right way and hope they'll choose to follow you. There's no leader in the camp; it's all about non-hierarchical, egalitarian society. Imagine it. Imagine if the whole world was like it."

Violet laughed. "It sounds fucking awful."

"You've got no faith in human nature."

"No," said Violet, "you're right. I haven't."

They were silent for a while. Ravi picked up a handful of pebbles and began to toss them into the sea. When he had finished, he looked at her for the first time since they'd sat down, and pressed his lips into something that might have been a smile.

"I'm sorry," he said, "I don't mean to take it out on you. You've shown me the way, if anything; shown me how an adult life can be free."

Violet couldn't help snorting at the absurdity of this. "Me? You've got to be bloody joking." She paused for a while, digging out a trench in the shingle with her cold fingers. "I used to be freer," she said eventually, in a small voice that wasn't quite her own, "but it all kind of seeped away over time. It'll be different for you; you're male. You'll be allowed to keep hold of who you are – your music and tastes and interests – whatever you do. Women can't do that; I don't know why. When I see Daisy, it terrifies me, because I know it's all going to get squashed out of her soon."

"Daisy? Is she that girl you were with last night? I see her all the time. She's fucking awful, a loudmouth. Always pissed."

It was a comment that she should have expected, a sentiment that she had already inferred from Ravi's reaction to Daisy the night before, but nevertheless Violet felt blood surge into her muscles as if they were readying to mount a very physical defence. She could have slapped him, then and there, hard across the face, for daring to criticise the object of all her affections, but she knew, too, that he wasn't entirely wrong. Daisy's brash nihilism couldn't be further away from Ravi's slow, philosophical optimism.

"You don't know her," she said at length, hoping he would sense the finality in her voice.

"No, you're right, I don't. And I don't want to. I've seen enough already. To be honest, I'm a bit surprised at you for liking a girl like that."

"A girl like that! Listen to yourself! You spout all this progressive bollocks, but when it comes down to it, you've not got away from being a little bit disgusted at girls who sleep around and get pissed. That old double-standard dies hard, doesn't it?"

"No." Ravi gripped her wrist as if he was afraid she would get up and walk away, "it's not like that. It's the selfishness, Violet, the unkindness. There's so many people like her, wrapped up in their own little worlds, not caring about the world outside them. Please don't get me wrong; it's not because she's a woman that I dislike her."

"Disapprove," interrupted Violet.

"Not disapprove. Well, maybe. Maybe I do disapprove of her. But it's only because she's part of a tribe, and they're taking over. Nothing matters to them. They're the people who are powerful, Violet, the people in charge. They're London, they're New York. They're destroyers."

Violet looked away and slowly shook her head. She found Ravi's idealism charming when it involved utopian fantasies about freedom and happiness, but childish and hectoring when they took the form of paranoid visions of an apocalyptic future. She hated the way he too easily took the moral high ground, chanting out Bogman's words verbatim, and judging all those around him from the comfortable solid ground of his privileged upbringing. She hated, too, the way she found that she couldn't argue with him. In a desolate part of herself, she believed he was right; the only area of disagreement was that, unlike him, she didn't believe that there was a solution. It was his naïve belief that he could solve the problem that infuriated her; it was surely already too late.

"Look," said Ravi after a while, "it's not just your friend Daisy. It's everyone. Look at Jason and Stephen. They're the best of a bad bunch at school, and they're awful, utterly moronic. In five years' time, they'll be starting company careers like their dads, and they'll forget that there was ever anything more important than paying the mortgage. They keep saying I've changed, but it's them. I still want all the same things I wanted when I was a child."

"You'll change too, eventually," said Violet. "It happens to us all. You'll get cynical; you'll grow a thicker skin." She let her words blow away from them into the sea. Ravi didn't reply.

"Hey," she said, levering herself onto her feet. "I'm hungry. Let me buy you lunch." They scrambled back up the steep bank of shingle, and crossed over into the realm of the black huts again. It seemed utterly still and silent after the violent blast of the sea wind, and Violet's cheeks burned in the wake of it. She could see for miles from here across a flat landscape with an enormous sky. The huts clung low to the ground, and the tallest thing she could see was the forest of telegraph poles that strung them all together, a network of marionettes. She noticed Ravi lifting his head and gazing sleepily around him, as if trying to see the good in the place; but his eyes kept being drawn back to the power station, and every time he looked at it, his delicate features would flinch slightly, as if assaulted by its ugliness.

"So you like this place," he said, smiling ironically.

"Yes," said Violet, "I feel at home."

TWENTY-EIGHT

There is a difference between aloneness and loneliness.

This mantra had served Violet very well over the years as she sat in her apartment every night, self-consciously filling the short interval between her return from the gym and the welcome oblivion of sleep. It was almost true back then, in a roundabout sort of a way; she may not have savoured her solitude, as her little catchphrase suggested she should have, but she certainly appreciated the absence of other people after a long day holding back the seething tide of politics and demands. Aloneness was a choice of sorts; it was just as well she had no-one to come home to, as she had no reserves of civility left to offer them at the end of a working day.

Yet today, the mantra was laughably ineffective, as Violet felt as though a raw, twitching void had opened inside her, longing to be filled by human company. She had said goodbye to Ravi on the steps of the hotel at five the previous afternoon, having first taken an hour to admire the smooth perfection of his knees, the tautness of the sliver of skin that crowned his navel, the way her own limbs glowed white against his. After he left, she had taken a long bath in the shared bathroom down the corridor, with the lights out and a single tea-light burning yellow against the watery dusk. Laying there, she had allowed herself to dream of Ravi's body, to leer like a man over her possession of this beautiful boy.

The remainder of the evening had passed quickly enough after that: she had eaten in the dining room of the hotel, which was open in honour of the half term and was surprisingly busy, full of serious-looking couples and fidgeting children. It was odd to see Antonia robbed of her leisure. She wove between the tables with blazing cheeks and a smile fixed on her face. Violet had appreciated the way that this freed her from Antonia's stifling attentions. She went to bed at ten.

The next morning was less accommodating. Violet woke early and skipped breakfast out of a shuddering aversion to sharing her space with the hollow-eyed families. She drank tea in her room, watched the news, showered, plucked her eyebrows, dried her hair, dressed slowly; then, reminding herself of the pleasures of aloneness, she strolled down to the end of the corridor to the guests' bookshelf, making a great display of the amusement that choosing a book was giving her. She waved her choice, a fat contemporary novel with a whimsical cover, at a passing family and said, 'What could be nicer? An afternoon's reading!' or something equally cloying; she couldn't remember the exact words but knew enough to be embarrassed by them. She gave up on the novel after reading the first page four times without retaining any clue as to what was going on. She smoked two cigarettes on the balcony while watching the sea.

At midday, she surrendered, and allowed the loneliness to spread across her like an ink-blot. Her brain craved the company of a friend, anybody. She calculated that she had only been alone for nineteen hours, and already she was overtaken by this craven urge for the society of others. Why hadn't she thought to arrange something with Ravi? He was almost certain to be at home. And yet, by now, the hole in her chest had solidified into something more desolate and self-pitying, which told her that she must not call on someone who had so signally failed to call her all the morning. If he had wanted her company, he could easily have summoned it. She would not intrude. He clearly had better things to do. She knew she could have salvaged her day by walking out into town and catching a bus to somewhere that interested her – one of the towns further along the coast, perhaps, or even Canterbury. But a gloom had fixed on her by then that recast these simple journeys as impossible feats, too complex and elaborate for her to contemplate. Instead, she managed to find the energy to seek out Antonia in the office, even though she resented this being her last resort. It would encourage that probing curiosity about her life that she so hated, but it was a lesser evil than an afternoon at the mercy of the four walls of her room.

Antonia, however, was not in the office. Violet found her in the dining room, repeating last night's sprint between the tables. After watching her lay plates on one table, deliver a bill to another and take an order from a third, Violet had still failed to attract her attention. When Antonia dived through the swinging doors into the kitchen, Violet followed her.

Antonia was hovering over a row of plates, garnishing each with lettuce from a deep ice-cream tub. She didn't look up as she counted three slices each of cucumber and three of tomato on to each plate; instead, she muttered under her breath, as if it were another ingredient in her salad, "Are you hungry Violet? I'll bring you something out. I got some lovely fish soup. Go find a table."

Violet obediently followed this instruction, wandering out to the dining room without a word, and taking a seat behind a women and her daughter who were bartering over whose choice of shoes the girl would end up with. The mother held the trump card, which was the arbitrary power to withdraw the offer of shoes altogether, but the daughter was slow to catch on to the weakness of her position, and whined tearfully against the injustice of low heels and wide fittings. *Fine*, said the mother. *My shoes or no shoes at all. It's up to you.* The girl fell silent, but Violet could hear the violence with which she was cutting her jacket potato.

A deep, steaming white bowl was soon placed in front of Violet, filled with a translucent, tomatoey broth from which protruded smart black mussel shells and the frilled heads of prawns. A little later, a fingerbowl arrived too, alongside a glass of crisp white wine so cold that it was frosted with condensation. Violet let herself be soothed by this quiet consideration, and felt sorry that she had ever allowed herself to construe it as an intrusion. She ate slowly, and waited while Antonia cleared away the last of the diners until the room was empty. Then, as she predicted, Antonia emerged from the kitchen with a tray containing cups of coffee, a jug of steamed milk and a packet of cigarettes. Violet found herself lighting up before she even poured the milk.

Antonia was very different company today, tired and distracted. It must have been boredom that made her so talkative and languorous before, as today the smallest stirring in the lobby made her pause their conversation and crane her neck around so that she could offer her benediction to each guest as they arrived or departed. They had only the time to talk about the weather's refusal to usher in the spring, the trials of dealing with the half-term flurry, and the even greater chaos that would arrive at Easter, before Antonia drained her coffee, sighed and said, "Okay, back to the grindstone. You going to have one of your swims?" It was an afterthought, the kind of activity offered by a mother to a restless child, but Violet was happy to accept her suggestion.

She could feel the coffee and the soup sloshing hot in her stomach as she eased herself into the cool water, and wondered if she might be sick, or develop the terrible cramps that were so ominously warned of during her childhood. As her body adjusted itself to the pool's temperature, though, the sensation subsided, and she wondered if this was just another lingering myth of childhood, like eating bread-crusts, that was essentially a meaningless warning, a symptom of anxious motherhood rather than a serious threat to one's health. After all, no-one warned you not to go to the gym after eating. Violet drew in a deep breath and corkscrewed into the water, allowing her body to flop against it, letting her arms and legs gradually find the full extent of its resistance. She didn't even pretended to herself that she came to the pool to swim anymore; she had surrendered fully to the purpose of playing dead, a quiet, meditative end in itself.

She could no longer conjure up the old wonder at the underwater world she was suspended in, the blue cube with its shimmering, distant limits. Instead, her mind defaulted to a kind of happy deadness when she drifted here, a feeling of numbness and an absence of the world, a sense of silent withdrawal. She savoured the way it stripped her back to basics, reduced her to a ticking hub of corporeality, nothing more than a beating pulse, a whir of blood in the arteries, a mechanical host of osmosis and mitosis. At moments like this, her brain was utterly empty – devoid, even, of its own company.

But by now, the link between she and Daisy had grown so strong that as soon as her own self had been pushed to the bottom of her consciousness, her double's thoughts and feelings surged up, filling her with their liveliness and colour. At first, Violet barely registered that she was intruding on the girl's private landscape again; their two worlds segued into one so effortlessly that there seemed to be no frontier between their two minds. But Daisy was in water too today, lying flat in a bath, the water cooling around her so it took Violet a while to untangle the two channels of sensory input. Before she could drag her thoughts away, Violet was party to Daisy's concerned survey of her thin body, her search for fat on the flat wastes of her stomach and her annoyance that the weekend's hair-dye must already have lost its brilliance due to the pink tint that the bathwater had taken on.

She was readying herself for something, without any particular relish. Her legs were smooth-shaven and her toenails freshly painted navy blue, and so were propped primly on the end of the bath, safe from the dangerous motion of the water. Violet felt the softness of bath oil in the water, caught glimpses of its floral scent, shivered at the chalky tightness of her face-pack as it leached the moisture out of her skin. There was an odd resolve about her, a sense that all this effort was to make a point; that she was perfecting herself because she believed she was above whatever this event was. It was an attitude that Violet recognised from her own past, the necessity of having to reinforce one's queenly status now and again by being magnificent for an evening.

Violet remembered one afternoon like this, when she passed four hours in the bathroom, working her way through a pharmacy of bottles and tubs that she thought would make her beautiful. She recalled the pleasure she gained from this careful process, the sense of taming and refining the body, but also an uglier will too, behind it all, a competitive desire to triumph over the other women in the room, to demand their respect and admiration.

She remembered arriving that evening, her skin tingling from her efforts, and standing in the doorway, taking a breath for a moment and feeling that the night was hers to win, if she wanted it…

Violet pulled her head above the surface of the water and gasped for air; it had been a long time since she had taken a breath. As her lungs ached and pumped to suck in oxygen, and the blood bloomed through her capillaries as if finding their outer reaches for the first time, another pulse came surging up in her, a realisation that rang like an alarm: this was it. She recognised the preparations, the expectations, the strange mood of prospective triumph, and she knew, too, how they would all feel like preparations for her own fall, the exaggerated primping that comes before an execution. Tonight, if she didn't intervene, Daisy would be changed forever. She had found her bookmark, the exact time and place it all went wrong.

This was it. Already.

Part Three

None of this is true.

You know that, don't you? There's not a single bit of it that's absolutely, objectively true.

Have you ever told a story so many times that it's become rounded at the edges like sea-worn glass? Sure, you started off including the mistakes and wrong turns; well, some of them, anyway. But then you got round to thinking that you were better off without them – no, scrub that; it isn't true either. You never meant to leave those things out. It was just that, the next time you came to tell the story, they just politely excused themselves from it. There was no deliberate choice to exclude them, no intention to lie, but they just got left out. You had no use for them. It wasn't a sinister thing, more a respectful omission; perhaps, if you thought about it, you would say that you left them out for the good of your audience, because the story ran smoother without them. The beginning, the middle, the end were the same, but the way you moved between them had been slightly improved.

Perhaps it was more than this; perhaps you forgot them altogether. Perhaps the brain has a way of deleting the inconvenient bits so that our life stories run more smoothly. Who knows why; I would suspect that a nice, clear story is much easier to store in those grey cells than a rambling, messy account of human life exactly as it is, with all its glitches and flaws.

And that is why, when you're telling your mates about the final, burning insult you spat at your boyfriend before you walked out on him for good (the one that was so perfectly-timed, so immaculately phrased, that all he could do was watch you, in speechless awe, as you picked up your suitcase and headed for the stairs), you can do so with the utter guilelessness of a child.

Never mind that you swore and cried and kicked and bit beforehand; never mind that you stumbled over your words and made a series of wild and irrational claims about his sexual activities outside your bed; never mind that he packed that suitcase for you and pushed you out of the door, and that you cried and banged for an hour before dragging your suitcase out to the car, and that you only thought of that final, perfect, crystalline insult then, when you were gripping the steering-wheel as if it would right you. Nobody expected it to be the whole and utter truth. We're all in it for the thrills, the chemical highs of a well-turned story, the buzz of tabloid excitement right on our doorsteps. We don't want to be embarrassed by your sticky emotional attachments, your guilty sense that you could have done more. We want a world painted bright and clear for us, free of doubt and ambiguity. We want heroes and villains, plot-twists, confrontations and denouements. We want to take sides. We want entertainment. You're cruel if you deny us these things.

It works the other way, too. We're prone to adding bits in, embellishing our accounts with little gems we've garnered from other people's lives, women's magazines, the TV. We're all expert storytellers these days, understanding the need for conflict, pathos, dramatic irony, identifiable characters and believable plots. We can make you laugh and we can make you cry. It's like each of us is born with a talent for it encoded in our genes, the ability to spin out a story that makes us look competent in this life.

I once told my college housemate a story about my great-granny having all her teeth pulled out as a twenty-first birthday present. They did that in those days, apparently. It was only after I told her that a cold sense came over me that the story I had told was not mine, but hers.

Don't shake your head and turn away. We only aim to please. We seek to fill the yawning holes that open up in our conversation with something that makes it all seem worthwhile. Be grateful that we do it, not disgusted. Without us, conversations would be a series of jolts and false-starts, hesitations and embarrassing silences.

Perhaps this is what a life is made of, a confabulated sequence of events, moulded into a kind of sense by its constant retelling.

We have – what? Seventy? Eighty? Ninety? – years on this earth to construct a narrative that's meaningful, that is progressive and reflexive, that builds towards something, a glorious crescendo, a graceful diminution. If we fail in this, our lives are ugly, ungainly, unpalatable, and our ending is nothing but an irritant, a tedious repeat-to-fade. But if we succeed, then we are remembered, and maybe even retold by posterity. They, too, will embellish a little, reconfigure the story to suit them, and so the cycle continues.

Why am I telling you this? Well. Why indeed.

It's because I feel I need to set the record straight. It's not just that I've tweaked bits – although I have, of course. It's that Violet's story and mine are so muddled up now that I can barely tell where I start and she ends. In telling our story, I've come to see the link between us less like a thread, a psychic umbilical cord, and more like a piece of Velcro, a network of hundreds of tiny hoops and hooks that bind us together so tightly that it's difficult to prise us apart.

I know myself and I knew Violet, in the real world, for a short space of time. And then, I knew her through her our link, a kind of dreamy friendship full of vague impressions and intuitions. But then, too, I knew myself through the window of her consciousness, a very obscuring kind of a mirror, although strangely penetrating. And I also know, more vaguely, herself back again, the view I had of her when she knew me, before I understood it all. And so the reflections continue, the call and response of two inexact mirrors placed opposite one-another, describing ever more shady impressions.

There I am in that mirror, eighteen; at my prime, I suppose. But not beautiful like Violet imagined me, nor nearly so exotic. Certain teenage girls have a force of attraction to them, a function of their fearlessness and their ageless flesh. I don't deny that I was one of them, but one out of a pool of thousands, millions maybe, who are just as luminous. Nothing special, or nothing much. I have written the view you got of me through Violet's eyes, and so I have been obliged to retain the imagined halo of my own radiance. I hope you'll understand.

And Violet, too, now I look back over my manuscript, had lost a little in translation. As I near the end of our story, I can see she's taken on the sepia tint of a brooding, romantic heroine, rather than the rangy, neurotic mess she actually was. A word in my defence: it's all been extrapolation, the majority of it, from her own patchy memories of the time, and she's been trying not to think about it ever since it happened. I've had to make it up, or patch it together from what little she's let me glimpse over the years. And more than that, she's always been a bit of a hero to me, that cool adult who gave me faith for a few short weeks one February. I couldn't do her harm. I understand her, after all. Over the years, I've even come to love her, the ghost of her presence jangling down the lines at me. I wonder if she knew that.

So none of this is true. I've written you a story, not a history. Not a single fact has been checked, not a single player consulted. This is her story, our story, as I see it. And I hope that, although it may look very different from the real thing, you'll understand: it may not be the exact truth, but it's a kind of truth, my truth and Violet's. It begins and ends in the right places, but the middle's all jumbled up. That's the only way it could ever be. It tells its truth as an average, a sum total of addition and subtraction that leads us to an honest kind of whole.

Anyway, enough of this. Let's get to the end.

ONE

Working out where to go was easy enough; Violet knew that if she hung around in Daisy's thoughts long enough, she would be rewarded with glimpses of her destination, and she was proved right, eventually, when Daisy started thinking through her route, wondering if she couldn't persuade her mother to drop her off in order to save her hair and makeup the trouble of the damp winter air. It was a sixth-form party in an old ballroom in town. So far, so similar.

What was harder for Violet was priming her own body to get there. After dredging herself out of the pool, she spent a long time in her room, going through the ghost of the routine she had observed Daisy undertaking, a grindingly slow selection of clothes and makeup during which her mind repeatedly wandered onto her strategy for the evening, so that she found herself several times standing half-dressed in the middle of the floor, her arms hanging at her sides, as her brain ploughed obsessively through its hopes and anxieties.

It was all too soon; she had expected at least some sort of warning, a run-up to the main event. She hadn't had enough time to decide where she stood, let alone to plan what she would do. She wondered many times if she should even go at all, whether her intervention was an ugly and unnecessary act that meddled with the natural line of Daisy's life, but then she would recognise the fear behind this concern which was leading her to trick herself out of action. Facing a rehearsal of the night when she lost her faith in her own robustness and infallibility, she was assailed by gurgling rattles of terror that made her immobile and unwilling to put herself in harm's way again. More than this, she longed to be able to continue to bask in the glow of Daisy's company; she wanted just one more night in which they drank and laughed together before all this happened. It was too soon. There hadn't been enough time.

She should have seen it coming, should have planned. If only she had mastered her link with Daisy better, had learned to somehow gain access to her future plans and not just her current thoughts. She felt that an interrogation of her own memories should have yielded more, but then it had all become so hazy lately, so elusive. The more she tried to access them, the less she knew about where her past ended and Daisy's life began. She could now only rely on her memories of the things that hadn't happened to Daisy yet; the rest were tainted with her own image, or occurred in places that Violet was sure were changed. There were moments when she believed that she was being overwritten like an old cassette. Daisy was authoring her life anew, updating and revising it, scattering it with a more contemporary set of clothes, technologies, locations. The basic plot was the same, the themes intact, but they were transposed into a newer, more modern life, as if someone had recoloured her footage to attract a younger audience.

She only partly resented this. It was strange to lose her own past, but she was convinced that Daisy was an improvement, a value-added beta-version of herself. Watching as Daisy lived through this part of her life, Violet was reminded of the ways that dry shingle is renewed by the first lick of the sea, its chalky colours restored to their original glow, the intricate markings of each pebble revealed. She never knew her own life had so much breadth or weight or depth. She was desperate to cling to it, to preserve its magnificent complexity; but she knew that the stones she took home in her pockets always faded, and only lent her the memory of their shoreline glories. She thought of the stacks of dusty boxes in her storage room in London, their cold, dry weight, their muted, displaced voices. She would wrap Daisy up like this if she could, encase her in white tissue paper, carefully folded, labelled, numbered, filed.

But this was not a solution she would be allowed. Change would come, whatever she did. People were not as still or passive as stones. They were unpredictable, reactive, random. To do nothing tonight and bring about a future in which Daisy was just like her, was unthinkable; if she got it right, she might produce an unknown future, a better one. She pushed herself through her various tasks – showering, dressing, applying her makeup – as if they were Herculean labours, conscious of the new impression she would make in those memories by the morning.

TWO

The room was darker than it needed to be, and already half-full of indistinct bodies clustering around the edges of the dancefloor, daring each other to make the first move. There was a DJ at the back of the hall looking utterly abandoned behind his makeshift table; from the voluminous hang of his tee-shirt and the way his hair straggled over his eyes, Violet guessed that he was someone's mate, one of them. He had no records or CDs with him, only a laptop which he hung over, afraid to look up, his flustered cheeks illuminated by the screen below him. He was playing a track that seemed to Violet to be nothing but a rush of uneven drumbeats, giving the sensation of catching a hurricane full-on in the face. This was the music the assembled sixth-formers clearly thought they ought to like, the stuff they would tell their friends was played after the event. They would never get up and dance to it, though; they didn't know how. They would sit it out awkwardly, watching from the sidelines and try to work out a way of indicating that they were enjoying it, all the while hoping to God that there would be a real DJ on the way, a balding man with a smoke machine and a mobile light show, so that they could dance to the same tired selection of Abba and Madonna that would have sent their parents crazy twenty years ago.

Violet's first glass of wine disappeared surprisingly quickly. She bought another and took a deep mouthful from it. No Daisy yet. She would be holding back, Violet knew, waiting to make her entrance. The wine and the noise made it hard to pick up on what she was doing exactly, but Violet didn't need any sort of a link to work it out: she would be lolling around Ruth's bedroom, drinking a bottle of something cheap, sweet and strong. It was hard to imagine her arriving before ten. An hour to go. Violet drained her wine, thinking how she ought to pace herself, and went to the bar to order another.

An extra barman had come onto shift, a tall man with cropped black hair and wide blue eyes. Violet held his glance as she ordered another wine, and offered to buy one for him, too.

"Maybe later," he said, and winked at her. Violet's stomach did a childish roll. A wink! What a glorious, brazen cliché! She tried to prowl a little as she walked back to her table in the corner.

She wondered if she should get up and dance, show all these foetuses lining the room the way it was done. There were a few girls now - the self-consciously uncool ones - up and dancing in the centre of the floor. They were the ones in strappy sandals and little black dresses, mincing to the feeble rhythms and singing along, eyes closed, as if dreaming of their spot on some reality TV show. Violet imagined the enthusiastic smiles that would greet her if she joined them, the tacit and desperate acceptance into their gang. She would stay where she was. She would hate Daisy to catch her anywhere near them.

She read the measure on the side of her glass as she finished it: 250ml. She must have drunk a whole bottle already. She really ought to slow down. She leaned over the bar so that her breasts pressed together as the barman poured the next one.

There was a jolt somewhere behind her hips a few moments before Daisy arrived. The sight of her made Violet shy; she hung back in the corner as she admired the sheer perfection of the girl's sense of theatre, the way she had chosen jeans, a man's suit jacket, a vest-top and a cigarette – the most under-dressed Violet had ever seen her – as her outfit in the end, a clear and deliberate signal of how little she cared.

But she did care. Violet watched her pause as she came through the door to rake her straggly hair over to one side and light the fag in her mouth, just long enough to make sure that everyone was looking at her. She caught no-one's eye, and looked in fact for all the world as if she wad walked into a room full of strangers, or at least people so monumentally unimportant to her that she saw no point in acknowledging them. She made her way directly to the bar, the very model of a woman with needs exceeding anything the rest of the room would understand, and ordered a double Jack and Coke with such an immaculate expression of ennui that Violet was sure she must have practised it. When the boy whose party it was inevitably tapped her on the shoulder and stumbled over his words asking her to put the cigarette out, she simply took a long draw on it, her eyes never leaving his, until the ash quivered at its tip like a catkin, and then shrugged and dropped it on the floor. She held his gaze as she ground it into the carpet.

Her poise shattered when she saw Violet, though. She did a genuine double-take, taking a moment for her brain to identify the mismatch between Violet and a school disco, and then hissed, "What the fuck are you doing here?" with such urgency that the whisky caught in her throat and she coughed.

Violet felt her neck redden. She had forgotten to make up an excuse, and now it was impossible to marshal her thoughts into inventing one.

"I didn't realise," she said at last. "I'd heard there was a bar here."

"Didn't realise? Jesus, what a fucking terrible disappointment that must have been. Nipping out for a swift glass and finding yourself amongst this kindergarten." A swig of her drink. "How did you get past the guard-nerds on the door?"

"Just walked in."

"And at no point did it occur to you, as you strolled past ranks of drooling children, that you'd picked the wrong place for your Monday night livener?"

Violet shrugged. "I didn't notice until I'd ordered."

A smile, and then a cackle. "That's what I love about you, Violet. You're always too fucking pissed to care. Come on, let's find our Ruthie."

It was easy, after that, to just follow her through the evening, allow herself to get churned up in it all. Violet wondered if Daisy's mystique was enhanced or diminished by her own presence, whether she was of an age that may have leant some adult cachet, or whether she just looked like a mother or a big sister, a sensible cap on Daisy's excesses. She was certain that the girl would waste no time in casting her off if she was some kind of embarrassment; the very fact that she was being publicly tolerated in this way must mean she was liked, admired, prized even. The thought of it made Violet glow. She had instinctively shied away from trying to discover this knowledge during her illicit wanderings through Daisy's mind, for fear of what it would mean to her if she was disliked; but this tiny shred of evidence, the idea that Daisy might even be proud to be seen with her, filled Violet up.

Tonight was not allowed to be a simple case of surrender, getting bound up in the ebb and flow of the night and allowing that familiar excitement to wash over her. Tonight, Violet had a job to do; she must remember that. She had to swallow back the urge to believe it would all work out for the best if only she was allowed one more night with Daisy, that nothing bad could ever happen to somebody this stellar.

She could actually feel Daisy's presence now, a warm tingle that engulfed her whenever she was near, as if Daisy trailed a golden corona behind her. As Violet waited at the bar to buy three glasses of red wine, Daisy stood so close to her that Violet could feel the adrenaline in her bloodstream, that intoxicating cocktail of defiance and sexuality that she had almost forgotten, but which now lit a slow-burning fuse in her gut. She filled her mouth with wine, washed its musty dryness around her tongue and swallowed it down. Nobody could tell her that this wasn't the right way to live, a level of perfection attained precociously and then, mysteriously, lost; all this adult soul-searching about how to live life was just a case of amnesia. This was rightness; this was home.

She watched Daisy light another illicit cigarette and felt the nicotine bloom in her own veins. Her hair was clouding across a shaft of disco light, glowing pink, green, pink, green. Her face was in darkness. Violet could smell her sweet-shop scent, a honeyed floral essence that seemed to drift around her; it made Violet smile when she identified it as Parma violets. A full circle. They were part of each other.

Violet's mouth was finding it difficult to move in time with her words. Her lips were numb. The music was too loud to think; it drummed around her head and confused her. She watched mutely as Daisy and Ruth shared frantic barrages of conversation and laughter; she followed them unquestioningly as they made their way out of the hall to the toilets. The chair legs and tabletops seemed to find Violet's limbs as she passed them.

THREE

The fluorescent light was shocking and flickered just enough to make Violet flinch. After the door swung shut, the bathroom was quiet, invaded only by the faintest hum of music from the hall. Violet's ears rang, filling the room with an endlessly mutating tone that made her dizzy. She steadied herself by sitting up on the sinks, immediately feeling the damp from the tiles seep through to her knickers. She pretended not to notice. Ruth was talking, rubbing her hand over her head and gazing at her ashen face in the mirror, while Daisy worked methodically through all the stalls, throwing each door open so that it banged painfully against its dividing wall.

"Right," she said, "coast is clear. Who wants some?"

"I don't know," said Ruth. "My head hurts. I'm not in the mood. What is it?"

"Cocaine."

"Cocaine? I thought you were getting Es. Who the fuck did you buy that from?"

"No-one." A sly smile. "A lady never reveals her secrets. Let's just say he gave me a discount."

"Jesus," said Ruth, "you're like some kind of crack-whore." A pause, and then a peal of laughter from Daisy that made it clear that this comment could have been taken either way. "I think I'll leave it to you."

"Don't be a chicken. It's no worse."

"Why didn't you just get pills like you said you would?"

"I wasn't exactly enchanted at the idea of becoming

all, 'hello birds, hello trees' amongst a roomful of people I despise. They might think I like them, and then I'd have to face them again on Monday morning. Come on."

"What do you do with it? Don't you snort it?"

"Yes you do, but we won't. So inelegant, don't you think, Violet? We'll rub it into our gums." She pulled a miniature plastic bag from her handbag, laid her compact mirror on the sink, and began to peel the plastic seal open.

"Don't do that here, someone will come in!"

Daisy looked for a moment as if she would berate Ruth for being a baby, but then glanced ferally at the door, and picked up the mirror and her bag before reversing into a toilet cubicle. She lowered the toiled lid with her elbow and sat neatly on it, before closing the door and locking it. Violet could hear her foraging about in her bag.

"Will you have some, Violet?" she heard Daisy call from the cubicle.

"Yes, um, sure. Why not?" The bathroom door opened and a small girl with a mass of curly hair walked in, dressed in a cheesecloth shirt and striped trousers. Ruth nodded at her.

"There you go, Ruthie; Violet will, so why won't you?" The girl's head darted round to see where the voice was coming from, before she turned into a cubicle.

"Not now, Daisy," said Ruth, her voice pressed into a whisper, "someone's here."

"Oh," said Daisy, "who's that?"

"Debbie Miles from my physics class."

"Oh hi, Debbie," called Daisy in a sickeningly cheerful voice, "You still fucking the boy with the knackered scooter?"

"Yes," replied a small voice, and there was silence after that, although Violet was sure she could hear Daisy sniggering. Ruth leant against the wall by the hand-dryer and massaged the back of her neck, which made the machine drone into life at intervals. Eventually, Debbie left after the merest rinsing of her hands and Daisy, who was clearly listening out for the sound of the door closing, sprang back into life again.

"Right," she sang, "come and get it while it's hot." The lock on her cubicle clicked open, and Daisy's head appeared in the crack. "Come on! We'd best do it in here."

"Not me," said Ruth. "I don't feel too good."

"Oh Ruthie," replied Daisy in a baby voice that made it sound more like *Wuffie*, "not that again. Come on!"

"No really. I'm not joking. I've got a headache. I feel a bit sick. I'm not bottling out. I just feel like shit."

"You should have thought of that last night when you were piling into that vodka."

"You were the one who threw up on her own feet."

"Well then, it just goes to show. Clearly you should have done the same."

As the debate continued in increasingly sarcastic tones, Violet battled to remember what she was supposed to be doing here. Did this ever happen on the night she thought it was? She didn't recall it. Maybe it had all changed already; Daisy and Ruth certainly seemed to be in so much more control than she remembered being. A thought occurred to her that was like a light blinking on: she wasn't here to change things, but to watch what would have happened if it had all gone right. This was why her memory seemed to be overwritten by each new experience; she was being made anew, the bad bits erased, the good bits brought freshly before her eyes so that she wouldn't make the mistake of forgetting them again.

"I'll give it a go, Daisy," she said, "I'm not bothered by it." She turned to give Ruth a sympathetic look, and was met with a glare of such scorn and fury in return that she felt as though she had mistakenly walked into a wall.

"No," said Ruth, through clenched teeth, "that's fine, Violet. I'm not bothered by it either. I'll go first." It had never occurred to Violet that Ruth might be jealous of her, and it took a superhuman effort for Violet to conceal the smile that was creeping across her face as she stepped back to allow Ruth into the cubicle first.

Daisy was crouched on the toilet lid, with the mirror laid open on the cistern, a tiny pile of white powder glistening on it.

"Glad you decided to join us, Ms Wallis," she said to Ruth, and gave her hand a discreet squeeze. "Now, watch and learn, children." She dipped her finger into the cocaine, bore her teeth as if presenting them to a dentist, and then rubbed her finger onto her gums in exact circles, the very model of correct dental hygiene. "There," she said at length, "easy." Her voice was blunted by the closeness of their bodies. Violet felt Ruth's shoulder rub past her arm as she reached across to take her own share, and she had a small impulse to nudge her, just to make her lose her balance a little. She could apologise after. But she didn't. She waited politely for Ruth to begin the frantic massaging of her gums, and then licked her own index finger and dipped it into the rapidly diminishing pile. Daisy went back for second helpings, and soon they all fell silent as they busily worked the gritty powder into their bare red flesh.

"Can you feel anything yet?" said Daisy.

"Not really," said Violet, "but then you can't expect a high like you would from a pill. It's more a general feeling of…confidence, like you can't do anything wrong. It'll take a few minutes."

"Get you," said Daisy, "Quite the narcotics connoisseur."

"It was a while ago," said Violet, and dipped her finger in again.

It was hot in the cubicle, all their bodies pressed tight together, their arms generating heat as they scrubbed at their gums. Violet barely noticed when the bathroom door opened again and two voices entered the room, singing along to the tune that drifted in with them. As the door shut, they fell silent, and Violet had forgotten they were even there before one of them rapped on the door, said, "Who's in there?" and giggled.

Ruth and Violet paused, and Daisy wiped her finger around the mirror before sucking it loudly and saying, "Queen Victoria."

"I can see more than one pair of feet in there," came the rushed voice in reply.

"And I can hear heavy breathing," said the other voice.

Daisy rolled her eyes. "That's because my friends and I have been having hot lesbian sex in here, clearly," she replied, her voice dripping with sarcasm.

"Really?" said one of the voices, and there was the sound of muted whispering for a moment, before the door opened again and footsteps faded into the music.

"Who was that?" said Ruth.

"Who knows. Who gives a fuck. We can rest assured that they won't suspect a thing, though. They'll be too busy spreading scare stories about the dykes in the toilets. Honestly, it never ceases to amaze me. They're a different breed."

Ruth unlocked the door, and they all piled out, relieved to breathe new air again. Daisy threw the plastic coke bag in the bin, and Violet couldn't stop herself from burying it under a layer of paper towels. Ruth washed her hands out of impulse, and Daisy checked in the mirror that she was maintaining the correct amount of dishevelment.

They walked out together. Violet's skin felt new, slightly shinier than it had before. It felt good that people were looking at them, like they were cowboys strolling into a paused bar. Daisy slumped down into one of the chintzy bucket chairs at the edge of the dancefloor and Violet ordered more wine. Ruth pushed hers aside.

"Don't tell me you've still got a fucking headache," said Daisy. "They used to sell that as a painkiller in Victorian times." Ruth turned away and watched the dancers, who were now crowded onto the parquet flooring, miming along to a song Violet had never heard before, but which now seemed to have adopted the actions to the Locomotion. She wondered whether any of them questioned what the piston-movements were supposed to signify.

Daisy was providing her usual commentary – how this girl would be pushing a pram before the year was out, and how that boy was blatantly gay and would be a much more interesting person if only he'd admit it – but Violet found it hard to listen amongst the noise and the darkness and the way the whole room seemed to have strayed from its moorings, and was prone to drifting across her line of sight if she didn't continually discipline it back into place. She gazed around to see Ruth talking into her mobile, a finger pressing her free ear shut. "I'm going home," she shouted over the music when the call finished, "I'm sorry. I feel really rough. My Mum's coming to get me." Daisy seemed oblivious, and she clearly had no interest in Violet's sympathy, so she pulled on her coat and simply walked out.

"Bye-bye, darling," said Daisy to her back, "hope you feel better," and she blew her three big, terrible kisses that seemed to burst on the inside of Violet's chest, muh, muh, muh.

FOUR

It was as easy as that, the beginning of it all. Violet had been distracted by the wine and the coke, by the complication of her own presence, by her desire for everything to be alright. But Ruth leaving must be the same as Sasha leaving all those years ago, and so this was where it all started.

Daisy was a model of dramatic irony, sloshing her wine and leaning in over the table to gabble at Violet, as if her own fall wasn't on its way. Maybe, thought Violet, she will still be able to do this tomorrow if I get it right tonight, but at that moment it seemed utterly hopeless to try and prevent it. Violet had a grinding sense of fate in action; the synchronicities were increasing. Those three little kisses, aimed at Ruth's back, had been her own, hadn't they, ten years ago? Violet tried to listen to what Daisy was saying, but by now it was agony: each word she spoke, each small gesture she made, carried its own drag of déjà vu, as if there were a series of invisible hooks stretched between them, and Daisy was operating Violet like a puppet. Or was it the other way round? Was Violet making Daisy do this, willing her to blunder into the same mistakes as she did? Could she stop it all, right here and now, if only she stopped imagining it?

But then, there it was, the face she had been scanning the room for all evening. She knew she would recognise him if she saw him, but it came as a surprise, a physical, visceral jolt, that he was already a part of the game. It seemed obvious now. He was fatter, more desperate-looking than she remembered, wearing the same sad Hawaiian shirt she had seen him in a week ago. Even as she watched him, she could feel the rough texture of his hands as he touched her, the hysterical sickliness of alcohol on his breath. And there he was, just standing there, looking around as innocent as you like. He hadn't even seen Daisy yet, but he had come back for her. Violet had thought she might lose her nerve when it finally came to it, but instead the act of rising from her chair and pushing her way through the bodies to get to him was almost involuntary, especially now that she saw something even more sinister in it. It was a premeditated attack, not just an act of drunken opportunism. She had always liked to believe that he had woken up the next morning, just as she did, full of regret and disgust; that he had made an idiotic, shameful, beer-fuelled mistake that would never be repeated. But that was not true. He had planned to do what he did to her. He had come back for more.

She could hear Daisy saying, "Let me know if I'm fucking boring you, Violet. Jesus," as she went, but she did not have time to turn and apologise; she was afraid of losing sight of him. There was anger in her now, an odd feeling of strength and weakness at the same time, an airy sensation of space cleared around her so that she could do what she needed to do. The music had all but disappeared.

She tapped him on the shoulder, and saw him smile as he turned towards her, the very embodiment of lechery.

"I know who you are," she said.

"Do you?" he replied, shifting his body to face her and raising a flirtatious eyebrow. "Lucky me."

"No, not lucky you at all. I know what you did to my friend the other week, and I know what you're going to do tonight. I'm not going to let it happen."

The man kept the smile fixed on his face, and glanced around him for support. "You know what I'm going to do tonight, do you? Are you some kind of psychic?"

"No." Violet heard her voice become shrill. Her arms were flying about her as she spoke. She wanted to lunge at him, to tear her nails into his neck, but he was broad-shouldered and heavy, and the small corner of her brain that was assessing her potential to do him harm was flashing her images of punches and kicks that barely made a dent, of his arms around her wrists to restrain her. Instead, she stamped her foot hard on the floor, an effort to channel some of the violent energy that filled her, which she knew seemed childish even as she did it. He ankle ached with the force of the jolt. "I know what you're going to do, because you did it to me, too. Not you, but someone like you. I'm not going to let you do it to her too."

"You're drunk," said the man, turning back towards his pint of lager on the bar. "Go away."

"No, I won't go away!" Violet was shouting now, forcing the words out so that they grated through her lungs. "I saw you at the World Underwater, with your filthy hands all over her. What's wrong with you? Can't you get it from someone sober? Have to pick on teenage girls when they've passed out?"

"Listen, love, I don't know who you think I am, but you can't go around making accusations like that." He put a hand on her elbow, a paternal, patronising gesture that Violet threw off immediately.

"Don't fucking touch me," she screamed, "Not again!" She swung round to see that a small crowd had gathered around them, a mixture of amused and startled teenage faces, and an official-looking woman in a skirt suit who she hadn't seen before, watching her from behind the bar. "This man," shouted Violet, addressing the woman, who seemed like someone who could help, "is a pervert who preys on young girls."

"I think you've had a few too many, love," said the man, a new hardness in his voice.

"Oh really?" said Violet, heady with her own righteousness and the space that seemed to have cleared for her around the bar. "So explain one thing to me. What are you doing here tonight? What business could a man of your age possibly have at a sixth-form party?"

"No," said the man, "I think I could ask you the same question. What you are *you* doing here?"

"I'm," she began, but then her words ebbed away as she glanced towards the door and saw Daisy strolling towards it, being led by the hand by the barman, the one she had been so enchanted by a couple of hours before. The blood retreated from her limbs. She had got the wrong man. Her brain had joined up all the dots in the story, but had made the wrong shape.

She pushed past the man and out through the crowd that was watching her, and which now cleared an obedient space to let her pass and followed her with amused eyes. The dancefloor was more packed than ever, seething with shirtless boys and unsteady girls who shifted obliviously in and out of her path as she tried to shove through. She heard a yelp as one girl's sandaled foot crunched under her own shoe; another girl teetered and fell backwards after Violet collided with her. Violet barely looked back; a part of her had the notion that they were doing it deliberately, weaving and swerving to block her path to Daisy. She could almost have laughed at it all now, this ridiculous scramble through a bewildered room, this stifling sense of her own stupidity, this knowledge that she had failed to recognise him the second time around, had even flirted with him a little, had draped her tits across the bar at him as if they were open doors. She hadn't learned a thing, and now, in this infuriating rush to get across the room, it seemed like a folly to ever have believed she could conquer the fates, that she could ever have been more than a bystander as the world repeated itself, endlessly.

But then she was at the door, pushing in the fire-bar and feeling the sobering cold of the night air against her bare arms as she made her way through the more sombre darkness of the outside. She shouted, "Daisy!" as she began to clang down the metal fire escape, her knees brittle beneath her. Later, should would taste the dampness in the air, feel the icy condensation drip from her fingers as she slid them down the rail, but here and now she felt nothing, tasted nothing, smelt nothing, only looked, searched everywhere, over the skip-bins and crates of empty bottles, to catch sight of her.

"Daisy!" she called again, as the stairs turned a corner and she swung round, slipping as she went, but miraculously righting herself, keeping on her feet as she hurtled down the last few steps. And then she stopped and looked around her, and everything was silent for a moment, until she called "Daisy!" again, into the void that the clanging of the steps had left.

There was nothing there, just a dark yard and a pile of rubbish, a few broken chairs, an eviscerated speaker. They had gone, moved on; he had taken her further away than he had taken Violet, somewhere quieter, darker, more remote. But then a sound, a small one, a shuffle and a slow, elongated, *Sssshhhhh*, the made Violet spin round on her heels and peer even harder into the darkness below the staircase itself. There was something there, a tall bulk concealed in the shadows.

She walked towards it, slowly now, hesitantly, afraid of what she might see. The two of them were there, with Daisy's back against the wall, and they were kissing ravenously, his mouth covering hers lazily. It seemed like an obscenity to interrupt them. Daisy was making soft noises, delicate whimpers that made him smile and roll his hands down her body, across her breasts, over her ribcage and onto her wrists, which he gripped and drew over her head, pressing them against the wall. Violet was close to them now, so close she could smell the woody tang of his aftershave, but she was nearer than that, watching from the inside, feeling the hardness of the wall against Daisy's wrist bones, the way her knuckles grazed against the bricks.

She was smiling, even as he drew away from her so that he could look her in the eye while he pushed both of her hands together and gripped them in one of his own. This was all a game, a little harmless bit of sexual play, and Daisy knew it, that's why she smiled and gasped and raised an eyebrow. But he didn't seem to know it; Violet watched him grip Daisy's hands harder, saw his thumb begin to dent the flesh; that would bruise tomorrow. And then his other hand crept down again, so that it seemed to drag across her cheek, and then pause at her left breast to circle, as if it were working its way up to something; and it squeezed, full-fisted, a little too hard…and an expression of surprise on Daisy's face…perhaps pain…

"Stop!"

Violet felt as though she had crashed through a plate of glass as she rushed towards them, had broken the rooted, fascinated horror of watching the past unfold before her eyes. She lunged towards them and put a hand on the man's shoulder, dragging him back towards her. "Stop! This is bad!"

She saw Daisy roll her eyes and catch his eye. "Violet, go home," she said, barely looking at her.

"No, you don't understand. I'm saving you. This man's…he's a bad man, Daisy."

"A very bad man indeed," said Daisy in a voice Violet hardly recognised, but which made the man lean in and kiss her neck.

"Daisy…"

"Go home, Violet. You're drunk. Party's over."

"But I can't. I have to save you."

Daisy shrugged, giggled. "Save me? What from?"

"I can't tell you. You don't need to know."

"Get some coffee, Violet. Leave me alone."

"No!" Violet could see Daisy's arms twining back around the man's, so she threw herself forwards and tried to insinuate her body between theirs. This seemed to make something break in the man, who grabbed hold of Violet's shoulders and pushed her out of the way, sending her reeling into the wall. "Haven't you already caused enough trouble tonight?" he growled.

She watched Daisy lean back into him, her hands pushed inside his belt, and so she grabbed at Daisy's arm and yanked her away. "Listen," she said, shaking and breathless, "I'll tell you why you can't do this. He'll hurt you tonight. You'll think it's alright, but then he'll grab you by the hair, and he'll push your face into the wall, and you'll feel the blood coming; your cheeks will be wet with it, and you won't be able to do anything about it, and you'll scream and cry, but no-one will hear and you'll have to explain it when you get home, your torn clothes and the cuts and bruises, and you won't tell, but they'll know, all of them, everyone." She paused to draw in a breath, feeling Daisy's wrist damp beneath her palm. "And when you wake up in the morning, Ruth will be dead."

"Fuck this," said the man, and pushed past the two of them so that he could run back up the fire escape. Daisy stared at Violet for a moment, so that Violet almost believed that she had understood, that she was scared, that everything was alright. But then she shook herself free of Violet's grip, and stepped back, as if she were afraid of contamination.

"You're disgusting," she spat. "Get some therapy if you need it, but don't go fucking up my life to try to solve your own." She picked up her bag from the floor and rushed away, brushing Violet's shoulder as she passed her.

Violet heard the gate slam behind her, and wondered how long she had been sobbing.

FIVE

Before Violet even got home that night, Daisy had turned off her phone. She had done it in temper; Violet knew this, because she had felt the violent electric surge of it when she called for the third time. Since then it had remained pointedly off-limits, its voicemail interrupting the second ring of every call. Violet had long since given up leaving messages anyway. After the first time, there was nothing more to add. She satisfied herself instead with imagining the missed calls tallying up on Daisy's phone, one for every quarter hour throughout the night.

Thirty-five, thirty-six, thirty-seven. Daisy was still asleep, or so Violet assumed from the dense mist that hung between them. Despite this, she felt the link more keenly than ever tonight; there were moments when she even believed that she could feel the tug of the girl's breath, drawing the air out of Violet's lungs so that her own could be filled. It hurt her that Daisy could give herself so easily to sleep while Violet herself spent the night fidgeting around her room, smoking cigarettes and gulping down cups of water from the bathroom tap. She had already drunk her way through the hospitality tray, the three sachets of weak Nescafe and two teabags of English Breakfast, which she had brewed to American tan strength, ignoring the tannic burn on her throat. The pastel pouches of camomile and blackberry she had ignored. She could no longer imagine stomaching their dilute sickliness.

She had been sick enough without them. Three times she was forced to rush to the bathroom and crouch over the toilet bowl, strange sweats and fevers flashing through her. She realised, tonight, what a necessary privilege it was to sleep off an evening's drinking, rather than feel each ounce of it pass out of your blood in thirsts and shivers. It was like getting drunk in reverse, with the complacent cocoon of the alcohol slowly making way for a more desolate world-view. Only here she was left worse than she was when she started, not least because of the headache that had rumbled into place behind her eyeballs an hour ago.

She had drawn the curtains to watch the sea at dawn, a white sun rising over an entirely monochrome scene. The sand, the low-tide seabed, the shuddering water, and the sky were all a steely grey. The town was so colourless before the people arrived that it almost frightened her. Now, with the light cutting into her vision and the people returning, she pulled the curtains again. The gloom suited her this morning.

Daisy was beginning to stir. Violet could feel the life coming back into her in flashes, and she imagined Daisy gradually working her way through a series of early-morning questions, just as she did. Is there anywhere I should be? Am I hung-over? Where was I last night? What happened? Violet imagined her rolling onto her side, remembering their argument, perhaps even feeling sorry for it; drinking from a glass of water by the bed; pulling the tangles out of her hair with her fingers. Would she now switch on her phone, check for messages? Violet could not work out whether the image she was receiving of this was fact or just a reflection of her own desires.

It was hard to battle past the headache to find her way to Daisy's consciousness. She caught snatches of sensation, the crumpled bed linen against Daisy's bare legs, the enervating chatter of the radio she had clicked on by compulsion, but little else. Perhaps it all meant nothing to her, another scene in a nightclub, another person put in their place by a barbed comment.

She rang Daisy's number again and this time it continued past the third ring, only to be cut off at the next, the premature termination of someone deliberately rejecting the call. "I know you're awake," she found herself saying to the voicemail, "pick up. Call me back. We need to talk." As soon as she hung up, Violet heard her own words repeated back in her head, desperate and sinister.

She fired off a text as well, something she could control the tone of a little more. *I'm v sorry abt last night,* she typed, racing against the speed of her own fingers, *I was pissed. I'm so stupid sometimes. Pls call me so I can apologise.*

Her phone buzzed into life almost as soon as the message was sent.

Fuck off violet. And stop calling me. It's weird.

Violet's first impulse was to dial the number again, but she hung up herself this time, after a couple of rings. She would call back later, give Daisy a chance to think things over. An hour, an hour and a half. She might have calmed down by then. The thirty-eight missed calls probably hadn't helped.

SIX

The dining room was busy, filled with older couples, the men in freshly-pressed shirts and neat sweaters. There was a young couple, too, their hair still wet from showers, who were making forced conversation as if the silence might destroy them. Violet found a table in the centre of the room and waited patiently at it for Antonia to notice her.

A young girl, clean-faced and pony-tailed, came and took her room number. Violet didn't recognise her. She tried to give her an imperious look, to convey that her room number ought to be common knowledge amongst the staff, and ordered a pot of tea. She was by now so hungry that she could have eaten the dusty cubes of sugar in the bowl on the table, unwrapping them one by one and shattering them between her teeth.

She felt a gentle hand on her shoulder, and Antonia leaned into her, brushing the hair away from her face. "You look awful, sweetie. Are you ill?"

"No," said Violet, "I just want some breakfast. A proper one. Bolstering." She watched Antonia's eyebrows rise in bewilderment.

"You don't want to brush your hair first, no? Or take off your makeup from last night?"

Violet's stomach dipped as she realised that there might be a contrast between herself and the over-presented guests that surrounded her, who had gone to great lengths to erase the suggestion that, just an hour ago, they had been shamefully dishevelled or even naked. She blinked and felt her eyelids tighten under the weight of encrusted mascara. Her own flesh was suddenly dirty, greasy under last night's clothes. It was all she could do to resist sniffing at herself to ensure that the only offensive thing about her was her appearance.

"I didn't think it mattered," she said quietly, reaching for her napkin under the table and unconsciously raising it to her mouth as if she could hide behind it. Antonia pulled out the chair beside her and sat on its edge, leaning in to her like a concerned mother.

"It doesn't matter to me, Violet, but do you really want other people to see you like this?" Violet turned her face away from Antonia, but this only made the elder woman move closer, so that Violet could not escape her gaze. "I can smell alcohol on your breath, honey. Did you even sleep last night?" Violet pushed herself away from Antonia and stood up, setting the table and its crockery rattling.

"That's none of your business!" she growled, and realised that she had said it too loudly when a noisy sort of concentration descended on the room around her, a proliferation of tea-pouring and plate-scraping accompanied by a discreet lull in the conversation. There was no point in sitting back down quietly, now that all eyes were upon her. She rushed away from the table, feeling her napkin fall and tangle at her feet, but kicked it away angrily, and shouted, "Fuck off! Leave me alone!" over her shoulder. She wove her way out of the room, swerving to avoid handbags and pushed-out chairs. As she neared the door, she clipped her thigh on one of the tables, and looked down by reflex to apologise, but then hardened when she saw the middle-aged couple sitting there conspicuously avoiding her gaze, staring into their fried breakfasts as if they had both lost a contact lens in there. Something about this look of abject embarrassment and terror brought out a testosterone-surge of aggression in her, a spark of butch pettiness that led her to poke out a hand and knock over the glass of orange juice that stood before the woman of the pair. The tartrazine-coloured stain seemed to spread over her own vision as she stamped, shaking, through the lobby and out into the cold street.

SEVEN

It was raining in hard, heavy drops that pecked at her face. She thought she heard Antonia call after her as she crossed the road and ran down the steps towards the promenade. Already, her thin blouse was clinging to her shoulders and arms, and she could feel runnels of water dribbling down the back of her neck. She caught the crossing just as the amber lights were flashing and the engines were revving, sending clouds of exhaust fumes puffing into the cold air. Violet barely noticed a people-carrier jolt forwards and stop abruptly, inches from her shins. She let her foot splash into the deep puddle of water in the gutter, and felt it fill her shoe, so that her foot slipped inside it. It made her smile a little, to be as drenched as this and not to care; she was barely even feeling the cold anymore, such was her fury and urgency. She ducked into one of the empty shelters that overlooked the sea and stood there for a while, savouring the meandering tickle of the rain running down her back, the entirely involuntary shivers that were passing through her body. Her teeth chattered between wet lips.

She ran her fingers through her hair and watched a glut of water plop down at her feet. Glancing up, she could see the Hotel Napoli on the hill above her, its façade grey against the pastel-painted houses that surrounded it. There was not, as she had almost imagined, an angry mob thronging its front steps, glaring out furiously towards her and waving their fists. Instead, the scene was disappointingly placid and still, as if she had been irrelevant to it. She leaned back against the steamed-up plexiglass of the shelter and reached into her bag for a damp cigarette, but could find no matches. The first man she called out to for a light ignored her, but the second, a boy in a painted leather jacket, struck his Zippo for her and shielded it with his hand while she drew on its flame, all the while looking out into the street as if he would prefer to be somewhere else. By the time he left, the cold was beginning to reach her, so she huddled into the corner of the shelter, hoping to derive some warmth from the smoke, and broodingly imagined Antonia working her way around the politely-ruffled breakfast tables, apologising for her guest's behaviour, saying she didn't know what had come over her, wouldn't have expected it, would be taking measures to ensure that the residents wouldn't be disturbed in this way again.

Violet dropped the cigarette onto the floor, and watched it glow against the dark cement for a few seconds before fading out in the damp. She couldn't go back, not this morning, maybe never. But she was cold and hungry, and overwhelmingly lonely, feeling an overriding, garrulous desire to share her catastrophe with someone, anyone. She pulled out her phone and dialled Daisy's number, but hung up as soon as she was diverted to voicemail. There was no point in begging.

Instead, she stepped back out to the kerbside and looked around for a taxi. Seeing none around, she suspended her handbag over her head, and made her way towards the taxi rank by the side of the station, jogging through the streets with her face angled downwards to prevent any more rain from running into her eyes. There was no queue at the taxi rank; she opened the rear door of the car at the front and climbed in, causing the driver to fold up his paper, and then swing round angrily when he saw the state of her in his rear-view mirror.

"Jesus," he said, "you can't get in here; you'll soak my bloody back seat."

"It's raining," said Violet, "everyone's wet. Gordon Avenue, please." The driver shook his head and turned up the heat, so that warm air began to billow around her feet, making her toes feel unnaturally cold by contrast. "There's no point tutting at me," she said, "I'm in here now."

"Any more of that and you'll be out on your backside," said the driver, punching the car into gear and swinging out into the road. Violet rolled her eyes and cleared a hole in the condensation to gaze out of the window. She had memorised Ravi's address weeks ago, as he had written it on the same scrap of paper as his phone number, and Violet had found this highly amusing, as if he expected her to send him love letters. She had never even considered using it to visit him before, disinterested as she generally was about his life outside the times his activities coincided with her needs; she had laid the scrap of paper on her dressing table, however, and had absorbed the address as she glanced at it every time she brushed her hair or put on her makeup. Today, driving in silence along the congested ring-road that led towards the residential area of town, she began, for the first time, to search her memory for information on Gordon Avenue, wondering if she remembered which street it was.

Her question was soon answered when the taxi turned onto one of the wide, quiet roads on the outskirts of town, where grass verges separated the ample front gardens from the road. Every house sat on its own plot, and the street seemed to have been built in fits and starts, perhaps whenever there was money in town. A row of expansive Victorian villas sat next to a series of low, wide 1950s bungalows, interspersed with kitsch new-builds, whose forms seemed to pastiche the kind of house a child would draw, red bricks and gabled roofs, a door that sat symmetrically between four large windows. Everything was smart, orderly.

Ravi's house, number 34, was a more tasteful affair, a tall Edwardian redbrick with a kaleidoscope of stained glass around the front door. She didn't wait for the driver to tell her the fare; instead, she flattened out a ten pound note and rested it on the handbrake compartment, giving it two smart, patronising pats to ensure he noticed it. Without a word, she got out of the car, and slammed the door behind her. She reckoned that she had paid double the actual price, but this suited her; if he'd asked, she would have told him that it was a lesson not to assume people are cheap, just because they're not dressed up to the nines. Everyone deserves a little respect. Secretly, even from herself, she also hoped the extra fiver would compensate for the wet patch she'd left on the back seat.

Ravi's front gate swung gracefully on well-oiled hinges. Violet rang the doorbell (original, bakelite) and tried to straighten out her hair and clothes as she waited for an answer. She was glad she had; the woman who opened the door was immaculately dressed in loose silk trousers and a knitted tunic, with a paisley scarf draped over her shoulder in the manner of a woman for whom elegance was an absolute entitlement. She tucked one half of her sleek, black bob behind an ear and said, delicately, "Yes?"

"Is Ravi in?" asked Violet, feeling every inch the ragged teenager, and hankering after a time when she felt at home with, even equal to, women like this.

"He's upstairs working," the woman said. "May I ask who's calling for him?" Her face changed a fraction, as if an obvious, distasteful fact had dawned on her. "Ah, it's Violet, isn't it?" Her eyebrows sank a little as she pronounced the name.

"Yes, that's right," said Violet, thrusting out her hand, noticing how red her knuckles glowed against her white hand. "Are you Ravi's mother?"

"Mmmm," said the woman, taking Violet's hand so lightly and unwillingly that she was embarrassed at having offered it. "*Doctor* Saira Kahn." She stood on the threshold for a few moments, discreetly taking in Violet's appearance.

"Oh, do excuse me," said Violet, remembering that she was good at winning these situations, making use of her hard-learned manners and her ease in the face of authority to charm people onto her side. "I must look a terrible state. I got caught in the rain. Completely misjudged the weather this morning. I don't know what I was thinking." She followed this with a forced laugh, and this seemed enough to elicit a weak smile from Saira, whose own manners were too acute not to reciprocate such a gesture without a very good reason. She moved back slightly to usher Violet into the hall and murmured, almost under her breath, "Perhaps I should fetch you a towel."

"No, please don't trouble yourself, Mrs Kahn. I'm drying out quite nicely now." Even Violet's voice was in on the act now, taking on the clipped, correct tones she could remember using on elderly aunts who gave out money.

"As you wish." No 'Call me Saira,' then. She hadn't climbed that far up the ladder yet. What was the point of this anyway? Why did she need to win this woman over? It wasn't as if she was going to ask for Ravi's hand in marriage at some unspecified time in the future; she was just dropping round for some company, perhaps company of a physical nature, the kind that might take her mind off calling Daisy for an hour or so. She imagined she and Ravi together, whispering, trying to stay quiet for the prying ears that they knew would be listening. "Shall I head on up to find him, then?" she said, trying to drown the impatience in her voice with cheerfulness.

"No, I'll call him down." Saira looked at her with suspicion, before taking hold of the newel post and leaning up the stairs to call Ravi; but before any sound had left her mouth, she swung back round towards Violet with a look of resolve on her face.

"No," she said, "I want to talk to you first. I've been wondering for a while if I'd get a chance to meet you ever."

"I'm glad we've had the chance," Violet began to say, but Saira waved her finger to stop her.

"No, this is not a social matter. Ravi has told me all about you, and I thought that perhaps he was exaggerating, but now I can see it for myself. You are a great deal older than him, aren't you?"

"I'm," said Violet, and faltered, forgetting for a moment how old she was, wanting to say eighteen, nineteen, twenty-one, twenty-four. "I'm thirty," she said, "next month."

"And do you know how old my son is?" Violet stayed silent this time, unwilling to risk offering the wrong age. She had an idea, but. "Have you ever asked him? I know he goes to all these pubs and bars and parties, but you know that he's not really old enough to be there, don't you? He's a mature boy, an old head on young shoulders, he always has been; and he thinks he's fooled you because you've never asked, but I don't see how he can be as convincing as all that. He's seventeen, Violet. Almost a child."

Seventeen. Violet supposed she knew that, really, from the clues he left, the way he spoke, the people he hung around with. He was certainly younger than Daisy, she knew that much, but he seemed older somehow, more robust and stable, wiser. Seventeen, spelt out in brutal terms, was appalling. She was old enough to be his mother, give or take a couple of years. Seventeen had been a time when she believed she was ready to take on the world, but of course she was wrong. In fact, these beliefs had only made her vulnerable, prey to zealots and flatterers. It was horrifying to think that she might be no better influence on Ravi.

"Yes," she said finally, "I sort of knew that."

Saira's face tensed, her voice jagged with anger, "Then can I ask what on earth you think you're doing with my son?"

There were footsteps on the landing above them, a creaking of the banister, and Ravi's dreadlocked head hung above them.

"Oh," he said, squinting at them both as if he had just woken up, "It's you, Violet. Are you coming up?"

Violet glanced at Saira, hoping for some final act of tyranny that would give her an excuse to walk out on this whole thing, but she seemed to still be staring up at the space where Ravi's head had been, as if she wanted to plead with his ghost. Violet muttered, "Excuse me," under her breath as she edged past her, and didn't look back as she climbed the stairs.

The whole thing was sordid, going up to a teenage boy's bedroom with his mother downstairs in the hall. What on earth had she been thinking? He was beautiful in the way that a child might be beautiful, not a man. The thought of the things she had done with him made her shudder now, like the thought of eating raw meat; worse still, she wondered what the others must have thought, who saw them and knew about them. Was it a police matter, an illegal abuse of trust? No, he was seventeen; it was more a matter of poor taste, of distorted judgement. There had been a few weeks when she had forgotten herself, had happily ignored her own age.

It had to stop. She would end it here, kindly. He had done nothing wrong; it was her mistake. He must have gained a heady prestige from it, telling his mates about illicit liaisons with a much older woman in a hotel room in town. They probably didn't even believe him. Seventeen year-old boys count themselves lucky if they can pull a fourteen year old, as far as she remembered. A thirty year old just smacks of a tall tale.

He had left his bedroom door open, and as she walked in, her folly was heart-sinkingly obvious. This was the room of an adolescent, with all its clichés: posters on the wall of bands she'd never heard of, a guitar propped in the corner, an over-prominent display of drug paraphernalia, a tendency for every trinket to carry a marijuana leaf. Granted, this was Ravi, and so the room smelt as clean as he did; his bed was made, and his shelves were stacked with copies of the Ecologist and political-looking books with apocalyptic front covers. But overridingly, the room made her droop.

She wheeled the office chair out from under his desk and sat down. "Well," she began, "I just had a right grilling from your mum."

"I know. I heard." Perhaps it was too conspiratorial a start; it sounded as though she was expecting confidences on how fascistic the olds were. She tried to gather her thoughts into a way of agreeing with Saira, but before she could speak, Ravi continued.

"We talked about it all last night. I tell her everything, you know. I guess she was just trying to save me from having to say it myself, but that's not her responsibility."

"Oh." Say what?

He sighed, bit at the skin around his nails. "She's right. I've thought about it, and it's not right, Violet. I started off thinking it was such a privilege that someone of your age wanted to be with me, but now I just think it isn't right. I mean, why would you be attracted to me? Unless you're a bit," a pause, while he detached his eyes from whatever distant spot he had found to fix them on for the duration of his speech, "weird." This word was delivered looking her full in the eye, a molested child challenging his abuser.

"Right," said Violet, "weird, right." She got up, and walked back onto the landing, down the stairs whose banisters smelt of beeswax polish, out through the hall from which Saira was conspicuously absent, through the stained glass door and out into the cold, damp street. And all the time, she had to clamp her lips together to stop her from shouting out the words that were rattling around her head: "It's not my fault! None of this is my fault!"

EIGHT

It was mid-afternoon before Violet accepted that she would have to go back to the hotel. She was too cold to walk on the beach, too wild for the shops. She drank lattes in a café for a while, but had to leave when she found the prospect of another coffee overwhelming. The exhaustion was setting in, making her eyes burn and her limbs stiffen. She was haunted by an uneasy feeling that sleep would come to take its due somehow, and would perhaps catch a single blink and draw her into unconsciousness, right here in public. Already she could see the dusky characters of her dreams massing in her peripheral vision, ready to surge onstage at a moment's notice.

For a while, she let herself imagine that she wouldn't go back at all, would find another bed in another hotel, and use it to sleep off this awful day and night before heading away somewhere, leaving all her possessions gathering dust in the room. It would feel good, clean, to abandon all the ballast that she had gathered, even in this short time. She imagined herself lighter without it, liberated. But then she knew it would not be left for long; at the very least, Antonia would come in to pack it all up once it was clear she wasn't returning; worse still, Violet knew that Antonia wouldn't be able to resist rifling for clues about her, hunting down the notebooks she kept in her bedside table, rooting through her drawers and carrier-bags, making deductions from the brandy bottles and pebbles that now cluttered every drawer and shelf. The thought of someone knowing about her like this was appalling. She had to return, if only to pack it all up and take it away.

More than this, every muscle in her body ached for the comfort of the pool, the blue cocoon in which she hoped she could insulate her body from the sickening feeling that her world was collapsing around her. She knew that it was impossible for her to just walk in through the lobby, risking being noticed by Antonia, or worse, recognised by the other guests. She was certain that she would no longer be welcome, would be forced to collect her belongings and leave, and if this was going to happen, she wanted an hour in the pool first, a little time to reset her exhausted soul before she had to cope with things again. She took the road out of town that led up behind the hotel, planning to let herself in through the residents' car park at the back of the building, and make her way straight down the steps towards the pool.

The door was unlocked to allow all those awful half-term visitors easy access from their cars. Violet padded quietly through the rear corridor, pausing at every turn and doorway to look our for Antonia. No-one was there. She descended the steps to the pool, and tried the door. It was open. A concession, she thought, to those visitors, who would be far too sniffy to make use of it. She closed it firmly behind her, and immediately felt the close air enfolding her.

Without access to her costume, she stripped to her vest and knickers, which were anyway already wet from the rain, and eased herself into the pool. The water was warmer than usual, and the damp smell of the room around her was soon overtaken by the intoxicating tang of chlorine. She breathed deeply, feeling the tight muscles around her ribcage give way to fill her lungs, and then she ducked under the water, letting her head lead the rest of her body before surrendering entirely to it. She let it carry her to the surface before tilting her head sideways to take in a deep gasp of air, which she released, bubble by bubble, while she let her arms float upwards, felt her vest slacken in the water and float out around her.

She wondered if she had been wrong, all this time, to call this playing dead; this afternoon, with her fear subsiding and a feeling of peace washing through her, it seemed more appropriate to believe that the water was bringing her to life, disconnecting her from the humiliations and hardships of the physical word, and allowing her consciousness to float to the surface along with her prone body.

Daisy was there, too, as she always was when the water filled Violet's ears with silence. When she focused her concentration, she struggled to pick up on where Daisy was, what she was doing. Instead, she could detect only a sheer, penetrating blackness, a violent sense of anger and oblivion. She was heartened, for a moment, that their falling out could have such a devastating effect on her. Surely such anger must indicate at least a small regard for Violet; it felt good to know that the whole thing meant something to Daisy. But then, as she continued to wade around the depths of Daisy's mind, something extraordinary happened. She was treated to a flash of Daisy's own memory, an image of Violet drunk and staggering in the darkness of the yard last night, drooling out incomprehensible entreaties. Delivered with it, in a compact package of emotion, was a sense of shame and rejection, a determination never to end up like that.

It was almost as if a moment of deliberate communication had occurred; that Daisy had sensed the intrusion of Violet's mind and had hurled an insult back at her. Violet's whole body felt the shock of it, an electrical repulsion that jolted the water around her, sending a fizz of bubbles rising to the surface. She raised her face above the water and gasped in some air, dizzy patches of grey light floating before her eyes. Did she know? Had she sensed Violet's intrusions into her thoughts and was now, finally, fighting back? Or was she just encountering the full blast of Daisy's contempt? It would be enough just to be hated by her, if that was the best she could get.

Violet plunged her face back in the water. She was as alone in here as she was in the outside world, just a single body drifting in the blue. That picture of herself as a drooling, staggering drunkard kept forcing itself back into her imagination, and every time it made her breath catch. Was that all she was, nowadays? She had found Daisy, had pursued and befriended her with the hope of offering her an alternative example of how to live, a demonstration of good adulthood that she believed would prevent the worst from happening. The life she had invented for herself down here was a sham; she had always known that. But it was an alluring sham, a tempting one; and anyway, she had stolen most of her new personality from Daisy in the first place; the crisp condescension, the concentrated energy. The self she had pursued was nothing but a carbon copy of the person she admired the most, and she had clearly not even managed this imitation. She felt that transparency of the whole act now, a humiliating misappropriation of that which didn't belong to her, the shameful mis-fit of borrowed clothes.

Best to pack up and go, disappear. Anything she did from now on would only shame her further, making her even stranger in Daisy's eyes, some kind of peculiar obsessive. She could no longer win, could in fact only do more damage. She wondered what life would be like, knowing Daisy was there, feeling her existence, but never being known herself, the eternal voyeur.

It was as though every live and pulsing thing had been taken from her: her heart, her breath, her stomach, and all that remained was the cavity that had hosted them, the hard, dry wilderness of spine and rib-cage. She could feel nothing without them, save for a certain desolate surrender in the limbs, a coldness in the veins. Perhaps that was why she could float here like this: she was hollow. There was not enough inside her to weigh her down. To her left, there was an explosion, a sudden disruption of the waters around her, and then a rush of sound and light, the sensation of her lungs drawing in dry air. The pain around her abdomen, she came to realise, was someone's arm gripping her tightly, hauling her out of the water, over the sharp edge of the pool. She scrambled against the arms, pulling them apart and falling onto her hands and knees on the rough tiles. When she wiped the water from her eyes, she saw Robert bent double beside her, his clothes soaked and his chest heaving.

"Jesus," he gasped, "you're alive. I thought you'd drowned yourself. Jesus." He put his hand to his heart, and flopped down beside her. "Are you alright? I came in here to clean the pool, and you were face down. Not moving. I thought you were dead."

Violet shook her head, waiting for her own heart to stop racing before she spoke. She had never considered before how she might look from the outside, her face in the water and her limbs floating freely around her. She had always imagined herself to be in total privacy.

"Had you fallen in?"

"No. I was just floating." For some reason, this made her cry, as if the jolt of too fast a transition between water and dry land was more than her body could take.

"You're in shock," said Robert, "I'll find you a blanket. I'll get Antonia to make you some tea."

"No! God, no!" Violet grabbed at Robert's sodden jeans to stop him from walking away. "She can't know I'm here! She hates me!"

"Not that I'm aware of."

"I showed her up this morning, in front of all her guests." Violet's words were as wet as she was, catching in the tears that were running into her mouth.

"Ah," said Robert, "that. She's been worrying all day that she's upset you. She'll just be glad to know you're safe and well." He looked her up and down, and Violet remembered for the first time that she was in her underwear. "After a fashion," he said.

"Wait anyway. People might see me."

"I think that's unavoidable, Violet, unless I pack you up in the dumbwaiter and haul you upstairs."

"I was thinking more of the laundry trolley," said Violet, and it made her cry even harder.

"Come on," he said, but before he got to his feet, Violet grabbed his elbow and pulled him back down next to her. "There's a girl that I've been seeing," she said, "and she's me. I know it sounds mad, but she's the same person I was a long time ago. We even look alike."

Robert shrugged. "I can well believe it. Nothing much changes around here."

"But she's really me, not just similar. Our lives are the same. I'm scared she'll make the same mess of her life that I did."

"You're feeling old."

"I'm not. Well, I am, but it's more than that. She's made me realise that I should have done everything differently. I feel like she's been put in my way so that I can make things better."

"You're after redemption?"

"Something like that."

"Isn't that what people have kids for?"

"I'm serious."

Robert snorted out a laugh. "So am I. No-one's allowed redemption. We just get the chance to make the same mistakes all over again. Did you know this was my dad's hotel? I said I'd never take it on, but of course I did, when the time came. I changed the name, decorated, put in a pool and an espresso machine, but nothing really changed. And now I watch the kids in town and think, there I go again. It's like there aren't enough personalities to go round, so we all have to watch our own mistakes paraded before us. No-one learns, even if we try to teach them. In fact, they just learn slower that way." He got to his feet and held onto Violet's arms as she stood up.

NINE

It didn't seem worth sleeping now. Robert had helped Violet into her coat, and they travelled haltingly back to the room, Violet fighting her body's conflicting desires to creep and run through the corridors, anything not to be seen. With the door safely locked behind her, she showered, running the water too hot, so that her skin felt scoured by it. This refreshed her aching eyes a little, as if tiredness were a physical substance that had only to be dissolved in order to find life again.

Once she was dry, she put on her old jeans, a tee shirt and a jumper, and started to methodically sort through her drawers, packing the more practical items, the things she would keep, into her flight case and a succession of carrier bags, and jettisoning many of the month's more ridiculous acquisitions into a pile by the bin. She was leaving; she wouldn't need them anymore, besides which she simply couldn't accommodate their bulk and their weight. She needed to travel light, to take with her only what she could carry in her own hands.

A plan was already forming in her mind. She wouldn't return to London. The thought of it was unbearable, a visceral horror that sent waves of panic echoing through her body. She would sell the flat; there must be somebody out there, some agent who could do it all for her, take the keys and make it all disappear, her magnolia walls, her miniature window, her wardrobe of grey clothes, her showroom furniture. Given three or fours months, there would be money in the bank, the inevitable profit made on London property. How long could she make that last: a year? Two? Five? Ten, even, depending on where she lived, how she lived.

She opened each drawer in turn, throwing out receipts and flyers, notes and tickets. She tucked her notebook away into the pocket of her flight case; if she was going to dispose of it, she would do so miles away from this hotel, where anyone who found it would be safely detached from her, unable to link the outpour of words to any name or face.

The thing she found the most of, in a quantity that surprised even her, were stones. They rattled and rolled in every drawer, gathered dust on each sill and table, and weighed down bags in the bottom of her wardrobe. Shells and worn glass jingled amongst them, shards of plastic and metal jutted out. She had been barely aware of gathering them, and there was no question of taking them with her, as much as she yearned to; they were heavy and useless, an absolute impossibility.

Instead, she hunted through the various bags and drawers until she found one stone to keep, a smooth, mauve pebble shaped like an egg, which she dropped into her pocket to soothe her on her journey. She arranged another handful of stones in a perfect vortex on her marble-topped washstand, their dusty colours reaching out into the room. Finally, she deposited the remaining stones onto her balcony, making a displaced beach of them. She initially tipped them all over the tiled floor, but finding them too sparse, she brushed them all over to one side with her hands, so that they piled up against the wall and drifted towards the floor in a curve, just like they did around the groynes on the real beach. As an afterthought, she squatted down and picked up all the various dog-ends she had left on the balcony, dropping them efficiently into a cupped hand.

Walking back into her room, she was struck by its bareness, its fundamental sense of absence, but for the untidy pile of bags by the door. It was chilling to see just how easily it reverted to being a hotel room, an innocuous, neutral space. Later today, she would be erased from it even further, the last traces of her skin and hair vacuumed from the carpet, the last traces of her scent laundered from the sheets The room would forget her in the clouds of bleach and furniture polish, just as the town would forget her, filling the space she had occupied with a bustling press of bodies. It had forgotten her once before, after all. Maybe it wasn't so different to London.

Her final gesture was to lift the Dansette and the box of records out of the bottom of the wardrobe and onto the bed, an act of defiance against the forgetful room. She couldn't resist dipping her hand into the records one last time to pull out a handful of singles, savouring their unruly weight. It seemed cruel that Antonia would relegate them to the attic again, as soon as she was gone. She unzipped her case and stuffed five records into the top of it, closing the lid before she could even see what they were. Perhaps later she would be able to take comfort from holding them again, turning their silken grooves in the light.

These tasks completed, she gathered up her half a dozen carrier bags, unlocked the long towing-handle of her case and transported the whole lot outside, making sure to lock the door behind her, feeling the heavy drop of the mortise, testing the handle three times. Then, she dragged the lot of it down the stairs to the reception, letting the case bump-bump-bump behind her.

Antonia was already waiting for her, as she had expected, but it gave her a small flip in the stomach anyway. She let the wheels of her suitcase fall onto the wooden floor from the final step, and their grumble filled the foyer as she approached the desk. She kept her eyes to the ground, unable to decide on an appropriate expression. Finally, when she reached the desk, she raised her gaze, and could see that Antonia had been unashamedly staring at her through the whole ordeal.

Violet coughed, a pathetic little noise that was supposed to segue into a conversation, but instead seemed to increase her sense of embarrassment.

Antonia smiled steadily. "Are you alright, Violet?"

"Yes, just a frog in my throat."

"No. Are you *alright?*" It was said with great solemnity, a downwards inflection on the word *alright*, to denote that it referred to one of the bigger problems in life – death, insanity, addiction, or perhaps all of them.

"Yes," said Violet, drawing in an airy breath and imposing a smile on her face, "yes I am. I'm checking out."

"You know you don't have to."

"Maybe. But it's time." She tried to return Antonia's laden look with an insouciant one, but was defeated by the other woman's greater determination, and her own poor acting. "I can't live here forever," she blurted out.

"Well," Antonia replied, and appeared for a moment to seriously consider it, "no, perhaps you can't. But you could stay nearby. You have friends here."

"Fewer than you'd think." Violet scrambled in her purse for her credit card. "Anyway, I need to get going." She snapped the card onto the polished wood and pushed it towards Antonia, who pushed it straight back.

"Don't be silly," she said, "it's been a pleasure having you."

Violet felt her face redden. "You have to let me pay."

"No I don't. Not at all."

"You've not exactly been busy."

"Come the summer, the place will be full again. We in the hotel trade are used to winter. Put your card away." She picked it up and pressed it in to Violet's palm, closing her fingers over its blunt edges. For a moment she cradled Violet's whole hand between her own, letting its reluctant weight hang in mid-air. "It's been like having a daughter, having you around."

Violet looked away, nervous of intimacies like this. Antonia continued to search for her gaze. "I know your mother, Violet," she said, almost whispering. "I still know her. But she doesn't know me. It's a shame. I see her every day, going about her business."

"I think you've got the wrong person. My mother lives in France."

"Yes," said Antonia, gripping Violet's fist ever tighter and intensifying her unblinking eyes on Violet's. "She lives in France, as you say. But I still see her every day. Do you understand?"

It was like being hit by the full force of a wave, this rush of understanding, as deep and intoxicating as the sea itself. "Yes," said Violet, who barely had any breath to say it.

Antonia loosened her grip on Violet's hand, let it ease down onto the desk so that she could steady herself. "She thinks about you a lot," she continued, "she thinks you're too grand and clever for her anymore. But I know differently, hey? It's been a pleasure, as I said. I always wondered if I'd get to meet you. A taste of what I could have had, hmmm?"

So she wasn't a singularity, a freak occurrence; she was part of a chain. Who knew how long it was. Antonia was, what? Three, five years older than Violet's mother? It couldn't have been much more. And yet the two women were unrecognisably different. Violet searched Antonia's face for signs of her mother's and thought, perhaps. She could discern a thinner, more glamorous version of her mother's plump face, but a more tired one, too, a more cynical, more cultivated face.

"You're so different," she said.

"Yes. We managed that all on our own. Our lives were the same in some ways, in some ways not. It wasn't just that we were born in different countries; we still ended up in the same place. But we also made different choices, small ones, big ones. Over the years, it added up to something enormous."

Violet was silent, stunned, muted by the way this knowledge rolled around inside her.

"Listen," said Antonia, "your mother never even knew I existed, because I never told her. She saw me around maybe, but I kept away. I was afraid of her; I loved her so much I knew I'd embarrass myself. Over the years it's broken my heart, Violet. Go and find your girl, the one who means the same to you. Tell her everything." She reached under her desk, and pushed her car-keys towards Violet. "Quick. It's getting late."

Violet looked at the keys for a moment, before grabbing at them as if she was afraid they would float away. She reached over and pulled Antonia's face towards her, kissing her on the cheek and then wrapping her arms around the frail frame. Antonia grabbed her briefly and then untangled herself, holding Violet at arm's length and saying, "It's funny how everything joins up in the end. Now go. Quick."

She unravelled slowly over months, maybe even years, before she died. I didn't recognise the signs at first, but I do now, a pointless kind of retrospect. There was nothing to be done, nothing I could have warned her about that she didn't already know. I felt, down the lines of our connection, the first, inexplicable weaknesses, the first spikes of pain. I thought little of them, imagined them to be the protests of an ageing body, a mistreated one at that.

She knew, though. Must have done. She started preparing herself, and me. More and more, I could feel her tugging at the other end of our chain, jolting me from my work or rest to share with me a little vision or insight, a fragment of her life. Over and over, she told our story back to me, endlessly cycling though the parts I knew, but dredging up new memories too, things I didn't know before, the minutiae of our courtship. With time, I became suspicious of these fresh details, wary that she might have been inventing or elaborating, ever conscious of my place as a character in her own history. I was afraid she wanted to show herself in a better light. She was too hard on herself, I think. She didn't need this blunting of her sharp edges to be redeemed. I left those bits out.

But then, by the time all that began, I knew too. She was falling out of focus, becoming dreary around the edges, and repeating herself endlessly, reiterating the same story over and over with its minor variations. It was as if she were trying to make a recording of herself, downloading her soul into me so that she could still, somehow, exist after she had gone. I began to take notes, although I didn't believe for one second that she could simply transfer herself into me this way, that her soul was nothing more than the sum total of her experiences. I would have said this to her, if I could have: we are not our souls, because our souls are things entirely without perspective; they are bigger than us. But I never could have conveyed a thought, a sentence, as exact as that through the static that fizzed between us. We only ever dealt in vaguenesses, suggestions, hints and traces. We never had the sunlight-clarity of actual conversation, of explanation and exposition. Perhaps it was better that way.

Still, the images came to me, drip by drip, over the final months of her life. I found myself assailed with little shots of insight, like snatches of film, a few frames at a time. Sometimes only the pictures would come, sometimes the sounds, sometimes the smells. It was like it had always been, receiving small packets of information seemingly at random, but I eventually came to discern the real memories, as they had a dusty quality to them, a grainy uncertainty, a certain judder and skip; the false ones were too bright, too smooth and primary-coloured. Later, much later, as she sank deep down into the machine-whir of her consciousness, the fragments she sent me became confused, jumbling impossible combinations of times and places, getting stuck in a groove like the old 45s she used to play, to create endless, lurching loops of the briefest moments. At the very end, it was just my name, over and over. Daisy, Daisy, Daisy, Daisy.

That night she came to find me, she drove out into the brown-dark just after dusk. She drove slowly, because she was afraid of her own awkwardness behind the wheel of a car. She ground the gears and stamped too heavily on the brakes.

She took a few corners too late, sometimes turned the wheel too far and almost swung a full circle.

She forgot about the de-mister, and so battled against the fogging windscreen with a balled up pair of socks from her carrier-bag.

She wondered if she would be able to find my house, but it turned out to be as easy as finding her own.

And then she sat outside, gazing at the light filtering through the drawn curtains as if it could tell her what to do next.

But these are the last things that I will pass on from her

perspective. From now on, it's my story. Of course, it was mine before that moment too, and not just as a life lived simultaneously. It was much more than that. Typical of Violet to assume that she was the only one in this relationship, the sole recipient of our strange twinning. I may not have had the same shock-revelation of her existence as she did of mine, the eureka-moment of enlightenment; after all, I didn't have the benefit of being presented with a version of myself that had already existed, and that was therefore recognisable.

There was something in its place, though, a slow-burn of identification, a repeated and mysterious conjuring of her face – no, not her face, her presence – in my mind's eye. I, too, encountered the funny little time-shifts, the sense of involuntarily flicking over to another living, breathing reality, and the odd impulses, the cravings to suddenly do this or that, drink black coffee or red wine, submerge myself in cool blue water, savour the weight of a stone in my hand. And all through this, she kept coming back to me, introducing herself into my thoughts unbidden. I wondered for a while if I was a lesbian, or pregnant, or both. It seemed like a rather devastating combination of things to face at eighteen. I drank the feeling away.

Then, there was the row in the backyard of the ballroom. I still, to this day, find it hard to believe that she was my saviour there, that she did anything other than intercept a perfectly pleasant notch on my bedpost; but Violet did; so proud was she of that moment that she played it back to me more than all the others, as if showing me a particular triumph, rubbing my nose in a woeful error. Towards the end, I think she forgot I was there entirely, and began to play fast and loose with the facts, like she did with everything else. In some accounts, she delivered a brutally-stinging verbal attack, making the barman shrink away into the darkness, a shamed Nosferatu confronted with a crucifix; in others, she physically attacked him, tore him away from me with her bare hands and threw him to the ground. Once, she erased it altogether, offering me an alternative history in which she picked on the right man in the first place, saving me from the appalling consequences of my own naivety before I even knew a thing. This was too much of a fabrication, even for her. She never repeated it. But she never understood, either, that she may have been wrong entirely; that my life was not her life. Another thing I'd have told her if I had the chance.

Either way, after that event, everything changed for me. As I walked away, I felt a kind of drag, like I was pulling against a magnetic force to separate myself from her. That night, she was everywhere, continually popping up in my thoughts, and, when I finally slept, invading my dreams. My head was full of her voice, whispering. I didn't understand what she was saying. I thought at first that it was because I was angry, upset by our row, but this level of intrusion seemed exaggerated even by the stands of my level of obsession with her by that time. By the next morning, I felt as though she were trampling through my brain. I was infested. I began to try to kick back against her, to push her out of me. For a while it worked. But I had other things on my mind that day, anyway, things that were just sinking in. A link had been established, whether I wanted to believe it or not. By the time Violet took Antonia's keys, she as already there. Her intention to find me that night registered somewhere in my consciousness, and I intercepted it as a certainty that she was coming, without understanding why. I felt with her the jolt of the brakes and the wet smear of the condensation on the windscreen; I heard the muted hum of voices on the radio, the croaking of the gears. I watched an ache grow in the pit of my stomach, like a physical kind of radar, as she got nearer and nearer.

By the time she sounded her horn outside, I had already known she was there for a long time. I was waiting at the front door, but it made me start anyway. I don't suppose she could have risked coming to the door, after what had happened with Ravi's mother earlier that day. I heard my own Mum say, "Who can that be?" and I didn't answer; she heard me take the chain off the door and called,

"Where are you going?" so I said, "Out." It was our usual level of exchange. Nothing much has changed since then. I closed the door behind me.

I remember I wasn't wearing a coat. The rain immediately stung my bare arms, but I wanted it to be like that, me appearing out of the darkness, cold and brave and unready. I had barely got up that day, hadn't even brushed my hair or put on make-up. I only had my jeans on because I'd spilt tea down my pyjamas.

I pulled the handle, got into the car. This time she started: did she think I wouldn't come? She didn't look at me; she watched my legs as I sat down, but she never caught my eye. "We can't do this out the front of my house," I said, and so she started the engine. I didn't want anyone to see. I found the cigarettes in the top of her bag, tried to light one with the car lighter. It was dead, cold. I shook it. Violet said nothing, kept her eyes on the road, but took it from me, pushed it into the dashboard, pressed in its button. I didn't thank her. We both reached for it when it popped out. I got there first, held its glowing end to my tab. I knew she wanted one too, could feel it in her urgent sideways glances, but I didn't offer. I knew she couldn't reach them. I wanted her to want them.

Neither of us broke the silence. Violet made the wipers go fast and then slow, fiddled with the air-con. I dragged on my cigarette, imagined its blue smoke billowing out to fill my lungs, watched the streetlights refracted through the rain-splattered window. The smoke began to fill the car, insinuating its way across the windscreen and creeping into the intimate void between us. I wanted her to react, to tell me off or fan it all away with her hands, but it was me who gave in first, when my throat itched so much I thought I would choke. Coughing would have broken my moral advantage of silence; I unwound the window a fraction, felt the cold, wet air blast onto my face, watched the smoke snake its way out. I threw the cigarette out behind it, knew she could see its glow in her rear-view mirror.

It was electric to be this close to her, a kind of agony. I encountered the proximity of her life in savage jags. I could sense her breathing and beating and feeling. I could almost hear the crackle and pulse of her nerves. I could nearly believe it would kill her if I held my breath. Yet she was mysterious, too, unknowable and separate. If I were party to her thoughts, it was only in flickers and glances. Here she was, so close that she had to fold in her elbow when she changed gear to avoid us touching, and yet I could read her no better than I could when I was at home. She sent me only black clouds and sadness, like sour wine. I suppose she was afraid, but at that time, in that car, driving God knows where, I hoped it was because I had hurt her.

The rain eased off; the wipers fell into a slow rhythm of sweep and pause, sweep and pause. Soon they began to screech when they crossed the windscreen. Violet switched them off, accidentally setting off both of her indicators in the process. I wanted to laugh. I didn't.

We had left the town. I could see no houses. The roads were dark and narrow, flanked by grassy banks. Violet flicked the headlights onto full-beam, and their white glow seemed to make a shield in front of us. Another pair of headlights approached, and she fumbled to dip her own bulbs. I watched the indigo light blink on and off on the dashboard. When she flicked them on again, we caught the red tail of a fox darting back into the darkness. It felt desolate when neither of us remarked on it.

A charge of wind and a vaster blackness to my left told me we were by the sea again. There were no stars tonight, not even the faint light of boats at the horizon. I thought perhaps I could hear the waves. There were houses to our right now, emitting faint, closed-curtain glows. Where there's sea, there's always people. I imagined that the row of bungalows had lined up to watch us pass, solemn and judgemental. I wondered where we were going. Should I be anxious, afraid? I wondered for the first time exactly how big Violet's obsession with me had grown, how dark. She could do anything to us out here, aim the car into the sea-wall or the path of one of those rare passing cars. I fastened my seatbelt. Surely I would know, wouldn't I, if she meant me any harm? Surely I would feel the knife or the rope in the boot, the matches in her pocket?

The road had begun to unmake itself. The houses were thinning out again, and the headlights showed that the road had frayed at the edges, its kerbless tarmac melting into grass and shingle. We netted rabbits in our lights, an amber flash of eye, a white flicker of tail, blackness. I never thought rabbits lived so close to the sea. I imagined them burrowing in the sand, the powdery walls caving in on them.

We passed small, low buildings, which looked like nothing more than shacks. They seemed to retreat from us as we approached. Up ahead, a beam of light swept through the black space. A lighthouse, then. The end of the road. As we got nearer, I could no longer see the light-beam itself, only its regular dazzle into the car.

Violet indicated before she pulled over, although there was no-one else around. She eased the car onto a patch of gravel, yanked on the handbrake, turned off the engine. I listened as the whir of the fan fell limp. Then it was ringingly silent in the car, save for the rush and thump of the wind around our windows.

"So," she said, and drew in a breath that I thought would burst her lungs.

"So," I said in return, but I couldn't let it hang there; I had to take possession of this space. "So you knew Ruth would die?" I felt the air absorb my voice.

"Meningitis," she said. "Yes, I knew."

"And you didn't think to tell me, or her, or anyone before it was too late?"

"It was inevitable," she said. "Just like before."

"No it wasn't!" I shouted. "No, it wasn't inevitable. There was a point last night when you could have saved her. You sat and watched her getting ill, and you did nothing. You could have saved her!"

"You wouldn't have believed me." Her voice was high, surprised.

"You didn't even try! How do you know we wouldn't believe you if you didn't try? You could have said, Hey, Daisy, get her to a hospital, just in case. Keep an eye on her. You could have taken her home, said something to her Mum. It would have been weird, but it would have been something. You didn't even try."

"Ruth wasn't any of my business; it was you I was trying to save." She said it looking straight at me, and I realised that she didn't understand at all, that as far as she was concerned, this was just about her and me; no-one else counted. In the years since it happened, I saw just how wrong she had got it; and she saw it too, eventually. She had been so busy constructing a narrative that explained her life away that she had wrung the humanity out of it. Her story, the one she made up to excuse herself of the bad choices she made, was the tale of a girl harmed, of malevolent male power. If she had stepped back a while, had deviated from the narrow path she selected, she would have told a different story altogether, a story in which a loved one was lost, a story in which the drinking and gigs and parties just didn't seem worth it any more.

But then, if there's no-one to blame, it's less of a story, isn't it? When we tell the stories of our lives, we want heroes and villains. And if we can't manage to be heroic, then we might as well be victims, feeble damsels in distress whose gallant knight never arrived. Perhaps Violet thought it was her turn to be the knight this time round.

Losing Ruth was the single worst thing that ever happened to me. I mean that. People think that, because you're young, your friendships somehow matter less; in time, they expected me to stop moping, move on, live a little. But I never did. I often wondered if, given time, there might have been more to me and Ruthie than just a friendship. I'll never know. But I'm almost certain that there was more between she and I than there was between Violet and her friend, Sasha. They were not equivalent. One of the many ways in which our lives were different. I don't think she ever really believed that.

We left on sour terms that night. We argued until my throat was sore, and then I made her drive me home. I didn't say goodbye when I got out of the car. I didn't want to see her again.

I never did, not in person. Violet drifted off after that, travelled to Brighton, Manchester, Edinburgh, then abroad. She did the world on the profits of that flat, scrounged off people whenever she could. She spent most of her time in Thailand, Goa, Morocco: wherever life was cheap and people were transient. They bought her drinks and shared their drugs; she pretended that she was like them, travelling, but with a life to return to. But there was nothing waiting for her. She wasn't like them at all. They tended to work that out fairly quickly.

Whenever it all got too much for her, when the locals were sick of her or she had embarrassed herself, she moved on. She had lovers, intrigues, passing friends. I know very little of it all.

Over time, things thawed between us. Her mistakes began to feel much like my own: distasteful and painful maybe, but understandable at the bottom of things, actions that should be judged on their intentions, however misguided, rather than their outcomes. More than that, I came to realise that I couldn't reject her if I tried. She hung around at the fringes of my consciousness, occasionally transmitting hits of emotion down the line at me. I couldn't ignore her for too long.

In time, we developed an odd kind of friendship, maintained through the flow of our respective streams of data. I never told anyone about her, although I suspect she told many people about me. I don't suppose anyone believed her. Who would?

And me, did I learn her lessons? Did I go on to live a freer life, to think for myself, to become a good grown-up? Of course I didn't. I did exactly what she did: threw myself into my schoolwork, got the grades everyone always said I was capable of if I applied myself, got a place in a big, stern university. I worked hard, kept my head down, avoided the student bar, the societies, the balls.

I got a First, just like Violet, and used it to get a job she found hauntingly familiar. I could feel her fury, her desperation at the other end of our link when she caught onto it. I ignored her.

But that's where the similarities ended. After a few years I got thoroughly sick of it. I hated all the same things that she did: the early mornings and late nights, the destructive levels of competition, the thick layers of artifice. Unlike Violet, I admitted it to myself. I took it all in and let myself detest it. If you see it all for the performance it is, work is a lot easier. There was no hurry. I watched and I waited, until I understood exactly what it was that I found so disgusting about it.

The city changed for me during that time. My vision adjusted. Instead of the place full of promise and excitement that I used to see, I began to see through its layers of silicon chip and air conditioning. Slowly, slowly, what emerged was a world I didn't understand. I would walk through the streets and allow myself to ask, What is this? What is that? What does that person do? I learned to assume nothing, to question everything. The world around me was suddenly made of materials that I couldn't even imagine being made. Where did it all come from, the veneers and glosses, the amalgams and composites? How did it all come into being? I read the labels on food packets and wondered what all the words meant. I interrogated people about their jobs, and found that most of them did little more than placate people with similar titles in different companies. My own job was no exception.

I began to apply the same bright floodlight to human beings. I started to wonder, if I weren't in a suit, would this person even speak to me? I never let myself get nostalgic, like Violet did. When I was eighteen, would I have been nearly so luminous (if Violet is to be believed) without the hair-dye and the eyeliner, the bottle of vodka and the packet of fags? Ugly girls with a loud mouth like mine are just considered rude – if anything, uglier for their acerbity. I wondered if I'd ever known authenticity in all my life.

I began writing about it without even knowing what I was doing. It was just a case of venting all these odd new thoughts, trying to make sense of them in some way. I used my computer at first, as I'd always done, but when I started to feel alienated by the neat spring of the keyboard, the dead-eye flicker of the screen, I switched to paper and biro, then fountain pen, then pencil. I let myself de-evolve, worked my way backwards until I found something real. By the time I felt ready to share my writing, I knew the sanitary distance of the blog wasn't for me. I distilled pages of my ramblings onto a couple of sides of A4 using my best handwriting, photocopied it, and handed it out on the streets. I left it in cafés and pubs, propped it behind public toilet cisterns, went into parks and secreted it in the branches of trees. I'll never know if a single person read that first edition, because I forgot to put my name or address on it. Probably for the best; I've since learned that my work has an extraordinary capacity to make people angry. It undermines their whole way of life, you see, sets them asking questions they don't want to answer. I was best off anonymous at first.

Still, even the experience of sending work out into the void like that gave me a taste for it. I could finally see a reason to quit my job, sell my flat, move out of London. As Violet discovered before me, the great benefit of London property prices is that they always go up. During my few years in the metropolis, I made enough to set myself up somewhere quiet, with a little to spare. I imagined moving to the country somewhere, to a house in the middle of a field, where no-one could bother me. While I worked out my notice, I began to take trips on the train at weekend, research trips. I bought a bike, carried it with me on the train, and spent the weekends pedalling around the countryside with an eye out for abandoned cottages.

I never found anything until, one Sunday, I ended up in Dungeness. It was an odd, dizzying experience the first time that strange landscape emerged over the horizon. I recognised it immediately, even in daylight, as the place Violet had taken me all those years ago. It was the peculiar sense of space, of thwarted light, that cowering confederation of wooden huts. The sun was setting as I made my way along the ragged tarmac, turning the sky a thick grey-blue. The power station was silhouetted black against it, a sinister, looming cube. I felt utterly alone there. It was perfect; and more perfect still was the 'For Sale' sign on a small, black hut with red window-frames, just beyond the reach of the sea.

I never believed in fate; Violet did. Maybe she was right about that, after all. There was my house, ready for me. I imagined it had sat there for years, perhaps since that rain-blasted night in the car with Violet, just waiting for me.

The house was a relic, the sole estate of a sea-fisherman who had left it to his bewildered nephew when he died. It had ageing electricity, a wood-fired Raeburn for heat and only four rooms: a kitchen, a sitting room, a bedroom and a bathroom with an enamelled bath and yellow tiles. The estate agent who showed me it suggested I'd be ripping it down and starting all over again, but I've barely changed it, save for the turbine that now provides most of my light and the shower I installed to save water. I wasn't planning on having visitors anyway.

The first thing I did was dig the garden, until I realised that the shingle continued for a long way down. I made raised beds after that, using anything I could find that was big enough: a dilapidated rowing boat, corrugated iron washed ashore, the fisherman's old bath. When the first tender plants broke through, they were scarred and ugly form the scouring wind; I built wind-breakers to shelter them, learned to drill these with holes so that they wouldn't blow away entirely.

It was here that the Notes from the End of the World were born. I wrote them between bouts of battling the Dungeness shingle and finding chickens hardy enough to withstand its eternal winds.

I hand-wrote the first few, just the same as my early attempt in London, and laid the text out in two columns, like an old-fashioned newspaper. I used them to record my struggles to live a better life, my hopes, my fears, the beliefs that were driving me. The battles with the vegetable garden were all in there, as were the disastrous interventions of the local rabbits, the difficulties of finding wood for the Raeburn with only a bicycle for transport, and the sturdy intrusion of the sea-kale that seemed to pop up wherever it pleased.

The first few months, when I photocopied Notes and sent it off to the small cluster of cafes and cooperatives in London that I thought might be interested, I heard nothing. But then, after the forth edition, something strange happened: I began to get letters, a trickle at first, but then hundreds, asking for a batch of newsletters to be sent to their own centre or café, passing on hints and tips to help me along the way to self-sufficiency, or just telling me how much they loved my ramblings, how it made them feel better about the world. Correspondence arrived from places I'd never even heard of, and I came to realise that people were photocopying Notes and passing it on. They told me that they laughed at my attempts to rig up an irrigation system for my used shower-water (I'm glad they did); that they felt with me the horror of losing my chickens to the local fox. They passed on recipes to deal with gluts of chard and swede, and even that sea-kale; they offered strategies for preserving my tomatoes into winter.

After the fifth edition, a man from the Lake District offered me the services of his antique printing-press, and I was glad to take him up on his offer, conscious that a photocopier was one of the high-tech trappings I was seeking to avoid. Soon after that, as our costs began to grow, we had to make a plea for paper, and it arrived, reams of it, and it still does to this day: letterheads of defunct companies, greens and blues with sun-bleached streaks, or packets of A4 that readers have bought and freely given as gifts, usually accompanied by a kind note or an expression of thanks.

More than anything, my readers tell me that my hunt for a more authentic way of life struck a chord with them. They understand my desire for the real, the urge to make contact with the actualities of life, its base components. They listen to my rambles and rants, nod sagely, and send back wise comments and perceptive interjections. They spread my words around like a new gospel.

I am, of course, not adored in all quarters. I am told that in the press, my name had become a byword for eccentricity and hyperbole. So be it. I gave up reading them long ago. Rumour has also reached me that I have been the subject of at least one television documentary. More disconcerting have been the leering pilgrimages that these unwanted pieces of publicity inspired, the men and women with rampaging children and plasticky clothes, who seem to hang by my desolate peninsular just to make loud comments about the state of my paintwork, and to squint through my windows to see if they can spot me. They only come at weekends. It's fine by me; perhaps they will learn something, or if nothing else, be haunted by the ghostly ruin of the old power-station, its brutal foreshadowing of the time when all cities will fall and decay like this.

Sometimes, if they listen closely enough, they might just hear music escaping from between the draughty wood-slats of my shack. My record-player, a gleaming white Dansette with a light-up badge and an air of having been treated reverently, arrived with an accompanying box of 45s a couple of years ago. No message, no return address, but I had a good idea who sent them. I play them after a windy day, when I can spare the electricity, and I wonder what Violet would give to hear their rusty, spacious charms again, their woeful entreaties, their commandments to dance, love, live, mourn, shake off the shackles, shake a tail feather. I hope they sound strange as they leak through the window frames, primitive and clumsy, liberated from the deep layer of gloss that encases modern life.

I played them all night when she died. I worked through one after the other, the good ones, the bad ones, the familiar and the obscure, as if hearing them could somehow reawaken her. Nothing, of course. Nothing forever now.

At the end of each song, the needle lifts smartly off the vinyl and returns to its plastic cradle with regimented precision, leaving an expectant silence in its wake. It's hard to stop; the space hangs there to be filled. We play the song again, learn the words, create dances to get us through it. But our familiarity doesn't change the facts; it just makes it more painful when the music stops, and we have to admit that we need it one more time.

We haven't got time to learn now. We're running out of life. A world that was created in geological timescales is unmaking itself faster than we can comprehend. On good days I think that at least I can make them angry, give them a searing consciousness to see them through while the world burns out. Other times I fear I'm no more than a diversion, a salve to desperate consciences, a distraction from the necessary business of making ready for the change.

But even if they understood, what could they do? At least in ignorance they can carry on making choices, and it's those choices that make us alive.

Acknowledgments

Thanks to all those who helped with the creation of this book, and in particular the insight, advice and support of Amy Barker, Dyfed Edwards, Peggy Reilly and Beccy Shaw. Thanks and love to Sue Gagie for just being so damned enthusiastic, and, of course, to Christopher May, who has had to tolerate an awful lot of whining to get here.

About the Author

Katherine May is an author with an interest in hauntings real and imaginary. Her first collection of short stories, *Ghosts & their Uses*, was published in 2006.

Katherine has taught writing and creative learning in various settings, including Tate Britain, the National Gallery and Creative Partnerships. She is currently an arts project manager with a particular interest in education, community engagement and festivals.

She lives by the sea in Kent with her husband and three cats.